A Crown of Thorns

Duncan Swindells

Acknowledgments

This book would not have been possible without the generous help of a huge number of people. If I have omitted anyone, my humblest apologies.

I simply couldn't have written A Crown of Thorns without Aleksei Kiseliov. He has provided incredible levels of information on all things Russian, has helped me create fictional companies where necessary and advised on everything from people's names to brands of cigarettes. Thank you, Aleksei.

Thank you to everyone at Green Aspirations and in particular my great friends Jo Edwards and Paul Cookson who allowed me to muck about with ropes and axes and showed me how to carve spoons whilst retaining my fingers and thumbs.

Thanks to Craig Steele from The Buchlyvie Pottery Shop for giving up his valuable time to explain slip and porcelain.

Thank you to Russell Schoof for fielding all my Glock related questions.

A particular thank you to my parents-in-law; Grant Boyd, himself an exceptional artist, for his encyclopaedic knowledge and Terry Boyd for gifting me the best sentence in the book.

Rob Williams for his excellent work on the cover.

A massive thank you to Georgia, Ruth Rowlands, Aleksei, Jo Edwards and my ever-patient mother for proof reading.

A Crown of Thorns was written during the global pandemic. I had wondered about sharing my feelings on this subject, but there has been more than enough said and written to last all our lifetimes. In any case, I prefer to look to the future. I would simply like to thank you for supporting me, wish you all good health and remind you that, however bleak things may appear;

"This too shall pass."

1

Marcus Bayer was not rash by nature. He was an intellectual, he liked to think, a patient considerer of the facts who only ever acted once each and every angle had been scrupulously examined and chewed over. Consequently, he was certain he'd never behaved quite so impulsively in all his twenty-five long years.

The quietly self-deprecating Tom Fratton sat sleeping, a pair of binoculars draped around his neck, their bulky mass resting awkwardly on an embryonic drinker's paunch. Bayer regarded him nervously. It was possible Fratton might not wake in the time it would take him. It was possible he would never know. He tiptoed across the tiny flat, away from the window and Fratton's supine figure. On the counter which separated the kitchen from their cramped living quarters Bayer found a set of car keys. There was just something about the man in the house opposite which had convinced him he should act. It wasn't uncommon, from their vantage point high above, to see him leave his house in the dead of night, not uncommon at all. But, as a rule, when the man did take a drive in the middle of the night, he would step purposefully from his beautifully appointed pre-revolution town house, not bothering with his hat, open the car door readily, ease himself in and drive off. After all, even in March Moscow could be fiercely cold. But this morning, at ten past two, Bayer had diligently recorded the time, the man in the house opposite had stepped onto his driveway, pulled his black fedora down over his brow, carefully found a Parliament and smoked it easily. If Marcus Bayer hadn't known, with the certainty of a professional snooper, that they could not possibly be seen in their hideaway across the street, he would have sworn that the man standing in the broad-brimmed hat, smoking so calmly, had fixed him through the lens of his binoculars. A long, lingering, open stare. He was appealing to Marcus Bayer. A very personal request to join him, Bayer was certain of it. He was allowing him enough time to collect his thoughts, together with his car keys, and make the decision which had to be made. And what else was Bayer to do? Perhaps there was another team who would follow? Perhaps he was breaking with all his training, but how often did the Deputy Director of the FSB extend such an obvious and personal invitation?

He looked at Fratton. There wasn't any point in leaving a note. What would he write? If he were lucky and whatever the Deputy Director had to say didn't take too long, there was always the chance he would be back before Fratton awoke. If he were unlucky, a note wasn't going to make the slightest scrap of difference. He would probably be fired, with or without Fratton's support. Bayer found a blanket and draped it carefully over his sleeping colleague whilst silently praying to the distantly forsaken Lord above that he didn't wake him in the process.

Bayer had been about to leave the apartment when he'd seen Fratton's gun. He disliked guns, always had done. He was a junior analyst, specialising in Russian politics and almost by definition, corruption. He had no use for guns and so subsequently, following his somewhat tortuous return to London and a debriefing which had lasted days and in which he'd been called upon to explain his actions almost hourly, Bayer had struggled to explain exactly why he'd taken the weapon. Perhaps it was, he'd insisted rather desperately to the three men in their brown brogues and matching ivory turn ups, that it had simply felt like the right thing to do under the circumstances. The sort of thing Fratton would have done.

With the Browning tucked in his heavy jacket pocket, Marcus Bayer left the apartment and climbed into the clapped-out yellow Mitsubishi The Service had so reluctantly supplied. In the distance, sat at a green traffic light, a set of twinkling red brake lights. He'd been right. The man in the Mercedes with the fedora hat and expensive taste in cigarettes was waiting for him. Buoyed up by nothing more than the reaching of a decision, he crunched the car into gear and pulled out.

Almost immediately Bayer began to doubt himself. *Follow procedure. Log the exit. Send a flash message if you really think it warrants it, but never break from protocol.* But then the man he'd decided to follow was deviating from his own routine, and hadn't John Alperton said that that was just one of the many things they should be on the lookout for? He should be praised for using his initiative, shouldn't he?

In all likelihood the man was just popping out for a fresh supply of cigarettes and Bayer would be heading back soon, colder, but none the wiser and hopefully in time to avoid any awkward conversations with Fratton. He was an odd little man, the man they had been tasked to observe. Seventy years old, short and round like a bear, thinning on top, moon rim glasses and a nicotine addiction the likes of which Bayer, as a non-smoker, had seldom witnessed. He looked up towards the end of the road as the two small dots of the car's brakes flickered before turning out of sight.

They drove for almost an hour, Bayer and the man he was following, weaving through the Khamovniki district of Moscow, and, Bayer realised to his disappointment, passing any number of late-night garages where, if the man he was following had been looking for cigarettes, he could easily have stopped and purchased them. Then they joined the Leninskiy Prospekt, leaving the city limits altogether and Bayer was forced to drop back as the Russian led them into the countryside. In spite of himself, as the endless flats and warehouses of the city dropped away to be replaced by tortured winter trees and rolling oceans of barren white fields, Bayer began to relax.

Then, for one terrible moment, he thought he'd lost him, immediately wondering again how he would explain his absence, first to the ever-dependable Fratton, then to their superiors. But, as the country lane they'd turned onto petered out unexpectedly, coming to an abrupt and unsatisfactory end and Bayer had been on the point of turning back to face the honourable Tom Fratton and pretend nothing had happened, two bright beaming headlights flicked on. They were trained directly at him and not far away. This wasn't what Bayer had been expecting at all. He brought the Mitsubishi to a halt as the other car's headlights flashed again, momentarily bathing the interior of his car in harsh electric light.

'This is not good,' he remarked to the empty car, acutely aware of his own inadequacies and eager in some small way to shift any blame for his actions. 'What the hell do I do now?' As if to answer his question the other car's headlights flashed for a third time.

Bayer was certainly not supposed to be in the company of the man they had been sent to observe, but then he had to assume, the man in the car opposite should not have been there either.

He flicked the stalk next to the steering wheel forward once before allowing it to quickly snap back into place. There was another pause whilst Bayer considered his position and then the door of the sleek black Mercedes opposite opened and the short, round man from Moscow's Khamovniki district eased himself out. Marcus Bayer watched as he halted, reaching back to withdraw his hat, before pulling it down, covering his eyes. He straightened his glasses and took a fresh packet of cigarettes from his jacket.

Cautiously Bayer opened the Mitsubishi's door and stepped into the freezing night air, glad to be out of the city but simultaneously wishing he'd brought a hat and scarf of his own. The other man, who had been walking slowly yet purposefully toward him, stopped halfway between the two cars. And then, without warning or ceremony, it began to snow. Large, heavy flakes, glistening in the car's headlights. When Bayer was about ten feet away, the other man spoke and Bayer suddenly realised that, whilst he and Fratton had been watching him for weeks, this was the first time he'd ever heard his true voice, uncorrupted by microphones or listening devices.

'Follow me.' Said as an order, not as a suggestion. But Bayer didn't need to be told they were fighting the clock. The Russian with the impeccable English and the disposable smile spun on his heel and led him away from the cars and the snow.

Ahead, out of the gloom, like a ship rising up unexpectedly in the night, a railway track, cutting east and long disused, divorced from the surrounding countryside, a relic of the man in the fedora's unhappy past. Neither spoke as Bayer followed the Russian, their feet the only sound in the soft, damp grass, until that too gave out and was replaced by the brittle crackle of gravel. They stood in the colossal shadow of the railway embankment. The Russian produced a flashlight from his jacket pocket and played its enquiring beam along the face of the escarpment. The beam bounced around merrily for a moment before being swallowed up by the entrance to a vast shaft running beneath the railway.

'Follow me.'

And then they were standing in the relative dry of a service tunnel and the short, stocky Russian turned to face him.

'Who the hell are you?'

'Bayer, Marcus Bayer.'

'Do you know who I am, Mr Bayer?'

'Aleksei Kadnikov, Deputy Director of the FSB,' Bayer replied, relieved to see the man standing in front of him nod his head, 'And you are Cheka.'

The Russian looked away, into the gloomy depths of the tunnel. 'And you, it would appear Mr Marcus Bayer of The Service, London, are a fool. Are you armed?'

'Why?'

From outside came the urgent crunch of gravel beneath feet indicating that they were no longer alone. Bayer turned back quickly towards the entrance to the tunnel as Kadnikov retreated deeper into its shadows. He struggled to release the Browning from the waistband of his jeans. A flashlight's blinding beam swept across his face and Bayer fired once. Then darkness and the deafening reverberations of a gunshot.

Kadnikov joined him and flicked open his zippo to light a fresh cigarette.

'What have you done?' he asked.

'You told me to defend myself.'

'*Nyet*. I told you I thought we had been followed, nothing more.'

The two men edged forward, toward the end of the tunnel. Illuminated by his own flashlight the face of a man Marcus Bayer knew all too well.

'It seems I was right,' Kadnikov said grimly. 'Try not to trouble yourself Mr Bayer. I will help you bury him. Dead men don't repent.'

✻✻✻

Wednesday, 4ᵗʰ March 2020 Kent.
In the United Kingdom coronavirus cases jump to 85.

'Sweetheart, have you seen my cufflinks?'

'Which ones?'

'Gold. Rectangular things. Have you seen them?'

'John, you're fussing. Please stop it,' Valerie Alperton said looking across the bed at her husband. 'They're there, by your side, where they always are.' She paused, allowing him his moment of discovery. 'I do wish you'd tell me what's going on.'

'Sorry, Val. No can do. The children will be here though, won't they?'

'Yes, John,' she replied, marvelling at him. They hadn't been children for years. 'Richard's getting a train down from London. I haven't heard from Steven, but he'll be here.'

'Good. I thought we might all go out tonight, together, like a family.'

'We are a family.'

'You know what I mean. Could you book a table? That French place in town's pretty decent.' By which he meant it employed a pretty decent wine merchant and if he was right about today he'd certainly be in need of a stiff drink later. 'I'll make sure I'm back by five or so and then we can go out.'

'Like a family?'

'Very funny,' he replied, slipping on his suit jacket.

'This had better be good John, whatever it is? I shall have to cancel my class.'

'We'll see,' Sir John Alperton said, forcing a smile.

He pushed the delicate gold rectangles through his shirt cuff. He was going to have to impart. Throughout his career in The Service there'd been little he'd felt able to share. Valerie had been understanding. She'd been kept appraised of carefully selected bits and bobs. His children had never known nor cared for his work. He'd often disappeared on a train into London long before they'd been awake and returned exhausted long after they were asleep. The absent father who was always there. His job, whatever it might have been, merely the cause of his abstraction, to be bemoaned and questioned for no other reason than its perceived complicity in his absence.

Valerie had for years been excluded from much of his career, but today, even though she didn't realise it yet, through necessity, John Alperton's job would be thrown centre stage and under the spotlight, to be subjected to the media's full pernicious scrutiny and all in the good name of The Service.

He'd been a member of The Service since its halcyon, men-only, smoke-filled-room days when records had been kept exclusively with paper and pen, agents had come predominantly from one of two universities and political ideology and not religion had been the prevailing enemy. British assets had been expected to behave like gentlemen, come from a certain social stock, and dress and speak accordingly. Now, with the relentless rise of social media and the endless glut of reality television shows and talent contests, all of that seemed a dim and distant memory. Anyone in a pair of jeans with a second-rate degree from an erstwhile polytechnic could and *had* to be considered for a job, Alperton reflected. The Service had even taken to placing adverts in the Jobs Column of The Evening Standard.

But this news, the news he'd been summoned to receive, this was news he could not rationally be expected to keep from them. There was every chance he would be in the papers. There might be photographers, perhaps even television interviews to be negotiated. Valerie, for her part, would dab away a tear from the corner of her eye and try to ignore the years of lies and infidelities as she told them just how proud she was of her husband. This morning was set to be an odd affair though, of that Alperton had no doubt. It had long been a commonly held belief around the water cooler that if and when Tobias Gray were ever to step down from the top job, Alperton would be his natural successor. And then Gray had gone and done the unthinkable and The Service's slow, clunking wheels of change had begun to grind inexorably to their own conclusion.

However, with the day of his long-awaited inauguration at hand, Sir John Alperton felt no joy, no pride. He would say and do all the right things, make all the right noises, but this day, this day which he had imagined for so many years, he already knew would be tainted. Things were not always as they appeared to be. He understood that better than most.

Alperton stood in front of the full-length mirror in their hallway and shot the waterfall cuffs, ensuring the requisite amount of shirt protrude. He straightened his tie, ran his hand over his hair, checked the polish of his shoes and, pleased with what he saw and having already pecked Valerie awkwardly on the cheek, selected an umbrella and set off on the ten-minute walk to the train station.

Whoever had booked the restaurant backing onto The Strand for their little gathering had unusually fine taste. Sir John had eaten there once before. He vividly recalled the roasted oysters and aged prime rib. If he remembered correctly, there was a rather exclusive bar downstairs where they might mingle, conducting blundering small talk before retiring upstairs to the restaurant's private function room and dining area.

A short invigorating clip over the bridge from Waterloo Station and he was handing his umbrella and overcoat to a demure young lady in a smart black and white uniform who proceeded to show him inside. A glass of champagne clamped in his hand he reluctantly discovered the only other person of his acquaintance to be Patricia Hedley-King, resembling a sack of potatoes in a woollen outfit secured around the waist with an outlandish belt which confounded even Sir John's usually keen sartorial eye.

'Pat,' he said amiably, gesturing to their surroundings as they moved away from the bar, 'This is all rather jolly. Your idea, I presume?'

'No, actually, although I wholeheartedly approve. I'm rather looking forward to this, aren't you?' she asked, shamefully. Alperton fought the overwhelming instinct to put her straight. He'd rarely heard King so enthusiastic, but today he understood her zeal, even if he was struggling to appreciate it. 'I think this is all going to be rather wonderful,' she continued to gush.

'And how are you, how's the house?' he asked, eager to drive the conversation on. 'Have they given you a date to move back in yet?'

'I'm fine thanks, just a few cuts and bruises. That bitch Gray sent to kill me, well it seems the bomb was badly made, not enough potassium nitrate, so they tell me. Anyway, I was lucky. As for the house, we'll see. To my untrained eye it all looks pretty devastating, but the insurance company, having been paid their pound of flesh for I couldn't tell you how many years, have taken it upon themselves to suddenly behave like the complete pack of arseholes I always suspected they were.' She paused long enough to take a drink of champagne and scour the room for more service. Sir John shuffled, uncomfortable at her forthrightness. 'Aside from that, things couldn't be better. A little fraught along the river at the moment. Everyone crapping themselves about some bloody virus which has come over from China. Mark my words, John, it'll never amount to anything. Never does. Be a distant memory by the summer. Do you suppose we're allowed to smoke?' she continued, producing a packet of cigarettes and a cheap plastic lighter.

'I highly doubt it,' Alperton replied, watching King throw her gaze skyward like a petulant teenager whilst replacing the redundant packet. 'Whilst it's always a delight to see you, shall we crack on?' Alperton asked loudly, watching more people arrive and catching sight of a clock out of the corner of his eye.

'We're not all here yet,' she replied, 'You shall have to wait.' And then King moved off leaving Alperton to watch as a door opens at the rear of the restaurant they'd requisitioned and a persecuted figure is noisily ushered in. Sandy Harper pushed a hand through his yellowing hair before glancing around the room in an effort to find his bearings. One of life's perennial overachievers but now with everything gone, the money, the house, the wife, his kids. Utterly out of place in such splendid surroundings too, picking at his scabby cardigan, his head roving languorously from side to side like a shoddily conceived wooden puppet.

Alperton watched Harper dispassionately, surprised he'd been invited until, finally, Harper returns his stare. His head stops moving and, with a rather dejected look he raises a hand, not in greeting but in simple acknowledgement. So, you're here too, it said. Had there ever been a time, Alperton wondered, when they'd got along? Perhaps, on the surface, to a complete outsider, they might have appeared to have had much in common, but, beneath it all, beneath the tailored jackets, the lunches at Lords and the accounts at Coutts, they were as different as different could be. Sandy had been born to it. He was, or had been Alperton reflected, old money. Somewhere in his ancestry there had been barons and baronesses. Alperton had always suspected his name and possibly even his family's inherited fortunes had bought him a place at Oxbridge. He, on the other hand, had battled for his education. The old man had looked quite horrified when he'd suggested university instead of following in his footsteps, taking on the family business and working intolerable hours at Billingsgate market. His father's exacting overbearingness merely serving to cement John Alperton's conviction that he shake off his working-class shackles at any cost. A degree in

French, seen by his father as utterly pointless, and his induction into The Service had followed. A job he could only ever refer to obliquely at best. George Wiseman had become his guru and someone to emulate.

Whilst Harper had felt instantly on an equal footing with the ageing spymaster, unintimidated and unimpressed by the old Jew, Alperton had respected and revered him, stopping just short of christening him a father figure. Whilst Harper had poured scorn on Wiseman's easy acceptance of all things American, had belittled his Hollywood persona and ridiculed his interests in baseball and the politics of The Hill, Alperton had embraced his mentor's passion for travel. Harper was a little Englander, reassuring himself with a pink empire upon which the sun never set, whilst Alperton and Wiseman had both seen the writing on the wall and were eager to forge new partnerships and build, what had long been considered by many, unbuildable bridges.

The irony, Alperton was quick to acknowledge, was that Sandy Harper, the old money conservative with the Bullingdon Club sensibility and permanently on the waiting list at the MCC was, in a world of fraudsters and fakes, the biggest fake of the lot. The money might have been old, there might even have been a title somewhere, but he'd never been invited to the Bullingdon Club, never become a member at Lords. He was a bag of contradictions in a world that was fast moving towards the horizon, leaving Sandy Harper fiddling with the brim of his panama, skating round bankruptcy and mounting gambling debts which were slowly eating their way through the last of his dwindling investments, shaking his head and rueing a broken marriage. Alperton looked at him now, a genuine fake and he hated him for it. In their imperfect world, a world of mendacity, of cheats and liars, not one person's duplicity offended Sir John Alperton quite so much as Sandy Harper's. For, when all was said and done, he was an imposter, completely lacking in any shred of honour or integrity and that terrified Sir John more than he cared to admit because he knew it could so easily have been him.

'Good afternoon,' Harper said, stretching out a hand.

'Sandy. How's life on the other side of the river?'

Harper decided not to rise to the bait, instead electing to change the subject.

'What's going on then?' he asked, throwing an empty hand at the room, 'Any ideas?'

'I have, as a matter of fact. Slightly surprised they've dragged you in to pay witness, but then I suppose the free lunch will be welcome,' and all said with a laugh and a smile and a flurry of reassuring hand gestures.

Harper shook his head and took a glass from the passing waiter.

'Are you going to tell me or would you rather we talk about Toby Gray?' he asked tiredly.

Alperton pulled theatrically at his suit's lapels. 'It's my understanding,' he commenced, 'that as of today I'm to be given total control of The Service.' When Harper failed to respond Alperton seized the opportunity to press home his advantage and deal with the secondary issue. 'As for Gray, I hardly think this is the time or the place to be raking over old ground,' he continued decisively. 'What's done is done. Can't say I wasn't more than a little surprised by David Hunter's handling of the whole situation, but then he always has had a rather unconventional approach.'

'Did you know?' Harper asked, clearly anticipating the answer.

Alperton nodded. 'I'd known for some time that Gray was in touch with the Russian. George clearly thought it best I handle the situation, do you see?'

Harper had to stop himself from laughing. 'Well, you didn't handle it as well as all that, if you'll forgive me for saying? To the best of my recollection we just stood there and watched him walk away.' He waited for Alperton to finish shaking his head. 'That day, in Bermondsey, at The Gate,' Harper said, forcing himself to recall his previous master's unforeseen betrayal and treachery. 'Were you armed?'

'Don't be so vulgar.'

'Gentlemen, there's someone I would rather like for you to meet.' Patricia Hedley-King has returned to Alperton's relief he was astonished to discover and is encouraging a woman in a smart business suit and some thirty years his junior to join them. He scrutinized her face carefully before looking questioningly at Sandy Harper, who appeared equally in the dark.

'This is Miranda Davenport,' Hedley-King cooed proudly.

'Delighted to meet you, Miss Davenport,' Alperton said, extending a hand with Harper barely out of the stalls.

11

'She will be taking over, after Tobias Gray's... since he left quite so suddenly.'

Alperton shot a look at Sandy and then to the smiling Hedley-King, and then finally at Miranda Davenport.

'This is Sir John Alperton,' Hedley-King put in quickly before either man could speak, and with a little more emphasis on Alperton's title than was necessary.

Alperton straightened his back and puffed out his chest. Harper's head swayed uncertainly on his shoulders. Both men prepared for her cardinal utterance, impressions already made.

'Sir John.' A soft, reasonable home counties lilt. 'To say that your reputation precedes you would be something of an understatement,' she continued, her hand still in his.

'You'll forgive me if I don't return the sentiment. Patricia, just what the hell is going on? Who is this young woman? I've never heard of her, and you're telling me she is going to be...' But John Alperton has run out of steam and words.

'Taking over,' Headley-King added helpfully.

'Taking over?! Is this some sort of joke?' Alperton spat, regaining his composure. He looked at Harper. 'Sandy, this is a bloody conspiracy. A poor publicity stunt aimed at redressing the balance in some misguided way I can only assume?' After all, they'd been down this path once before, or tried to, with the appointment of Angela Chisholm and that, Alperton was forced to reflect more than a trifle imperiously, had not ended well. Chisholm, rising star of the sisterhood, last seen boarding a train to Vienna, passport in one hand, a list of every Service operative east of Smolensk in the other, never to darken their door again.

He turned on King, Davenport conveniently forgotten. 'How dare you. How bloody dare you,' he hissed.

'I was warned that you might be a little... resistant to my appointment, Sir John,' Davenport said, relinquishing his hand, 'but I do hope we can find a way to work together, going forward,' she continued before moving on to Sandy Harper and abandoning Alperton like a spurned lover.

'Ah, it's Mr Harper, isn't it? I'm ashamed to say I haven't found the time to read your file quite yet, but rest assured, I shall.'

'And are we to be permitted to know anything about you, Miss Davenport?' Alperton snapped.

'Certainly, Sir John,' she replied, playing her part for all it's worth. 'For one thing, I'm married, so you may call me Mrs Davenport.'

Alperton and Harper stared at her, the former in slack jawed amazement, the latter with a smile of begrudging admiration.

'Is that it?' Sir John asked, catching his breath whilst Pat Hedley-King continues to smirk wildly.

'Yes. Yes, I believe it is,' Mrs Miranda Davenport concluded. 'Sir John, if I may be permitted a moment of your time? Although I think you may prefer it if we continue this conversation in private.'

Alperton glanced at Sandy Harper for any fraternal support he may choose to offer but Harper and Hedley-King have already moved off, deep in conversation with King doing most of the talking whilst Sandy Harper continues to shake his head. Davenport took Alperton by the elbow as she might her own father and steered him into the centre of the room.

'May I suggest you take a vacation, Sir John?' she offered kindly, her head on one side as if talking to someone else.

'By vacation I can only assume you mean holiday?' Alperton rasped.

'Have it your own way. Take some time off. Talk to your wife. You have a family I understand. Why not talk to them too? Work out just how much you want to be here and how much you want to return from your holiday.' She sipped unhurriedly from her glass. 'I hope you don't mind, Sir John, but I took the liberty of reading your file.'

'I should bloody well hope so too,' he retorted.

'And I'm only too aware of the set of circumstances,' she gave a mildly embarrassed smile, 'which led to my appointment.' John Alperton looked about to cut in, but Davenport beat him to the punch. 'I don't believe in mincing my words John, so you'll forgive me if I say, I know you had your eye on this job, and I understand how pissed off you must be.' Davenport checked herself, perhaps surprised by her own vulgarity. 'So, take some time.' This last is said not as a suggestion or a request, but as a flat, unequivocal statement.

'Am I being suspended?' Alperton gasped, aware that a small group of co-workers have gathered and are pretending not to listen to their conversation.

'I don't know. Do you think that will be necessary?' Davenport didn't wait for an answer, perhaps also aware that there are people hanging on her every word. 'Get your head around my appointment first,' she said laughing gaily, 'and come back with your batteries recharged, refreshed and raring to go.'

'Raring to go?'

'Unless you'd rather not, of course?'

Alperton decided to skip over Davenport's last remark and endeavoured to take a new tack.

'And Scott Hunter, David's boy, what's to become of him?'

'I don't know David Hunter, never met him, but his son interests me. He's young and intelligent, I'm told. I feel no need to punish him for Michael Healy's failings?'

'Healy's failings?'

The group, which had stopped to listen, turn to one another in shocked silence.

'Yes. I've reviewed his file too. Michael has had a fine career, that goes without saying, but as of late has overseen some sloppy work, I think you'd have to agree?'

'I most certainly would not.'

'I shall be suggesting he hand in his resignation before the end of the day and hope he does not compel me to more drastic measures.'

'Good God, woman, there won't be a department left,' Alperton bellowed.

'Pat and I are only too aware of that.'

'Pat and I? What the hell is this, some unholy cabal of bloody feminists determined to restructure The Service from the inside out? I won't have it. If you're intent on sacking Michael Healy, well you can jolly well sack me too. In fact, I'll spare you the trouble. You'll have my resignation on your desk first thing tomorrow morning.'

'As you will,' Davenport replied calmly, aware that, with this latest revelation, the small group of onlookers has suddenly dispersed. 'Shall you be present when HR clear out your office?'

Another waiter, carrying another silver salver weighed down with champagne flutes passed between them and Davenport firmly yet politely declined his offer of a drink. Alperton called back the lad in the black waistcoat and matching bow tie and helped himself to glass. It's probably too late to phone Valerie and suggest she cancel their table for the evening.

Davenport smiled an executioner's smile, amazed at quite how successful her meeting with the infamous Sir John has been and moved off to speak with Sandy Harper, leaving Alperton to lick his wounds. The knight of the realm nursed his glass, looking around defiantly whilst determinedly failing to catch anyone's eye and steadied himself. Pat Hedley-King watched on from her vantage point on the opposite side of the room. She almost felt sorry for him. Almost.

✳✳✳

After Gray's departure, Sandy Harper had found himself in a somewhat invidious position. He'd been boxed in, subject of an unkind draw and in danger of being brought down early, when, quite unexpectedly, Patricia Hedley-King had called. He'd seized upon the opportunity to remain a member of their inherently flawed yet highly influential inner circle. There was to be a meeting, she'd said. It wouldn't take long, she'd said. He'd put his plans for the day on hold. The pub and the bookies at the end of the road could wait. In truth, Harper had been delighted to close the door on the tiny two bed flat in Forest Hill he'd been forced to rent since the divorce and make his way across the river. Now he was being courted by The Service's newest and most controversial appointment for many a year and so far he was enjoying what he was hearing.

'Mr Harper,' Davenport began, 'it appears we share a common problem, going forward. John has just announced his intentions to leave us, as I'm sure you will have heard.'

He had heard, and from the horse's mouth no less. Alperton, the bane of his professional life, to quit on a point of honour, naturally. Sir John, with his flair for the puritanical, had resigned and in such a public and unforeseen fashion that even Harper, the inveterate gambler, would never have predicted. Well good riddance to bad rubbish. 'Damned awkward timing for us of course,' Davenport continued, 'but it can't be helped I suppose. I did wonder if, in his absence, we might take the opportunity to join forces?'

Harper drew himself up to his full height and tugged at his cardigan.

'I'd like you to put a team together,' she said. 'You'll be answerable to me, naturally.'

'Naturally,' Harper interjected, too hastily.

'Use young Hunter. I hear good things and I'd like to see what he's capable of.'

Harper briefly considered voicing his concerns about Scott Hunter, but there had been something quite unambiguous in this new woman's tone and it was simply too soon to be rocking the boat. He'd take the opportunity to work on Hunter a little. It might be fun to push the novice around for a while, and if their relationship took a turn for the worse he could always go to Davenport and explain that he'd tried, really tried, but that Scott Hunter, like his father before him, hadn't been up to it and so should, reluctantly, under the circumstances and in everyone's best interests, be let go. With Alperton and Healy already out of the running, the field was definitely opening up, leaving plenty of room for Sandy Harper, no longer the outsider, to seize his position by the rail and make his move. He nodded his assent and looked to Davenport for her next instruction.

'Pat's just been bending my ear about Oleg Lobanov.'

'Russian billionaire. Owner of some of the most expensive real estate Europe has to offer,' Harper trots out obligingly.

'And British citizen, yes. I'd like you to look into this recent influx of Russians. Where's their money coming from exactly and, perhaps more importantly, where is it winding up? Everyone seems to agree that there's little or no point in going after Lobanov himself, he's pretty much untouchable even by the Home Office, but we were wondering if you might not have a nosey round Dmitry Patzuk.'

'And he is?'

'Oleg's shadier partner. A lot less slick than his boss and generally seen as something of a blunt instrument. A who's who please. Usual data. See what Hunter can find on him and keep me up to speed with where it takes you. You'll be aware I'm sure that the Home Office haven't been exactly ecstatic with the background checks performed on some of our most recent arrivals, so if you were to stumble upon a reason, however small, that Mr Lobanov lose his British citizenship, that might well be viewed as an added bonus in the current climate.'

Harper nodded. He was aware there'd been a colossal shitstorm round the corner in Whitehall. Articles were appearing in the papers, which no one liked, and then questions had been asked across The House, which was a massive pain in the arse for all concerned and could almost certainly have been making the new girl's start in life unnecessarily complicated.

'How would you like us to proceed?'

'Intelligence gathering please. Once we've got something concrete, I'll push it on and under the noses of our cousins up the road and then hopefully, providing you've done your job of course, they'll leave us alone for a while to get on with more pressing matters.' Davenport paused dramatically but wasn't quite done. 'We'll leave the dirty work to them for a change, shall we?'

She flashed Harper a conspiratorial smile. If he were to be brutally honest he'd never really expected to replace Gray, but then John Alperton had been passed over. That would take a little while to come to terms with, like a big win on a rank outsider. A female boss was certainly disquieting, but he was warming to her and all the signs were that things might be swinging in his favour. Davenport appeared well spoken and intelligent. Perhaps she could be made to tow his ragged line? She was suggesting digging dirt on the Russians whilst at the same time keeping The Service's hands squeaky clean. Well, nothing would give him more pleasure. For years Russia had been Harper's sworn enemy until quite suddenly, following the pillaging of their own country for its natural resources, they were being welcomed into the fold with open arms. A state of play he had never condoned. Yes, Sandy Harper's life was beginning to look a little rosier. He thoroughly approved of everything he'd seen of his new boss thus far. Get those pencil pushers at the Home Office to do the dirty work, how fabulous. He'd happily follow her suggestion and stick David Hunter's boy to the task. If the papers were still sniffing around and everything looked in danger of turning to shit, he'd gladly throw them Scott Hunter.

'Now, I wouldn't want you feeling unable to investigate *every* aspect of our friends out of the East.'

Davenport looked away, suddenly fussing with the tiny clutch bag which dangled from her shoulder.

'Every aspect?' Harper asked.

'Yes. Look, Sir John has been a dedicated servant of The Service for years now, as I hardly need remind you. He has, in that time, been involved in countless operations. Consequently, it isn't inconceivable, you would have to agree, that during your investigations his name may well crop up.' She looked hard at Sandy Harper to make sure she was being understood. 'Whilst I'm not suggesting for one second that he would ever have done so deliberately, there is always the possibility that an action of his, unintentional I'm quite sure, might not show him in the most flattering light. And let us suppose that evidence of such a nature were to float across your desk, I wouldn't want you to feel, because of your previous position and friendship, that you were in any way... conflicted.'

Conflicted? What was she suggesting?

'I hope we understand one another. It might be better, for the sake of The Service, if this investigation not cause too many ripples.' Davenport's smile might have led a lesser man to doubt himself. 'John's had a good run and although he's seen fit to prematurely call an end to his career, I see no reason to make his departure any more,' she thought on the next word carefully, 'traumatic than it needs be. So, report directly to me if you wouldn't mind, particularly anything of a sensitive nature, and we can spare the good Sir John his blushes, do you see?'

Sandy Harper did see. He thought he saw extremely well.

'If you decide to use Hunter, impress upon him the importance of his discretion. I don't want him running off bothering his old boss unnecessarily.'

'Of course.'

'And we shall hope that Sir John's reputation, along with your own naturally, remains as unblemished and pure as the driven snow, as I'm certain it shall.' She shot him that smile again. 'Dear me, Mr Harper, I have kept you far longer than I intended. Shall we make our way upstairs? I hear the seared scallops with Serrano ham are simply to die for.'

✳✳✳

Later the same day, Bermondsey SE1

Following Tobias Gray's ignominious midnight flit, Sir John Alperton had hauled Hunter over the coals. *I can't say I'm not disappointed, and Michael had such high hopes for you too, but it seems that, when the chips, as our American cousins are so fond of saying, are down, you don't produce the goods. If it weren't for your father, I'd have had nothing more to do with you.*

He'd tried to plead his case, but all explanations had fallen on deaf ears. Alperton had shaken his head and stared moodily at his gleaming toecaps leaving Hunter with the distinct impression he was living on borrowed time and were it not for the fact that Sir John seemed destined to finally secure the position he'd so brazenly coveted, Hunter would have been out on his ear. Alperton, for his part, had left him dangling. Hunter still had the flat in Harrow and money periodically appeared in his account, but he felt he had taken many a retrograde step. None of his sizeable collection of mobile phones rang and no texts were received from Sir John or Michael Healy, and so Hunter returned to the quasi-monastic life he'd been living before his adventures in Hong Kong.

Initially he'd brooded, unsure as to his future. Then there'd followed an intense period of internalization, angry frustration and long sleepless nights in front of the television. The only silver lining, suddenly with time to spare, an incipient relationship with his father. After a brief bout of shadow-boxing they'd slipped into a comfortable routine with Scott spending his Sundays in the sleepy little village of Sarratt, often arriving before his father returned from his morning walk. He'd let himself in with the spare set of keys David kept under a pot of geraniums, sit with a fresh cafetière of coffee and wait. If the sun was up, he'd take a walk around his father's garden. Even though Scott had little interest in shrubs or flowerbeds, he made the effort to spot a new plant or hanging basket aware they might prove useful topics of conversation later. Bandages for the years of misunderstandings and mistrust. Added to which the contents of David Hunter's borders were about as far removed from Michael Healy or Sir John Alperton as Hunter cared to imagine.

Once his father returned, they would sit together and drink coffee whilst determinedly refusing to discuss The Service or anything to do with it, killing time until The Boot at the bottom of the lane opened and they could wash down a Sunday roast with a couple of pints. Scott was delighted to see that every week his father was in ruder health and higher spirits than before. It appeared the morning walks really were doing him good, although Scott couldn't help but feel there was something else. Recently, when he'd phoned on a Saturday evening to make sure their arrangement still held, his father had been unavailable. Then, when Scott had asked where he'd been, his father had fobbed him off.

Scott wondered if he'd strolled down to the pub but was too embarrassed to admit he'd been drinking alone.

And then, just as his life without The Service was settling down and totally out of the blue, he'd received a text from the most unexpected of sources. *Your Uncle Archie would like to buy you a drink sometime in The Gate and have a little chat. Topic of conversation, unspecified.* For *Uncle Archie* read Sandy Harper. For *sometime* read get your arse down here immediately and your feet had better not touch the bloody floor.

Walking from the station Hunter passed Michael Healy sat in his black Audi, deep in conversation, his ear clamped to a mobile phone. Hunter was surprised not to be acknowledged. As a rule, Healy was alive to every sound and movement. Hunter could only assume that his normally laconic mentor would be joining them once his call had finished.

He crossed the road to the pub's curved front doors, anticipating the first person he would see. Hunter tried to prepare himself for the encounter. This, he acknowledged, was going to be awkward. The last time he'd seen the landlord of The Service's public house of choice Hunter had unceremoniously booted him, his trousers around his ankles, into a collection of old cardboard boxes and empty bottles. It was unreasonable, he supposed, to now expect anything other than the frostiest of receptions.

As he pulled open the door Hunter shot Healy one final glance, but his mentor seemed quietly determined not to return his approach, perhaps as disappointed in him as Alperton had been? At the bar, the rangy blond figure of Sandy Harper, striving to unravel the mysteries of the universe from the bottom of what Hunter had to assume was a not insignificant gin and tonic. His face a middle-aged outpouring of nasal hair and ruptured arteries. An injurious turkey's neck nature's cruel reward for observing the rest of humanity down his nose. A lifetime of barely concealed snobbery and condescension. Sandy Harper, the almost man. Rarely invited, never thanked or promoted and always just one bet away from redemption. Harper hated The Traitors Gate, its obsession with football, its cheeky chappie, salt of the earth culture, its dropped consonants and its devil-may-care attitude towards punctuation. The Gate, as he would insist upon calling it, was tawdry and bellicose in equal measure and represented everything Harper despised about the un-aspirational working classes. Behind Harper, Shoeshine Ian, whose immediate reaction upon seeing a fresh customer was a broad Pavlovian smile of greeting followed by the briefest flicker of recognition. Then Shoeshine's cheery South London demeanour settled as quickly as a flat pint. He glared at Hunter across the bar and Scott looked to Sandy, the least likely of allies, for his support.

'Hello, Unc.,' Hunter opened, badly misjudging the room. Harper, returning from any secrets his drink may have held and only barely managing to restrain his eyes from raising to the ceiling, gestured for Hunter to join him. Hunter looked expectantly between boss and bartender but neither seemed inclined to offer him a drink.

'Why don't we take a seat?' Harper said, indicating a disreputable looking table by a long stretch of worn-out pews. A despicable setting for a despicable clientele. Hunter drew back a chair whilst Sandy Harper slumped wearily into the thinly cushioned pew. An unsure man, uncertain of his place and position and possessing all the worries and anxieties of a small child but wearing the anaemic disguise of forty years of coping mechanisms.

'Let's get one thing absolutely straight right from the off, Mr Hunter. I don't care for you. I never thought that much of your father either as it happens, unlike some who clearly thought the sun shone from his base fundament. You have been foisted upon me, like a bastard foster child. You are clearly unready for work in the field...'

Hunter opened his mouth to object.

'As was made abundantly clear from your handling of...' Hunter watched as Sandy Harper struggled to ejaculate the name, 'Tobias Gray.'

Was there any point in trying to correct him, Hunter wondered, to try and expound upon the nuances his father had explained to him? Was there any sense in trying to point out that he too had been shocked by the decision to allow Gray to walk free? Almost certainly, from what he had witnessed of Sandy Harper to this point, not. Hunter frowned, pushed at a vacant beer mat which might have born his drink but didn't and elected to take it on the chin. His silence was long enough for Harper to launch into another scathing attack on his juvenile career.

'Sadly,' he continued, 'the decision to keep you on or not wasn't mine for the taking.' Harper sipped distractedly at his G&T whilst Hunter sat patiently, like a child waiting to be caned. 'So, as you are regrettably under my jurisdiction, I suggest we begin afresh and see just what can be salvaged. They tell me you're bright, for a Tab, and that you show possible aptitude in both cryptology and analysis.'

Suddenly Hunter was liking what he was hearing.

'I propose we take a stroll up to the archives on floor four. I'll introduce you to Julian Palgrave. I would get Michael to do it but sadly, after your most recent escapade, we will no longer be able to call upon his services.'

'I beg your pardon,' Hunter asked, genuinely confused.

'Oh, have you not heard? Michael Healy resigned, about thirty minutes ago actually.'

'What?'

'Have you gone deaf, Hunter? Healy handed in his notice. There's a new boss in town and she wasn't too chuffed at what she found when she read through his file. No thanks to you, I might add. So, John Alperton's last task was to ask Healy to resign and save him the embarrassment of being pushed. You and your sanctimonious father can add that to the long list of your achievements. Personally, I'm amazed she let him go and not you, but that's just life I suppose.'

'What about Alperton?' Hunter asked.

'What about him?'

'You said, "his *last* task".'

'Oh, Sir John, God help us all, has seen fit to hang up his boots as well and so you are to report directly to me,' Harper said, having the good sense to allow time for Hunter to think on it before continuing. 'I would like you to find out everything there is to know about the increasing number of Russian criminals seeking safe haven in the United Kingdom. In particular one Oleg Lobanov.'

'The mafia boss?'

'I think he prefers to see himself as a philanthropist and entrepreneur, but yes, I believe we are talking about the same individual. It's been suggested to me from upon high that you save yourself the bother of actually investigating Lobanov himself and instead concentrate on his number two, Dmitry Patzuk. Who is he? Where's he come from and where is he going? Etcetera etcetera.'

'Why?'

Sandy Harper slowly closed his eyes and when he finally reopened them seemed disappointed by Hunter's continued presence.

'It's part of a much wider on-going investigation into foreign nationals, predominantly Russian, with, shall we say, somewhat dubious credentials, coming into the country and exerting their influence where it is not wanted. I would like you to look into Dmitry Patzuk. He's a particularly unpleasant individual who seems to be operating here without a care in the world.'

'Do you want something on him?'

Harper let out a long sigh. 'Try not to be quite so uncouth, Hunter. Rest assured the Home Office will be well ahead of us in that regard.'

'Why am I compiling a file then?'

'Just do as you're told please. Find out, put it in a dossier, have it on my desk as soon as you like. Don't ask fatuous questions.'

'How long do I have, or is that a fatuous question?'

Harper closed his eyes again and spoke deliberately and plainly to himself.

'Just like the father. I expect it by the end of the week, Hunter. You will no doubt need help. To that end, I believe you've already met Samantha Fairchild?'

Right on cue, emerging from the corridor which ran along the back of the bar and, Hunter knew, to the basement below, the blond girl who had first drugged him and then almost blown him to pieces. He leapt from his seat.

'No,' he said, shaking his head furiously, 'absolutely not. No way. She nearly got me killed, not to mention trying to blow up my father.'

'Hey now! That's not fair!' the blond came back, 'I never did that.'

'But you would have done, if Bennet had told you to, you'd have done it, wouldn't you?'

Fairchild shrugged a silent maybe and fiddled distractedly with a hairpin.

'Sit down, Mr Hunter,' Harper snapped, as if addressing a recalcitrant dog, 'you are causing a scene.'

'Yeah, come on Scott,' the girl said, pulling up a chair on the opposite side of the table, 'or would you like me to get you a drink?' she laughed.

Reluctantly Hunter sat down, aware that several of the pub's patrons, not to mention its landlord were staring at them.

'What's she doing here?' he asked Harper, ignoring Fairchild.

'You'll be working together on the Russian project. It goes without saying that your discretion is paramount,' Harper continued, looking at Hunter. 'You are not to discuss this with anyone, previous employers, Michael Healy, even trusted family members. Do I make myself clear?' Hunter nodded. 'Good. I expect you will have seen Michael waiting outside?'

'Oh, great,' Fairchild put in unhelpfully, 'laughing boy's here is he?'

'Young lady,' Sandy started, intent on admonishing her, 'you are to have nothing to do with Michael Healy, do I make myself clear?'

'Okay! It was just a joke,' Fairchild replied looking to Hunter. 'I'll be very happy if I never see him again.'

'I should get to work immediately if I were you. I'm told, by greater powers than me,' Harper said, as if the mere idea of such a thing were an aberration, 'that should you both prove to be useful in some way, we may consider keeping you on. If it were down to me, which it isn't... well that's a different matter. Miss Fairchild, I take it you can be relied upon not to blow anything up?'

Fairchild replied with a withering look and Hunter was only surprised when she didn't stick out her tongue.

'You see, I can joke too,' Harper continued, the spiteful schoolmaster. 'Mr Hunter, you have considerably further to go to redeem yourself. So, girls and boys, off with you and play nicely together, otherwise...' Harper happily left the threat dangling, like a modern-day Dionysius. He rose the table, squeezed past the girl, leaving his glass for someone else to deal with.

'Oh, come on Scott,' Fairchild said, after an unhealthy silence, 'I didn't kill you.'

'That's not the point,' Hunter replied, getting to his feet, 'you tried to. Twice!'

'Where are you going? Don't you think we should sit down and talk this through?'

'No, I do not.'

'But we have to work together, Scotty. Come on?'

Hunter was at the doors now. 'I don't want to work with you. I'm going to speak to Healy and try and find out just what the hell's been going on.'

He left the pub and walked out into the muggy London air. Michael Healy remained seated in his car on the opposite side of the road, staring into the middle distance. Hunter tried the door. It opened and he sat down.

'What happened?' he asked.

'What do you mean, what happened? They let me go. Too many cock ups, too long in the tooth, take your pick.'

'But...'

'But nothing, Scott. It's the way The Service works so you better get used to it. Anyway, I shouldn't have to explain it to you, not with your family history.'

'What will it mean, for you?'

'Hand back the car, the phones. I suppose I should probably give this back,' Healy said patting his gun, 'and go and sign on. I really hadn't thought about it.'

Hunter could hardly believe what he was hearing and the idea of Healy signing on would have been comical had it not been quite so tragic.

'What do we do now?' Hunter asked.

'*We* don't do anything. You're to forget *we* ever met. Someone'll be sent to replace me, no doubt. Don't misunderstand me, you're going to be fine, Scott. You've the makings of a good agent with a good brain, but you're not there yet.'

Hunter knew that better than anyone. He'd been banking on Michael Healy's years of experience and caustic words of guidance to get him through. Now all he had was Sandy bloody Harper, who he didn't trust further than he could throw. No boss, no monosyllabic mentor and all the signs that any blame for The Service's latest self-implosion were being laid quite squarely at his door.

'What will you do?'

Healy ran his powerful hands over his face, where they came to rest, his thumbs under his chin, his hands covering his nose as if deep in prayer.

'Not sure. The Mrs is delighted of course, but we'll see how she feels about it once I've been under her feet for a week or two.'

'I'm so sorry,' Hunter said.

'Don't be. It happens. I expect Sandy's already put you on a fresh assignment,' Healy continued, eager to change the subject. Hunter was about to speak when Healy stopped him. 'Best you don't. Now, I'd offer you a lift but I have a feeling we're headed in very different directions.'

Healy fired up the Audi and gestured for Hunter to get out. No emotional farewells, no real speeches of any kind. Michael Healy, business-like to the bitter end.

***

1995 Royal Borough of Kensington and Chelsea.

George Wiseman walked up Lansdowne Terrace, weaving his weary way between the rusty bollards and trying to convince himself he'd done the right thing. Tobias Gray might not have been everybody's first choice to succeed him and he knew there were people who would point at his background whilst raising a cautionary eyebrow, but George had been forced to make a decision and so Gray it would be. He paused at the bottom of the twelve steps leading to number 23 and, as he had done for more years than he cared to remember, brushed back his long fawn Mackintosh, searching for his keys. It would be tough on John Alperton but he was pig-headed and obstinate enough, George had decided, to get along with or without his help. And it wasn't as though George was leaving The Service for good. He was simply moving onwards and upwards to a position where he might keep one eye on Gray, Alperton, Sandy Harper, David Hunter et al. But at the same time he was glad to be away from them and their insidious little world. He loved the notion that he would never run for another tube train or be late for another meeting ever again. The grand overseer, able now to contemplate his army of worker ants from on high, where time was as abstracted as his position, his sole responsibility the guardianship of his school of secrets. As long as his charges, even the ones he knew to have worrying leanings to the left, behaved themselves and continued to be as predictable as they ever had been, Wiseman's life ought to be an altogether simpler affair. After all, they'd all done things, he conceded, thinking about his wife. Sometimes under the weighty banner of politics and personal beliefs, sometimes in the name of love. Even his unimpeachable predecessor, Jack Forester, and his predecessor before him, all the way back to the honourable Percival Blackmore, linchpin and cornerstone of The Service, they had all done things. He was simply the next in a long line of secretive men who had been relied upon to make awkward and difficult decisions. Yes, there would be summons to Whitehall to explain his charges' behaviour every now and then but from now on his position was almost titular, little more than the figurehead of a chaotically skippered ship, the occasional mouthpiece or reluctant lobbyist for The Service. All of which aligned pleasingly well with his gentle easing into retirement. A time to write, meet new friends and old enemies at his club and enjoy long, sleepy afternoons in The Lord's Pavilion.

Because, for the first time in his long and illustrious career, George Wiseman was growing concerned. Concerned he had forgotten. Forgotten how to connect, to empathise with his fellow man. For although it might appear counter intuitive to the chap in the street, in the rich world of lies and dissemination he inhabited, the ability to commune with the people he worked with, and against, was paramount. Without this talent he was little more than a kite without a string, blowing fitfully in the wind and forever destined to a graceless and violent end. Wiseman had reluctantly admitted, if only to himself, that he was in danger of being consumed by the process, by the very machine he was so uniquely responsible for having created. He knew this to be true because he had witnessed it in others. Years of unquestioning devotion to The Service had stripped many acquaintances back to profound and emotionless husks. Wiseman was resolved to avoid such a fate both for himself, and for his family.

He inspected his door keys and scaled the dozen steps to the apartments. John Alperton would get over it. He and Sandy Harper were young enough to still be useful in the field. As to their obvious hatred of one another, they'd have to learn to rub along. Gray, by contrast, was calm to the point of indifference, but George was confident the others would follow him in spite of that.

Wiseman listened to the security door shut behind him and began looking for the other key, the key that would open their front door. He'd just found it when he heard the latch turn and Galia was standing in front of him, smiling.

'How was it?'

'It was fine, Gali' he said, kissing her gently on the cheek.

'Can you talk about it?' his wife asked, already knowing the answer. Wiseman smiled and took off his jacket. He knew she was only enquiring out of kindness and not because she expected to be told.

'Drink?' she asked, moving into their sparsely appointed sitting room and shooing away a lazy black and white cat.

'What have we got?'

'There's the end of a bottle of gin. I can see if we've some tonic somewhere?'

The real worry facing Wiseman wasn't the handing over of his department, nor the selection of his successor and his troubling yet potentially rewarding relationship with Aleksei Kadnikov of the KGB. Upon George's promotion fresh information had been revealed to him. Information, the existence of which had been hinted at throughout his time in The Service but never corroborated. Now he'd seen the evidence with his own eyes. There was no disputing the documents he'd been bequeathed in that nasty little pub in South London and which currently lingered perniciously in his briefcase. The question now would be, what the hell was to be done with them?

'Have we got any Scotch, Gali?'

His wife looked at him.

'Scotch, George? Oh, dear, it must have been bad.'

He smiled his smile again and regarded the empty space in front of the bay window overlooking Lansdowne Terrace.

'You know, I think I'll pick up a table tomorrow. Put it there, where the light's good.'

'George?'

'Do a spot of writing. What do you think?'

'Memoirs?' she teased.

'Perhaps,' he shrugged.

'Oh, George, it *must* have been bad,' she smiled, handing him his tumbler.

2

Friday, 20ᵗʰ March 2015 Paris.

Clive Somerset had a list. A list of paintings in which he'd immerse himself. Armed with nothing more than his bag of jotters and sketch books, pencils and pens, he'd gently interrogate them and, through time, grow to understand them, their form, their structure, their intent and then, by the end of his time in Paris and if he were truly successful, he would inhabit each work as if it had been his own. Some he'd seen many times before, but always in his capacity as a teacher, which had tended to tarnish the experience. He'd visited Paris regularly of course, but this was the first time he'd been there alone. Alone and with one intention, to immerse himself in the world of Parisian art one painting at a time. Then he'd move on to Florence, where roles would gratefully be reversed and he would become the student. Like any good teacher, Somerset was happy to concede, he still had much to learn, despite his age. And wasn't that so often the problem with even the best of his students, even if that thought remained rarely if ever insinuated? They felt they'd mastered their craft from a handful of books, a magazine subscription and a weekly visit to his evening class.

On the cusp of retirement, Somerset was at a point in his life where he'd been forced to acknowledge others simply weren't interested in who he might have been or what he might have done. Once overweight but now, following a salutary afternoon with his doctor, unhealthily gaunt and forlorn. His hair was starting to thin, though had retained much of its colour, unlike many men of a similar age. He didn't walk quite so easily and had taken to swimming three times a week to try and keep on top of his weight. And yet, despite all that, in his mind's eye, he was still a young Robert Redford.

He'd found a hotel on the rue Saint-Honoré, as close to the Louvre as his meagre budget would allow. Once he'd braved the overzealous security guards and found his way through the museum's labyrinthine corridors, Somerset would take up position for two hours in the morning, break for lunch and a much-needed stretch of stiffened limbs, then back, sometimes until six o'clock in the evening when the building closed.

At the end of a long day, Somerset would retreat to a wine bar he'd found halfway between the Louvre and his hotel where he was on nodding terms with a cute young lad who worked the early evening shift, order a demi-carafe of *vin ordinaire* and a *croque madame* and sort through the day's sketches and observations. Then he'd flick through a guidebook or peruse one of the arts magazines left scattered around the café. When he returned from his enforced sabbatical, Clive Somerset determined he would start afresh. A new beginning for a new man.

But today Somerset had already decided he'd allow himself to go slow. His hand was sore from sketching and writing and his head hurt from the after-effects of the previous evening's wine and the medication he was taking. He'd risen late, sending housekeeping away, his bed unmade, and treated himself to a long soak in the room's barely adequate tub. He considered having room service prepare him a late breakfast but, unwilling to put his French to the test, elected instead to take a leisurely stroll down by the river. Perhaps he'd follow the north bank for a while to the Chattelle and Notre Dame where he could sit and people watch before crossing Pont Neuf. He might drop by Shakespeare's the bookshop before grabbing something to eat on his way back to the hotel, or just keep walking and simply see how the mood took him. Either way he was determined to have an early night so as to be fresh for the following morning. Selfishly he'd planned a trip to the Musée d'Orsay where he would bask in the splendour of Paul Cezanne's *Apples and Oranges* without ever feeling the need to put pen to paper. Then, perhaps, treat himself to something needlessly extravagant and which he could certainly ill afford from Sennerlier's the art shop around the corner.

Standing in the window of his tiny hotel room looking out over the bustling rue Saint-Honoré below as he secured the last buttons on a fresh shirt, Somerset casually eyed the entrance to the block of apartments opposite. A steady stream of tourists and visiting businessmen blinking in Paris's keen morning light. Amongst the weary families and joking backpackers he watched a man exit on the far side of the street. A tall, handsome man with a straight back and solid chin, strangely out of place in his surroundings. Not a young boy, not an Apollo or a Tadzio, but a real living man, of Somerset's own age, with a lifetime of beautiful flaws and beguiling imperfections no doubt. The man carelessly lit a cigarette and Somerset found himself closing his eyes and inhaling. And the longer he stared at this man the surer he became that he knew him. Somerset adjusted his glasses. Paris was a busy metropolis, home to millions of people and hundreds of thousands of visitors. What was he saying, that he knew this man from all the others? He flicked open the plastic lid of the tablets the doctor had prescribed and went to the bathroom to fetch a glass of water.

When he returned to gaze out of the window, the man had gone, leaving Somerset with a profound yet inexplicable sense not of loss, as he might have expected, but of reassurance. A city of two million people and already he knew one of them or at least felt as though he did. He spent the day as he'd intended, but the memory of that tall, distinguished gentleman smoking so casually outside the apartments opposite would not leave him.

The next day he honoured his obligation to the Musée d'Orsay but not before he'd stood in his window for far too long willing that enigmatic stranger to return. His trip to the converted railway station was frustrating and only a partial success. Somerset couldn't say why exactly, but he'd found it difficult to concentrate, had not even been enthralled by the Cezanne. Perhaps it was the lack of air? The Lorazepam he'd been prescribed to steady his nerves and help him come to terms with his loss? Or perhaps it was the haunting memory of that man and, behind the confusion, the possibility that he was not, as he had secretly feared, entirely alone in the city?

The next day Somerset made a bold decision. He would introduce himself to this perfect stranger and they would become friends. It would be as easy and as simple as that. He made no plans for the morning. If by lunchtime he'd not seen and at least said hello to the man living opposite, then he would take some lunch and maybe manage an afternoon of sketching. But he would not give up, of that he was quite determined. After all, the Louvre would be there tomorrow. He was about to gulp down another couple of pills when the apartment's entry doors swung open. Somerset observed, enthralled, as the man stood by the front of the block, uncertain of which way to proceed. Then, as Somerset continued to watch, Daniel made up his mind and started off west towards the 8th and the Arc de Triomphe. Somerset's jacket lay on the bed. He grabbed it, found his sunglasses, picked up his wallet and room key and left as quickly as he was able, now more resolute than ever to make this perfect stranger's acquaintance. It would be an exhilarating little adventure and offset all the study and the culture.

The rue Saint-Honoré at midday was chaotic. The surrounding offices had disgorged their staff who were happily chatting whilst looking for somewhere to eat. Everywhere there were huddles of tourists amongst the street cleaners and tradesmen and suddenly Clive Somerset's idea seemed an incredibly foolish one. There was no way on earth he would be able to keep up, even if the man he'd chosen to follow weren't already halfway down an escalator and heading for the metro by now. He looked along the street, following the direction he'd taken, but there was no sign of him, just row upon row of bobbing heads and sun hats. Then a puff of smoke caught Somerset's eye as the man negotiated his way through the throng. Somerset's immediate impulse, to call after him, but already he was far too far ahead and moving off at speed, with his long purposeful stride. Somerset was having to half-walk half-run just to maintain the distance between them and then, quite suddenly, the man disappeared, departing from view so abruptly it put Somerset in mind of a theatrical illusion he'd seen once as a child. He continued to jog a little longer but his quarry had gone, vanishing into thin air as effortlessly as any magician's assistant. Somerset resigned himself to returning to the hotel. But as he retraced his steps, he decided that the next time he followed Daniel he would be better prepared. He shook his head. No, it couldn't be Daniel. It couldn't be Daniel, because Daniel was dead.

***

Thursday, 5th March 2020
The United Kingdom maintains a "moderate" risk level.

Floor four took up the whole of the top storey of 20 Bedford Place, a terraced Regency town house in Bloomsbury, off Russell Square. No plaque, no name plate, no distinguishing features of any kind, just a house number and a functional yet discreet entry buzzer. Everyday hundreds of people walked past the chaste marble steps and black iron railings and never gave the building a second thought, blissfully unaware as to its purpose or significance. And that, of course, was just the way The Service preferred it, although there wasn't a cab driver north of the river who didn't know exactly who worked there or to what end.

Hunter found a front desk occupied by an elderly gentleman, modestly attired in sombre grey uniform and exacting peaked cap. Were it not for the metal detecting arch and x-ray machines at his side, he could have been in any block of apartments or exclusive flats. Samantha Fairchild was waiting for him. She nodded a hello.

'He's called up to Harper,' she said, eyeing the doorman, 'who's on his way down. Needs to sign us in apparently.'

On the other side of the metal detectors a lift door opened and Sandy Harper emerged, ill-tempered and fractious and plainly unhappy at being dragged away from whatever lofty pursuit he'd previously been engaged in.

'Quick here will give you a pass,' he said, gesturing to the gentleman in the cap. 'It'll allow you access to floor four and nowhere else.'

Quick produced two plastic security tags on lanyards and watched as Fairchild and Hunter signed for them.

'Would you mind emptying your pockets into these trays, please?' he said, somewhat matter-of-factly.

Hunter watched Fairchild empty the contents of her pockets into the grey plastic tray provided. A tin of lip balm, a half empty packet of tissues, a small collection of keys on a silver keyring with a capital K at its heart and a promotional laser pointer from a music festival Hunter had never heard of. The briefest glimpse into the life of someone he barely knew but was now being forced to work alongside. And then Quick replaced the tray with another and it was his turn. He found his cigarettes and a cheap plastic lighter.

Fairchild and Hunter did as they were instructed and walked uneventfully through the security arch, whilst Quick scrutinized the contents of each tray. Once they'd collected their possessions, Harper ushered them into the lift. He extended the cord on his lanyard and pressed his pass over a sensor which beeped obligingly.

'You'll need to do the same when you come back down,' he said as the lift doors slid shut.

Floor four was every university library Hunter had ever set foot in, if you'd replaced the books with box files and the endless rows of shelves with dilapidated filing cabinets. As they stepped from the lift, another counter and behind this a gentle looking middle-aged man with thinning red hair, fine freckled features and wearing a pair of round, wire-framed spectacles, a maroon cardigan which had seen better days and a pair of mustard yellow corduroy trousers. Hunter thought he detected the blind insouciance of someone casually working out their time. The redhaired man was dealing with a smartly dressed thirty-something in a motorway-grey suit and shiny black Oxfords which had been polished so hard they would have made any sergeant major proud. He was waiting for something to be returned and gently kicking at the counter with the toe of his shoe. Finally the redhaired man withdrew a mobile phone from beneath the counter and handed it over.

The other man stopped tapping with his shoe, pocketed his phone and headed for the lifts, leaving a vacant space for Sandy Harper to step into.

'This is Julian Palgrave,' Harper sneered. 'He oversees our archives and has done for as long as any of us care to remember.'

Palgrave looked up from the papers he'd been examining. He pointedly ignored Harper, choosing to squint dramatically over the desk before removing his glasses and smiling down benevolently upon them. 'And who have we here?' he asked, as if addressing an overanxious parent at Christmas.

'Scott Hunter,' Harper said. 'David Hunter's boy,' he added unable to hide his disapproval.

'Oh, yes,' Palgrave replied, still unwilling to meet Harper's eye.

'And this is Samantha Fairchild. They are both working for me, so make sure you let them see anything you deem appropriate.'

'What level of clearance do they have?' Palgrave asked, as though both Fairchild and Hunter were invisible.

'They're working for me Julian. *De facto* they have my level of clearance.'

Palgrave busied himself with some more paperwork, continuing to purposely avoiding Harper's glare. 'I'm sorry Sandy,' he replied, barely able to look up, 'but I don't think that's going to wash. I'm going to have to run it past Davenport.'

'If you think it's worth the bother,' Harper replied, 'although I suspect she'll only tell you what I've just told you.'

Sandy Harper watched as Palgrave lifted the receiver and asked to be connected. Fairchild and Hunter continued to stand in an embarrassed silence. Hunter took the opportunity to scrutinize their surroundings. At the far end of the room, sitting on an old school desk with a dull red finish and which someone had rescued from a skip the previous century, one solitary computer. Next to that a row of microfiche machines which appeared not to have been used in anger since the 1970s and walls and walls of sensible boxes and bound files. It wasn't hard for Hunter to imagine his father sat hunched over the microfiche machines late into the night. The shelves disappeared into an uncertain horizon and Hunter was struck with an irrational urge to pitch himself into the records, to drown himself in the endless sea of intelligence, until he'd absorbed every last detail, however minute, however archaic. Like a gigantic computer programme, he supposed that in some almost microscopic, esoteric way, each one of these files, each story, each incident, from whichever bygone era or location, had to be inextricably linked to the next, forming in Hunter's mind an almost infinite spider's web of lives and lifetimes, crimes and recriminations. Hunter realised that the room had become eerily quiet and that both Harper and Palgrave were staring at him. Julian Palgrave smiled a knowing smile. Sandy Harper did not.

'Daunting, isn't it?' Palgrave said putting down the phone. 'I'm not overly happy about this, and I shall,' he continued, finally able to address Harper, 'when the time is right, be bringing it up with Davenport, but as things stand, I will grant you both Sandy's level of clearance.'

'Tomorrow,' Harper said, above offering Palgrave his thanks. 'I shall expect to see your report on my desk first thing tomorrow. Let them see everything you think is appropriate,' Harper said again, ignoring Hunter and wheeling back towards the lift. 'Oh, and I'd make sure to keep an eye on the pair of them, if I were you,' he suggested casually.

'Will do,' Palgrave replied to Harper's retreating form.

They waited as the lift transported Sandy Harper to more important affairs. Hunter was interested to note that, once it became clear he would not be returning, Palgrave became an altogether different individual.

'Right, first some ground rules. The information held on these shelves here,' he said gesturing with an open hand 'and those filing cabinets there, is mostly reference. Much of it's already in the public domain, newspaper cuttings, tax returns, registrations at Companies House, that sort of thing. All the juicy stuff is back here,' he said, indicating a locked door behind him. 'If you need any files from in there, you have to come to me and we fill out the requisite form which releases that file. Internal communications, for instance from a station abroad, should have the following information: the name of the station, the time and the date, and the sender of course. Any of that should be enough for me to find the original transcript. Once you've filled in the correct paperwork I go back there and find the relevant file. You will then sign for it here,' Palgrave dabbed uncompromisingly at the blank form on his counter. 'Once you've finished with it, bring everything straight back to me and I'll record its return in this space here,' his finger tracked across the form and he tapped several more times at a second box. Fairchild and Hunter both nodded their understanding. 'Not all files are available to you, despite what Sandy Harper may say to the contrary, and you are not permitted, under any circumstances, to remove or copy any documents from this room. Is that understood?'

'Yes,' Hunter replied, with Fairchild nodding vociferously by his side.

'And to that end, I will need your mobile phones, please,' Palgrave continued, holding out a hand.

'Why?' Fairchild asked.

'He's worried we're going to take photographs,' Hunter put in, saving Palgrave the bother.

Fairchild reached into the back pocket of her jeans and found her mobile. Hunter placed his on the counter next to hers. Palgrave picked them both up and withdrew two metal boxes from beneath his counter. The phones were placed carefully inside and the boxes locked. Each box, as well as a tiny carrying handle, had a number taped to its lid and Palgrave handed them both a small rectangle of disreputable card on which was printed the corresponding number. With both phones accounted for, he slid the boxes back beneath his desk and smiled for the first time.

'Now, what can I get you? If you can't find *everything* you're looking for right away, we'll try the microfiche. That goes all the way back to the year dot. We started scanning everything into the computer in the seventies and we've been slowly going back through the old files ever since.'

Fairchild nodded sympathetically. 'And if we're after information on a particular individual, we...?'

'Put their name into the computer's search bar along with any additional information you may have. Name, date and place of birth, current abode, that sort of thing. Then the system will find any relevant matches in our database. If there's anything of interest, come back and tell me and I'll see what I can do.'

She looked at Hunter. 'Where do you want to start, filing cabinets or that thing?' she asked pointing contemptuously at the computer.

'I'll make a start here,' Hunter said firing up the iMac and happy to put some distance between himself and Fairchild. Seated uncomfortably in front of the desktop, he started trawling through floor four's comprehensive records. Initially, and in stark contradiction to Harper's advice, he concerned himself solely with Oleg Lobanov. Whilst Fairchild produced box after box of fresh information Hunter began slowly broadening his parameters to include potential business partners, work associates and family members, all of which only helped confirm what he already suspected. The Russian was a recluse. Camera shy and evasive, he preferred to stay out of the media's spotlight as much as his huge fortune allowed.

'That's everything I could find on Lobanov going back nearly ten years,' Fairchild said, heaving another pile of boxes onto the table.

'Anything interesting?' Hunter asked, pointing at the files.

'Precious little really. Mostly glossy double spreads from Sunday colour supplements. A decade of lazy journalism. The same tired old article rehashed ad infinitum but with slightly different photographs. There's nothing of any substance. Even our snoopers can't get into his place. And he keeps his family as far away from the press as he can. For instance, it's almost impossible to say from these exactly how many kids he has. Some say two girls and a boy, some say two of each. From what I can gather his eldest was briefly at boarding school, until the press started nosing around, trying to put his kid's private life under the microscope. Lobanov moved them all back home from where they've been privately tutored ever since. He has a modest staff who are almost exclusively Russian and who all live on his estate. When the family travels, it's by private jet or helicopter. The paparazzi have been trying to get a decent picture of his wife for years,' Fairchild concluded, sliding a grainy black and white photograph in front of Hunter. 'Oksana Tchaikina. She was a pop star in the 90s. A handful of minor hits, but nothing you could whistle. This was taken by one of ours seven years ago and is the last photograph we have of her.'

'What about him? What about Lobanov?'

Fairchild flicked through some articles taken from a variety of magazines. 'These are older. My guess is that when they arrived, Lobanov and his wife thought it might be sensible to be seen in the right company.'

'Very pragmatic,' Hunter said.

Fairchild laid a succession of cuttings in front of him. 'Here he is attending a dinner at the Russian Embassy in Kensington. That's him glad-handing the former Prime Minister and again at a fundraiser for the promotion of Russian culture, of which he is an extremely active yet silent honorary patron. You'll notice there are never any shots of his kids and only a few of the lovely Mrs Lobanov.'

Hunter looked through the collection of photographs. Mrs Lobanov had long flowing hair and the easy smile of one accustomed to photographers. In the last picture of her, Hunter picked her at late forties or early fifties. She'd kept her figure well he noticed, with just the slightest suggestion of surgical assistance. Her eyes seemed unnaturally drawn he thought, her brow inanimate, her breasts a touch unyielding. But behind the plastic surgery Hunter was pleased to see kind eyes and an open face.

Oleg Lobanov, by contrast, was an inch shorter than his wife. His jet-black hair beginning to thin. He wore a cropped beard and two tiny black eyes stared back challengingly from each and every photograph. There was nothing of him physically, yet his body language was fierce, highly charged and confrontational. His clothing was never ostentatious, an open-necked white shirt, belted trousers and black patent slip-ons, no matter the occasion. Lobanov's only concession, a trio of delicately intertwined Russian wedding bands suspended elegantly from a tightly wound gold chain around his neck.

'What about you, how've you got on?' Fairchild asked.

'There's the bare bones,' Hunter began. 'When he came over, some financial masterstrokes in the City, high profile stock investments and the propping up of a couple of everybody's favourite ailing companies, but since then, very little. He maintains an office in Mayfair from where the bulk of his empire appears still to be run, but which he rarely if ever visits. Maybe Harper's right? Maybe he is untouchable? He looks dodgy as hell if you ask me, but on a first pass there's nothing obvious. I think, if we're going to get anything truly significant on him, we'll have to pay his number two a visit?'

'I've made a start already,' Fairchild said, producing a significantly thinner folder. 'Dmitry Patzuk first crops up in Kiev calling himself Dmytro Panasuk. We're pretty sure it's him and the Ukrainian Police files seem to corroborate it.' She slid the manilla file in front of Hunter. At the top right corner of his criminal record, held in place with a heavy steel staple, a passport sized black and white photograph of a boy, thin, with a full head of unruly dark hair and the apparent air of one for whom prison holds few challenges.

'We're going to need to get this translated,' Hunter said.

Fairchild nodded, 'I'll see if Palgrave can help us out.'

'Do we at least know what he was in for?'

'Nothing major,' Fairchild said, turning a page. 'Racketeering mostly. According to The Service's report,' she added quickly. 'Just did six months.' Six months in a Russian prison sounded like an eternity to Hunter. 'Then there's a couple of years in the wilderness.'

'Any sign of a family?'

'Later yes, but not yet. He sticks his head up again aged seventeen. Got his wrist slapped for selling illegally imported jeans and knocked off electrical goods, mostly laptops that kind of thing. Oh and he and his cronies developed an interesting side-line distilling vodka from technical spirits. That's cleaning fluid to you.'

'Jesus!' Hunter said.

'Yep, that stuff'll send you blind and stupid.'

'And he only got a ticking off?'

Fairchild nodded. 'Even at that age it seems Patzuk had at least one of the local police in his pocket.'

'What's he doing here then, if life back home was so profitable?'

'From what I can gather,' Fairchild said flicking forward a couple of pages, 'his luck ran out. There was an incident involving the local mayor.'

'What kind of "incident"?' Hunter asked, already suspecting the worst.

'They found his body in the district park,' Fairchild said holding up a grisly black and white police photograph. 'There was no going back after that.'

'He's on the run then?'

'I don't think so. I should get Palgrave to take a proper look at these,' she said, waving the police reports at Hunter, 'but just based on what I can make out and the newspaper cuttings I've seen, nothing was ever proven and the case was dropped.'

'Before or after Patzuk left the country?'

'After,' Fairchild replied.

The pair looked at one another, both understanding the implication. Dmitry Patzuk might not have beaten the mayor to death with his own hands, but he'd certainly been responsible for having him killed, and then, with the local police no longer able to protect him from prosecution, he'd fled the country. No sooner had he left, and lacking its prime suspect, the case had collapsed. 'Left in a hurry too. His wife and kids are still in Russia,' Fairchild continued.

'But even though the investigation was closed, you'd think it would be enough to have him deported?' Hunter said.

'You've never been to Russia, have you?' she joked.

'And you have?'

Fairchild pushed awkwardly at the files in front of her.

'Okay,' Hunter said. 'Where's he based now?'

'That is an excellent question. That we know of, he has the obligatory flat in Chelsea, a house in Tuscany and another flat in Paris. But he never stays in the same country long enough to call any one of them home.'

'Or pay the taxes,' Hunter said.

'Or pay the taxes,' Fairchild confirmed.

'How's he managing that?'

'Lobanov's jet mostly. Currently in a hangar at Mandelieu Airport outside Cannes undergoing its annual D-check.'

'How the other half live, eh?' Hunter said, picturing a sleek white Gulfstream.

'That's not the worst of it, Scott. The reason Patzuk's in Cannes is because it's where he has a permanently moored luxury yacht. He bought it at the Boat Show in 2016. I'm surprised you missed it,' she continued with a grin, 'it was in all the society columns. He more or less walked in off the street, had the whole place cordoned off from prying eyes, spent about ten minutes looking around, which I'd have thought was barely enough time to walk from one end to the other, and then just stumped up the cash.'

'How much?'

'Eight and a half million. Rumour has it he signed the cheque on top of a case of Héloïse Lloris.'

'Classy. And all that from selling knocked off jeans and T-shirts?'

'Don't be a dummy, Scott. Anyway, he's not big money.'

'He isn't?'

'No, not really. He's a glorified nightclub owner. There are probably premiership footballers who make more than he does. The real money guys, guys like Lobanov, they *own* the football clubs. Patzuk's small fry.'

Deep down, Hunter knew she was right. 'Have we got enough, do you think? For Harper, I mean?'

'I should have thought so, yeah, although it's going to need some typing up,' Fairchild said.

'I'll do it,' he offered. 'It shouldn't be too big a deal. I used to churn this kind of thing out regularly at uni. I'll see you in the morning.'

'Okay, if you're sure?' Fairchild smiled back. 'Thanks, Scott.'

Hunter spent the remainder of the evening on floor four. In that respect at least it was utterly different from the university's library. No one bothered him and he felt under no obligation to leave. He worked methodically through all the boxes Fairchild had brought him, scouring each one for any fresh piece of information which might bring a smile to Sandy Harper's otherwise splenetic face. He procured an A4 pad from Palgrave. By midnight he had a brief résumé of Oleg Lobanov but the makings of an excellent report on Dmitry Patzuk, tracking his life from his formative years in Kiev all the way through his criminal youth, a short stint in prison and the resultant building of his modest empire to his final brush with the law and subsequent inauspicious departure.

With Palgrave's expert linguistic skills and copies of Patzuk's police records, Hunter was able to catalogue the extortion, the fraud and the suspected murders right up until the point when he'd left Russia and arrived in London. Hunter asked Palgrave if there was any chance he could help print the document off. But as he watched Palgrave do battle with The Service's recalcitrant printer, Hunter had the overwhelming feeling that, whilst his report seemed thorough enough, it was still missing something. He was happy to concede that it didn't shed much light on Lobanov but Sandy Harper had already suggested there simply wasn't enough known about the man. Eventually, after some whispered threats, Palgrave persuaded the printer to cooperate. Hunter shoved the report into his bag, retrieved his phone and headed for the lift.

He strode through the metal detector whilst Quick x-rayed his bag. Hunter was about to pass the front desk when Quick called him back.

'Phone please.' Hunter looked at him. 'Put your phone on the table please and be ready to unlock it. I'm going to need to take a look in your bag as well, I'm afraid.' Hunter put his shoulder bag down and then Quick was holding up the report, its ink barely dry. 'What's this?' he asked rhetorically. 'I'm sorry, sir. I understand this is your first day and all, but this document can't be allowed to leave the building. Frankly I'm surprised at Julian.'

'Well what am I supposed to do? Harper wants to see it first thing.'

Quick leant in towards him. 'It's a bit irregular, sir, but I could hold onto it for you. You can pick it up tomorrow morning.'

Hunter thought for a moment. 'Thanks very much,' he said, seeing no alternative.

'Now, I'm going to need to take a look at your phone, please?' Quick continued. 'Please put in your password, sir.' Hunter did as he was instructed. 'Now, open your text messages, please.'

Again Hunter did as he was asked before handing back his phone.

Quick scrolled through some texts, asked Hunter to open his email account, had a cursory look in there too, apologised for having to do his job and wished him a good evening.

As Hunter walked down Bedford Place towards Holborn Tube, and praying he hadn't just missed the last train north, his phone beeped with a fresh voicemail. Negotiating his way through Bloomsbury

Square Gardens, he listened to his father's answerphone message. 'Just checking you're still free on Sunday? There's someone I'd like you to meet,' and then the message came to an abrupt and rather inglorious end.

Someone I'd like you to meet?

He flicked the mobile off and tried not to worry about his father, the ex-spy.

Wednesday, 25ᵗʰ March 2015 Paris.

Clive Somerset did not see the man over the next few days. He returned to his exhaustive studies in the Louvre, but there could be no doubt that he was distracted in his work. When he was preparing for the day he would gaze down at the entrance to the apartments opposite hoping to see that tall, urbane physique again. The same was true when he emerged at street level, into the city's whirling hurly burly. He caught himself scouring the heads of passers-by, but the man he was searching for had disappeared, leaving Somerset with nothing more than the overwhelming sense that he knew him but not from where or when. They were of approximately the same age, he figured, nearing retirement, so perhaps they had been at school together all those hundreds of thousands of years ago, or attended art college at the same time? That, Somerset was comfortable admitting, if only to himself, had been a wild time and remained in his memory as little more than a blur. Then there was the chance that they were on a similar pilgrimage, except that the object of his most recent obsession, in his fine suit and tie, looked more like a businessman or executive than an art scholar.

It was as Somerset looked out over Paris's rooftops and steeple towers, sadly determined he would never again see this man who had left such an acute and lasting impression on him, that the tall oak doors of the apartments opposite swung open and out he stepped.

Somerset saw him check his watch and adjust his tie. This time there was no panic, no second-guessing or indecision. He walked from the room, looked briefly at the lifts, but instead bolted down the stairs as quickly as his outraged knees would allow.

As Somerset emerged from the hotel, there he was. He'd moved off down the street but, unlike the previous occasion, was still tantalizingly within reach on the opposite side of the road. Today he seemed in less of a hurry and Somerset kept up with him easily until they both arrived at a busy junction and suddenly the opportunity to cross the road presented itself. And as quickly as the lights changed the lunacy of his situation struck home. Was he really going to approach a total stranger, or at least someone he took to be a total stranger, and say what? *Excuse me, you don't know me, and I may not even know you, but I have the strangest feeling that we've met before.*

A curly haired student, clutching a bottle of wine in one hand and a trio of learned books in the other cut across his path breaking the spell and Somerset laughed to himself at the absurdity of it all. What a thought and at his age too! He couldn't even be certain the man spoke English and yet there was something about his body language, the way in which he held himself, wore that expensive suit, that was quintessentially English. How fascinating he was to Somerset. But where was this man that he felt such an immediate and powerful affinity with leading him? He continued to follow through winding crowded streets. Every now and then he noticed another puff of thin grey smoke. Daniel didn't smoke, did he? But then this man wasn't Daniel, Somerset reminded himself. Daniel was dead. He'd buried him himself. Stood by as his sister had thrown dirt and a single white rose onto his coffin. Daniel hated roses and he had never smoked.

At the junction the man swung left, heading south on rue du Louvre and a route Somerset knew all too well. He smiled to himself as the man turned right onto rue de Rivoli. It crossed Somerset's mind that perhaps he'd been right all along and this was an old acquaintance from art college, possibly with a similar agenda to his own. But then the man pressed on, past the crowds queuing for admittance, past Pei's extraordinary glass pyramid, towards the Arc de Triomphe. He continued on, ignoring the Musée des Arts Décoratifs, before ducking into the Tuileries Gardens. Somerset was struggling to keep up, his breath coming in short, shallow gasps. And then, just as he was about to give up and turn back, having abandoned his exercise and still none the wiser, it dawned on him. At the far end of the gardens, by the banks of the river, in the shadow of the Place de la Concorde, stood the Musée de l'Orangerie. It had been on his list but only if there had been time and now he was being led there in this magnificent act of happenstance and fate. It was beautiful. Of course, The Orangerie. The only reason it had not featured more prominently on his itinerary, that he had seen Monet's Waterlilies so many times before. But he'd never seen them with Daniel and that had been a lasting regret. A lasting regret he now saw the perfect opportunity to redress.

He turned to face the Musée de l'Orangerie just as the figure he had pursued all the way from rue Saint-Honoré disappeared inside.

Somerset followed, through colonnades and marble halls, down grandiose corridors. There is an exhibition of Pierre Bonnard. It *is* Daniel. It *has* to be. At first he had been unsure, but now he has to stop himself calling out Daniel's name in the quietly echoing hallways.

And there he is. But he is not alone. He's standing with another man. Somerset watched them furtively embrace. The paintings faded away, empty rectangles of other people's misfortune, and in that instant he was heartbroken. *Daniel, I don't understand.* They sat together, close, in the way that he used to, and he heard a deep, hearty laugh. Then this other man, he is brutish and coarse, like an old, worn tree trunk, with no neck, his head sitting atop his shoulders, an uncarefully balanced cannon ball, his hair dark and unkempt. He hasn't shaven, a livid port-wine stain descending from beneath his ragged hairline to cover the portion of his face above his left cheek. *Oh, Daniel, what have you done?* Somerset stifled a cry. A scruffy old jacket and thick denim jeans. He'd even brought his wretched shopping with him. A thin blue plastic bag resting incongruously at his workman like boots. He was every inch the navvy, or at least how Somerset imagines a navvy must be. Dull and lumbering.

And so Somerset found himself doing what he believed any self-respecting, well raised Englishman would do under similar circumstances. He pretended to have seen nothing, made to look as though he'd inadvertently stumbled into the wrong room, quietly admonished himself, apologising to no one in particular, turned on his heel and removed himself as quickly as he could, all thoughts of impressionist karma, Daniel or anything else other than acute embarrassment instantly forgotten.

The first death from coronavirus in the United Kingdom is confirmed

As they waited for Sandy Harper in the foyer of 20 Bedford Place, Hunter fished in his shoulder bag and pulled out the report Quick had kept for him. He handed it to Fairchild.

'What's this?' she said.

'You should give it to him,' Hunter replied, waiting for her to take it.

'No way, Scott, this is your work.'

'I'm pretty sure Harper hates me. You take it,' he insisted. And then Sandy Harper was standing on the other side of the metal detectors, his key-card in his hand, scowling at them and there was no more time for discussion. They joined him in the lift and moments later were standing in his office on the third floor. The room was simply too small to accommodate three people comfortably, despite all Harper's elegant attempts that it appear otherwise. Harper went to sit behind his desk, pushing away an unwelcome cup and saucer of half-finished tea. The cup clinked merrily as it slid across the desk's tired leather inlay and Hunter wondered if he didn't detect a hint of something stronger.

Harper was about to speak when Fairchild theatrically dropped the bulging grey file onto his desk.

'And what the hell is this?' Harper asked, his stare never leaving Hunter's.

'It's everything there is to know about Dmitry Patzuk,' Fairchild said rather too proudly.

'Rubbish,' Harper replied, not even deigning to open it. 'I could have learnt more from a badly penned article in *The Observer*. Where's the *real* information?'

'But you haven't even looked at it,' Fairchild began before Harper cut her off.

'Please try and remember to whom you are speaking. This,' Harper continued pushing at the file with one long outstretched finger and wilfully ignoring Samantha Fairchild's protestations, 'is a worthless pile of crap. The chatter off the parade ring, when what I asked for was the dirt from the weighing room. They said you were like your father,' he continued, eyeing Hunter, 'and how right it appears they were. Take it away, dispose of it in some dark and faraway hole and start again. You have,' Sandy's gaze finally shifted from Hunter's as he awkwardly pushed up his sleeve, exposing an old and sentimental wristwatch, 'you have twenty-four hours to produce something worth reading and not this overwrought pile of horseshit. Remember children, this is an exercise in intelligence gathering, not an end of term assignment. Short and to the point please. Not too many long words and just the right amount of filth. Off you go, and take that with you,' Harper concluded, nodding at the unopened file before replacing his cuff and giving the watch beneath a reassuring pat for good measure. He pursed his lips, preparing to speak, looked up at Hunter, who had remained recalcitrant throughout, considered him for a long, uneasy moment, then broke away as if abruptly remembering something of *real* import.

Hunter, who was silently shaking with rage, picked up the report and turned as calmly as he could to the astonished Samantha Fairchild.

'Come on then, we've got some work to do,' he said.

'You're not serious? You're not going to let him get away with that?' Fairchild said.

Hunter grabbed her elbow and steered her out of Sandy Harper's office and toward the lift.

'Forget it, Sam. It wouldn't have made any difference what we'd written, he'd have found fault in it,' Hunter said, jabbing at the lift button.

'But he didn't even bloody well open the folder.' Fairchild was fuming.

'He's trying to provoke us,' Hunter continued, 'or, more likely, *me*. So, what we can't afford to do, under any circumstances, is rise to it.'

'Rise to it? Scott, he didn't read a single word of the report.'

'That's because he didn't have to.'

'What do you mean, didn't have to?'

Hunter jabbed the button again and they listened to the lift approach.

'He was right,' he said, holding up the file, 'this *is* a newspaper article not an intelligence report. All the information in here is stuff anyone could have dragged up.'

'Well thanks very much!' Fairchild said as the lift doors closed behind her.

'You know what I mean,' Hunter replied, shaking his head and smiling at her. 'Let's go and see what Julian has to say about it.' The doors opened and Hunter approached an unresolved Julian Palgrave.

3

'Is everything alright, Mr Hunter?' Palgrave asked.

'You keep a record of every file signed in and out of your collection back there, is that right?'

'It is.'

'And can anyone see who signed and what they signed for?'

'In theory, I suppose so, yes.'

'And you'd remember if someone came to inspect your little black book, wouldn't you?'

'I most certainly would,' Palgrave said, pushing at his glasses.

'Say, this morning,' Hunter continued, 'before ten o'clock?' Palgrave didn't answer. He didn't have to. Instead, he closed the book in front of him. 'Perhaps there is something else I can help you with, Mr Hunter?'

'No, I don't think so, thank you. Come on Sam, we've got work to do.'

He led her off towards the computer terminal at the far end of the room.

'What the hell was all that about?' she asked.

'Harper was up here before we arrived, checking which files we'd been through. That's how he knew we were only scratching the surface and that means there must be other information which he thinks we ought to have been looking at.'

They drew up two chairs in front of the computer and Hunter was surprised to see Fairchild pull on a pair of glasses. He'd forgotten that the first time they'd met she'd been wearing them, perhaps assuming that, like everything else he knew about her, they too were a lie. But now he was taken with quite how different they made her look and just how well they suited her. And then she was staring at him quizzically and Hunter had to quickly look away and dive back into his work.

'Do we agree we've exhausted everything there is on Patzuk?' he asked, after a morning retracing their steps and reading and re-reading the same old reports.

'I suppose so,' Fairchild replied.

'Then I think it's about time we look more closely at the people he's surrounding himself with.'

Hunter typed *known associates* into the computer's search engine and a list of names began to appear.

'We'll need to whittle this down a bit, otherwise we'll be here forever,' Fairchild said. 'What about *known associates, London?*'

Hunter typed. This time the list was significantly shorter. At the top, the untouchable Oleg Lobanov then Dmitry Patzuk himself, followed by Leonid Katz, Yuri Sklepov and Evgeny Tikhonov.

'I'll go and ask Palgrave what he's got,' Fairchild said, scribbling down the names on a scrap of paper. She returned a few minutes later. 'Patzuk's working a team,' she said, proudly sliding two police profiles in front of Hunter. 'Right here, in London, or was. Sklepov, he's a glorified chauffeur. Used to do a bit of dealing out the back of his car, the odd handgun, that kind of thing.'

'Used to?' Hunter said.

'He's no longer in the UK. Went back to Russia in 2015. The other guy's a little more interesting. Leonid Katz, he's the money man. Russian born Jew from St. Petersburg and still working for Patzuk from what I can tell. I'd imagine that's quite a cosy little relationship. Katz knows where all the cash is hidden...'

'And Dmitry knows where all the bodies are buried.'

'Exactly,' Fairchild said, leaning in close to Hunter as she placed Katz's folder on the top of the pile. 'He's a little older than Dmitry, straight down the line, maths grad.,' she smiled, 'just like you! Except he went to the dark side.'

'And we haven't?'

'Point taken,' Fairchild said, smiling. 'These days he splits his time between Moscow on the Thames...' Hunter raised an inquisitive eyebrow. 'That's Chelsea to you, and Milan where he's built an impressive villa stroke party venue stroke fortress.'

'What about the third guy, Tikhonov?' Hunter asked, consulting his computer screen and struggling with the pronunciation.

'This is all Palgrave gave me,' Fairchild replied, shaking her head.

'Okay, but I still don't think it's going to be enough, and I'm certain it's not what Harper's looking for.' He tapped the folders Fairchild had brought. 'Harper wants us to look at Russians coming into Britain. So far, we've been looking at Lobanov and Patzuk and their lives, we've never actually spent much time looking at how they got here. I think it's time we shine a light a little closer to home, don't you? The Foreign Office? Home Office? Even here, I guess?'

Was it possible, Hunter wondered, that Sandy Harper, in his own uniquely oblique way, was trying to push them towards investigating a connection between the British Government and Oleg Lobanov and if so, wasn't Hunter potentially about to upset some extremely important people? But then that was for Harper to deal with, wasn't it?

Hunter made quite certain that Fairchild was busy, checked that Palgrave was behind his desk and found the Home Office's website. He quickly assessed the site's external perimeter before launching his attack. Less than five minutes later he was calling her over.

'Sklepov's visa ran out after six months so they sent him home, but what about the other two?' he asked Fairchild.

'Where does it say Sklepov's visa ran out?'

'In the Home Office records,' Hunter replied sheepishly.

'In the what?!'

'Never mind. What happens when a foreign national wants to come and live in the UK? Legally, I mean.'

'They'd need to get another visa from the Russian embassy.'

'Could be tricky couldn't it, especially if they've got a criminal record?'

'Says the man who's just hacked a government department.'

'Okay. But as far as you know...'

'As far as I know, the visa would still only be valid for six months and then they'd have to reapply or leave.'

'Unless in that time they've disappeared off the grid.'

'Which we know they didn't,' Fairchild put in quickly.

'Okay. So how are they still here then?'

'Not as refugees requiring humanitarian aid, that's for sure,' Fairchild said.

'They have to be here as British citizens. Is that right, like Lobanov?'

Hunter went to work on the computer again, surprised by his own conclusion.

'Sklepov went back to Russia in February, so we can discount him. Katz seems never to stay in the one country for very long, so let's look at Dmitry's records. Let's see if we can't find out when *his* visa was due to expire. You might want to look away now,' Hunter said, starting to type.

'I'll see if Palgrave's got anything else on him. Just don't get caught.'

Hunter pulled up the relevant information and Fairchild went and signed for the files. Five minutes later she was back with a photocopy of Dmitry Patzuk's recorded flights in and out of the United Kingdom over a three-month period.

'He arrived on 7th January. The next time he travels is on the 14th February when he returned to Moscow. He's only there for a couple of days before he's back. But look at this,' Fairchild said pointing to the last flight Patzuk had taken. 'He got out of the country the day before his visa expired on the 29th March.'

Hunter had been tapping away at the computer keyboard whilst she had been talking. 'But it says here he was back in the UK less than a week later,' he said. 'Would that have given him enough time to get a fresh visa from the Russian embassy in Moscow?'

'That's the thing,' Fairchild said triumphantly, 'He didn't go to Moscow, he went to Paris.'

✳✳✳

Thursday, 26th March 2015 Paris.

Somerset watched the pair lunch together from a café across the street. The other man, the man with the dark red birthmark who ate as though he'd never seen food before, was shovelling down some soup whilst Daniel, having tackled a mussel, was elegantly washing his fingers in the bowl provided. Somerset was transfixed by the stockier of the two men. He tried to imagine an artist who would have used such a robust model. Peter Howson, he thought, at a push, or Goya perhaps? Somerset smiled to himself. Yes, he could be one of Goya's monstrous Black Paintings, or even one of Van Gogh's grotesque Potato Eaters. And the way that he devoured his food, as though he were competing in a race, anxious that at any moment his plate might be removed. Somerset had never seen anything quite so disgusting. Why then were they lunching together, this ill matched pair? He was struggling to imagine what they could possibly have in common, although the conversation did appear to be free flowing. Added to which there was something else. He ordered another *pression* from the bar and retook his seat. Somerset consulted his watch and began padding down his coat. In the last of his pockets he found his tablets and briefly considered asking at the bar for a glass of water before slipping two into his mouth and washing them down with the light, frothy beer. There was something about the other man. It wasn't simply that he possessed all the social graces of a wounded rhinoceros or that his bearing put Somerset in mind of a Wagnerian dwarf, although it *was* something to do with his appearance. He took another pull on the beer and felt the first waves of euphoria hit him as the Lorazepam started to kick in. His gaze drifted back to Daniel and he shook his head. This man, the man in the expensive suit speaking easily and joking with their waiter, this man was obviously British. Somerset was prepared to go further. He was English. There was something about the way he held himself, his body language, which Somerset, as a Kentish man, instantly associated himself with. He took another mouthful of beer and called over to the bar in his schoolboy French for one more. That was it. That was what had so troubled him. The man he had chosen to take lunch with was, by all the same criteria, definitely not English, British or, Somerset concluded looking at the charming young waiter with the olive complexion and the careworn smile of all Parisians, French. Neither was he, like Goya, Mediterranean. *Never.* So, where the hell *was* he from, Somerset wondered? He was starting to enjoy this social experiment. He'd spent a lifetime trying to draw out people's characters as he'd painted them, so surely he should be able to divine something from this man's appearance. Somerset started working his way around the globe, eliminating countries and whole continents on the way, until, with pride in his abilities at least partially restored, he concluded that the thick set man ordering a coffee and a shot in the café across the street was most probably eastern European. He wasn't prepared to commit to anything more specific than that but yes, he could certainly be one of Ilya Repin's broken Barge Haulers. The next question naturally, as he watched both men light cigarettes and briefly disagree over the bill, was why was his new English friend having lunch with him?

Somerset settled up, leaving as much of a tip as he was able and in a month when he was determinedly taking charge of his life and making difficult decisions he should never have been called upon to make in the first place, made another. He was going to find out more about this Eastern European. The two men said their farewells, the Englishman picked up his plastic bag and set off in the direction of the Louvre and, Somerset supposed, his apartment on rue Saint-Honoré, whilst the other man headed west but did not follow the river.

✳✳✳

The following morning Somerset woke late. His head was foggy and he felt queasy. He picked up the little pill bottle from the nightstand next to his bed and gave it an exploratory shake. It wasn't empty but, judging from its pathetic rattle, there couldn't be many of the small white Metformin tablets left. Soon he would be forced to find a *pharmacie* in Paris and negotiate a fresh supply. Perhaps, he reasoned, today would be a good day to swear off the pills and the booze altogether and be kind to himself for a change. He reached for the can of coke he kept close at hand for just such an emergency and cracked the ring pull. Slowly, as the sugar went to work, he began to recall the extraordinary events of the previous evening.

Out of bed, Somerset slipped into his morning routine. He was far too late for breakfast of course, but he would need something to eat and soon. He showered, found a crisp white shirt and decided that, in the spirit of fresh beginnings, a tie would be in order. He stood and looked out over Paris, jerking the length of burgundy from side to side in the window's reflection. He considered his daily routine and just how different his current life was from the one he'd left behind. Satisfied with the knot, Somerset took the lift down to reception and was just about to attempt to ask the concierge where he might recommend for a late breakfast when he spied the same tall, distinguished figure he'd followed the previous day, leaving the apartments opposite. Immediately any ideas of brunch, lunch or anything else were put to one side. This man had a routine of his own. He would take his time, stand outside and smoke a cigarette before moving off for the day, and these few precious moments gave Somerset just the time he needed. He did his best to thank the concierge and collect himself, only momentarily confused when the man turned right and into town instead of left towards the Louvre as he usually did.

After walking for twenty minutes and with a clear head and the kaleidoscopic light streaming in through Gothic stained glass, Clive Somerset suddenly saw clearly for the first time. He did know this man. Not his name, and not him personally, but he knew his wife and rather well and he was now certain that they had met on at least one previous occasion.

❋❋❋

'What the hell was Patzuk doing in Paris?' Hunter asked.

'Hard to say isn't it, but don't forget, he does own a flat there, so perhaps a spot of housekeeping?' Fairchild glanced over her glasses, embarrassed by her own glibness. 'He returned to the UK six days later,' she continued more earnestly. 'How did he manage to do that if he didn't go back to the motherland and sort his visa out first?'

'I don't know,' Hunter said.

Fairchild went to talk to Palgrave and returned a few minutes later with the passenger lists for the flights for both Heathrow and Gatwick airports. Hunter took one set and Fairchild the other and they sat in relative quiet not quite knowing what they were looking for, until Hunter leapt up.

'There he is. D Patzuk came into Heathrow on the 12:10 flight from Paris Charles de Gaulle.' He ran his finger to the end of the column. 'As a British citizen!'

'What?'

'It says here, Dmitry Patzuk arrived on BA 309 from Paris to London Heathrow, travelling on a British passport.'

'What happened to Lobanov's private jet?' Samantha asked, taking the printout from Hunter.

'I don't know. Perhaps *he* was using it. Anyway, it wouldn't have been necessary. If all your paperwork's above board and you're trying to appear like an ordinary, law-abiding Joe, you hop on a British Airways flight along with everyone else and blend in with the crowd.'

'I still don't see how that's possible? How did Patzuk suddenly become a UK citizen?'

'I don't know,' Hunter replied. 'A forgery?'

'I suppose...' Fairchild said, sounding less than convinced.

'With this guy's background it'd hardly be a surprise,' Hunter said. 'He's bound to know someone who could hook him up with a dodgy passport. Can't imagine why he went for a British one though, especially right now. Bit high profile, don't you think, and under his own name too?'

'Can open a lot of doors, a British passport,' Fairchild countered, 'or could.'

'Yeah, sure, but you'd imagine if he's making a fresh start, he'd change everything, wouldn't you? Plus, what are the chances of a counterfeit making it through Heathrow? You'd go for one of the smaller airports, like Southampton or Bournemouth.'

'Nope. Says here it was a legit passport,' Fairchild said. 'His name, his place of birth, everything on the level as far as immigration's concerned.'

'Really? Well if he's suddenly obtained a British passport which he's not worried about using, then on a purely practical level, Heathrow does make a lot of sense for his place in Chelsea.' Hunter tapped away at the Mac. 'Look, I found the last time he left the country. It was just a few weeks ago. Customs pulled him over, presumably thinking the same as us, I suppose. From what it says here, they really put him through it, too. Everything but the rubber gloves. Upshot is, his passport checks out. It's genuine.'

'I don't see how it can be, unless he's got a granny in Wales that we don't know about,' Fairchild said. 'Can you look up the agency's records?'

'I'll try,' Hunter replied. 'Do we know the number?'

'It's here in the immigration department's report.' She read it out and Hunter keyed it into the passport agency's database.

'Well?' Fairchild asked impatiently.

'It's there all right, although it sort of isn't,' Hunter said, genuinely confused. 'An authentic UK passport which the UK passport agency has no record of and doesn't seem to remember issuing?'

'What do you mean "doesn't seem to remember issuing"?'

'Look at this one, the one issued immediately prior to Patzuk's. There's the location, UK Passport agency, Durham, the time and date, even the name of the person who dealt with the paperwork and rubber stamped it. Look,' Hunter said, pointing at the screen, 'that must be their personal ID there. Now look at Patzuk's. All his information's there, right down to his shoe size and how he takes his coffee, but no one issued it. There's no issuing address either.'

'Perhaps they forgot to fill those bits in?' Fairchild suggested weakly.

'Let's see, shall we?'

Hunter scrolled through all the passports which had been processed that day. Each one had the name and number of the person responsible for dealing with the application. He went back further. Day after day of new passports issued to hundreds of people, and never once was that information missing.

'This is something worth putting in front of Sandy Harper wouldn't you say?' Fairchild asked, determined that their next encounter be a more successful one.

Hunter nodded. 'Let's have another look at that flight list?'

Fairchild handed Hunter back the sheets which Julian Palgrave had helpfully stapled together. 124 passengers, 2 pilots and 4 cabin crew had travelled from Paris to London that day. There was D Patzuk, in 14C. Hunter scanned through the rest of the pages, running his finger carefully down the list of names so as not to miss anything.

'I knew it,' he said. Fairchild looked up from what she'd been doing. 'When Patzuk came back to Britain, he wasn't travelling alone.'

❋❋❋

Friday, 27th March 2015 Île de la Cité, Paris.

John Alperton, the lapsed Catholic, allowed himself to smile as he approached the Cathedral of Saint-Chapelle. Just another thing the French did so well; cheese, wine, clothes - my God the clothes were exceptional - and cathedrals, scattered across France, dozens of them, beautiful, sparkling in the glorious mid-day sun like the jewels they contained. Following the previous day's rendezvous he'd put his foot down, perhaps even overstepped the mark a little. Alperton hadn't been able to say quite why, but he had felt uneasy over lunch, so today he'd insisted they meet somewhere new, not a restaurant or an art gallery. They would mingle with the hordes of tourists and that would be when they would make the exchange. He hadn't enjoyed feeling quite so anxious and about such a nothing, run of the mill operation too, collecting bags of intel. Alperton was sure there would be a pay off somewhere, there always was, but he was content to have nothing to do with it and play the messenger boy. He was enjoying this little break in his favourite city, being away from Valerie and the kids. He was particularly enjoying not having Toby Gray breathing down his neck every five minutes. But what he wasn't enjoying was the sensation of being watched.

Alperton had his own reasons for visiting Saint-Chapelle. An in-joke the Russian would never understand but which gave him huge pleasure. He'd taken a little convincing, leading Alperton to suggest that perhaps, on this occasion, he not think quite so much about his stomach for a change.

He'd never understood why so few people knew of its existence, drawn as they were to the infinitely guileless Notre Dame less than half a mile away. He was happy he'd suggested the cathedral. It had all been extremely last minute of course and bad tradecraft, but it was still a welcome change. They'd agreed to meet under the creation of Adam and Eve and, when Alperton arrived, he was delighted to find the Russian craning his thick neck to admire The Legend of the True Cross, the now familiar skimpy blue plastic bag at his feet.

What was the kickback from all this, he wondered? What was the price one paid for hundreds of Russia's finest state secrets? Money? Lives?

Alperton joined him and they sat, comfortable in each other's silence for a while, gazing simply at the panels of stained glass surrounding them.

'This was excellent idea,' the Russian said flatly.

'Good, I had a feeling you might like it.'

And then the other man was rising, and Alperton greedily looked down at the bag of Russia's treasures nestling at his feet.

'Nice to see you, Henry,' the Russian said before nodding politely and walking towards the nearest exit empty handed. John Alperton stooped to retrieve his bounty and when he stood again, ready to return to his apartment and the time-consuming task of copying all of the documents, before sending them back to London, found himself face to face with a quite different man. But a man he was sure he knew.

4

Christ, the chap from Valerie's Wednesday night watercolour classes. What the hell was he doing here?

Alperton looked at him more closely. The man he remembered had been a Beadly looking article and many pounds heavier, with a rounder body, and a fuller, plumper face. This man was half that size. Could he have heard what they'd been discussing, him and the Russian? What in fact had they been discussing other than the beauty of their surroundings? A couple of tourists then, in thrall to the majesty of Saint-Chapelle and nothing more.

Get a hold of yourself, man. The Service had checked him out thoroughly when Val had decided on her hobby, in the way in which they checked everybody out, from his wife's hairdresser to the thirteen-year-old monkey who delivered his *Telegraph* so carelessly every morning. There had, to the best of his recollection, been no clear or obvious concerns. There'd been a brief period in the sixties when he'd lived in a squat in Camden and the report conjectured that some of the people he was rubbing shoulders with might not have been the most wholesome. Not merely socialists, they'd said, but full-blooded commies. But there was never the suggestion that he had anything other than the wateriest of political convictions.

The man was obviously a queen, had a partner to boot, if Alperton remembered correctly. But then there had been a time, he reminded himself, when every other member of The Service had been gay. If memory served, the man opposite him had attended a number of marches in the late eighties demonstrating against Clause 28 and, whilst Alperton didn't share his sentiments, the marches themselves were no cause for concern. Valerie seemed to enjoy his lessons and it was just bad timing and a bloody shame that he should pop up right here and, more inconveniently for John Alperton, right now.

Alperton had been along one year to see her class's work. Mostly amateurish daubs by women of a certain age, whose children had left them for higher education and whose husbands had abandoned them for the golf course. He'd been obtrusively polite about Valerie's efforts. To Alperton's eye they'd appeared no better nor worse than anyone else's. She'd spend days, he recalled, finding just the right field to paint or flowers to arrange. For his part Alperton had pursed his lips and nodded deliberately in a way he hoped expressed deeply considered and rational criticism before praising her work to the heavens. This chap, whatever his name was, had been waddling around in the background, a fag dangling from his bottom lip, like an overanxious mother hen, straightening frames and tutting and simpering.

'It is you. I said to myself, there's Valerie's husband! I've forgotten your name, I'm so sorry. I said, there's Valerie's husband, but then I thought, Clive, don't be such a silly-socks, I mean really, what are the chances? Well, you would, wouldn't you? But it is you, isn't it? John, am I right? I am so terrible with names.'

'That's right. What a pleasant surprise,' Alperton said, sticking out a hand and painting on a smile, a bag of Russia's most sordid secrets clutched in his other hand. 'How lovely to see you, Clive.'

'And is Valerie with you? Where is she? I must say hello.'

'No actually, I'm here on my own.' *What to say?* 'In a sort of business capacity.'

'Really? A sort of business capacity, how exciting.'

'No, not particularly. Quite dull in fact. But I've never been one to pass up the opportunity to spend some time in Paris.' Alperton surprised himself with how close to the truth this latest pronouncement was.

Somerset nodded his approval and waited for his newfound companion to expand on the statement. Instead, Alperton eased back a perfectly ironed cuff and inspected his wristwatch.

'You're looking well,' he said, suddenly uncharacteristically unsure of himself.

Clive Somerset laughed as loudly as their surroundings permitted.

'Thank you,' he replied, and then, perhaps sensing Alperton's confusion and not wishing the other man feel uncomfortable, 'It's the diabetes, you know?' Somerset patted his now meritorious stomach with both hands. 'Doctor told me I was to cut out the ciggies and lose 10 stone! I'd have said it was impossible but then Daniel passed away and suddenly not eating became the simplest thing in the world.' He stuck his head forward and shrugged all at the same time. 'Ciggies took a little longer!' he whispered.

Alperton was racking his brains. Who the hell was Daniel? It took a moment. 'I was so sorry to hear of your loss,' he added in the nick of time.

'Did you ever meet him?' Somerset asked, slightly taken aback.

'No, I'm ashamed to say I didn't.' Sometimes, on rare occasions, the truth could be the best option, Alperton thought. 'But Val always spoke very fondly of him.' Back to another comfortable lie.

Somerset nodded slowly. 'Of course,' he said, and Alperton wondered if he wasn't on the verge of tears. Somerset was aware of it too now and stopped himself. A brisk change of subject would spare them both the embarrassment.

'Incredible here, isn't it?' Somerset said, waving a hand around to generously encompass the interior of the cathedral.

'I have a friend who believes this to be the single greatest artistic achievement of the Western World,' Alperton replied.

Somerset sniffed and dabbed beneath his spectacles with a handkerchief. 'I think perhaps da Vinci might have had something to say about that but yes, yes it is pretty extraordinary.' Alperton glanced at his watch again. 'I don't want to hold you up, if you have somewhere else you need to be? It has been lovely bumping into you though,' Somerset said, now that he could see this man for who he really was. 'Small world, eh? Listen, I hope I wasn't interrupting anything, just now?' Alperton stared at him, agog. 'You were meeting a friend?' Somerset continued, gesturing at the empty seat Alperton had just vacated.

This was John Alperton's worst nightmare and all because he'd decided to change what had been a perfectly satisfactory arrangement.

'No, no,' he said.

'Oh, it's just I could have sworn I saw the pair of you talking.'

Alperton shook his head listlessly.

'And then he called you Henry, I'm sure he did.'

'It's dreadfully noisy in here, I think you must be mistaken.'

Somerset nodded. 'Yes, yes I expect you're right.' Perhaps he had misheard, after all? It was terribly boomy in the cavernous cathedral and anyway, why on earth would the other man have made such a mistake?

'Never seen him before,' Alperton continued. And as the words fell from his mouth he knew he'd overplayed his hand. It was, in a lifetime of deception, a particularly poor lie and he could see from Somerset's face that he knew it too and so each man took a moment to examine their surroundings again in the hope that Alperton's ghastly fabrication might die on the wind like a falsely whispered prayer.

'I tell you what,' Alperton said, looking at Clive Somerset, this tragically broken man whom he had so shamefully attempted to circumvent. 'What are you up to tomorrow? If you've no plans, we should definitely meet up for lunch.' Alperton smiled. 'It'll give us a proper chance to talk and you can tell me all about your plans and what you really think of Valerie's paintings,' he joked.

Alperton's mind happily clouded with bistros and brasseries. Julien, a stone's throw from Saint Denis, would have been lovely, but far too formal for this occasion. Au chien qui fume, on the southside of Les Halles, was well known for its seafood and close to his apartment but a little too public, whilst L'Écluse overlooking the river, too intimate. Au Pied de Cochon came to mind, but he worried that the menu might have taxed his guest too greatly. Le Felteu then. Alperton realised he'd been looking for an excuse to visit the tiny bistro in the heart of the Marais since his arrival. It was cosy without being sentimental, off the beaten track certainly and, whilst at first glance the menu might have appeared a tad *simpliste,* it was in truth merely honest and well cooked. It was never good to dine alone, added to which it would give him an opportunity to discover just how much Somerset thought he'd heard.

'That would be lovely,' Somerset replied, a little unsurely.

'Good, that's agreed then,' Alperton said, writing the address on the back of some glossy literature from the cathedral's museum.

'Although I'm worried I shan't be able to afford your prices, John.'

'Trust me,' Alperton joked amiably, 'You can pay, you can pay.'

***

Fairchild stared at Hunter. 'What do you mean, he wasn't travelling alone?'

'Look there,' Hunter said, pointing at the bottom of the flight manifest, 'Right at the back of the plane. E Tikhonov.'

Samantha Fairchild thought for a moment and then began desperately rifling through the pile of papers next to her.

'There,' she said, holding out an almost identical sheet to Hunter's. She quickly ran her finger down the list of names on her manifest, flicking through the pages. 'That's what I thought. Patzuk travelled to Paris on his own. I was sure I hadn't missed Tikhonov's name. So where the hell was he all that time?'

Hunter shook his head. 'I don't know but I agree with you, we need to find out a little more about Evgeny Tikhonov. How did he manage to slip back into the UK?' Hunter tapped quickly at the iMac. 'I can't find any record of him ever applying for a visa, which is weird, and I'm guessing he's not travelling on a UK passport like his boss?'

'No,' Fairchild said staunchly, 'he most definitely is not.'

Hunter looked up, sensing immediately that she'd found something. 'Well?'

'He came into London on the same flight as Dmitry Patzuk.'

'Yes,' Hunter replied, 'we know that.'

'On a blue passport,' Fairchild announced, waiting for Hunter's reaction. 'A *blue* passport, Scott.'

Hunter shook his head and shrugged. 'I have no idea what that means.'

'Russian passports are red, with two exceptions. Diplomatic passports are green and Service passports are blue.'

'Service passports?'

'Like, civil servants, judges or,' and now she paused for dramatic effect, 'members of the armed forces.'

'Shit. But there's never been anything to suggest that Tikhonov was in the army. I've never seen his service record, have you?'

'No.'

'We definitely need to find out more about this guy.' Hunter looked at Fairchild and then at Julian Palgrave.

'Oh no, come on Scott, I spoke to him last time. It's your turn, although I wouldn't get your hopes up. He told me he'd given me all the information he had.'

Somewhat reluctantly, Hunter rose and went to speak to Palgrave. 'Could I have anything you've got on Evgeny Tikhonov?'

Palgrave scrunched up his face.

'As I told Miss Fairchild, I'm unable to release that file, I'm afraid.'

'Oh,' Hunter said, not wishing to fall out with Palgrave. He'd understood from Fairchild that they'd seen all the information he possessed on Tikhonov but now it seemed as though there was more which he simply didn't want to share. 'Why's that?' he enquired.

'I'm not convinced either of you has the clearance for that material, Mr Hunter.'

'But Sandy said...'

'I recall only too well what Mr Harper said. I have seen the file, he has not. I am not releasing that file to you or Miss Fairchild. That's the end of it.'

'Could you call him, please? Or someone else?'

Palgrave shifted uncomfortably and fiddled with his spectacles. 'I could, but I really think that...'

'Please make the call,' Hunter interrupted, eager to stamp what little authority he had on proceedings.

Grudgingly Palgrave picked up the receiver, leaving Hunter to stare at his boots.

'Well, Mr Hunter,' Palgrave said finally, having sullenly returned the phone to its cradle, 'it appears you may see that file after all.' He didn't afford Hunter the courtesy of a reply but stormed off, returning moments later and reluctantly relinquishing Evgeny Tikhonov's file. Hunter could see immediately that it was half the thickness of the other two. He thanked Palgrave profusely and went to share his findings.

'I'll start wading through these two if you like,' he said, picking up Sklepov and Katz's files. 'You can have Evgeny Tikhonov,' Hunter said, checking the name on the outside of the file. 'Looks pretty skimpy to me, so it shouldn't take too long, although I had a devil of a job prising it out of old Palgrave.'

Saturday, 28ᵗʰ March 2015 Paris.

Never having been to Le Felteu and anxious he didn't know his way around the Marais particularly well, Somerset arrived early. A vibrant part of town, its thin strips of pavement constantly in motion, streets lined with cafés, bars and bistros. Even with the first drops of rain heralding the onset of a brief spring shower, Clive Somerset was content to stand outside the modest establishment John Alperton had selected for lunch and watch the world go by. From the pavement Le Felteu appeared unremarkable, even second-rate, but Somerset was reassuringly impressed by the steady flow of locals making their way inside. Someone had pinned up a rudimentary menu. Somerset didn't need his spectacles, the dishes, writ large, were indeed reasonable. As Somerset was methodically translating the *Menu du jour,* John Alperton pulled up in a taxi.

Somerset turned to observe as Alperton paid the driver, a beautiful cashmere overcoat draped over one arm, a Lockwood brolly dangling from the other. Valerie Alperton wanted for very little too, Somerset thought. If he'd suggested to his class for instance, that such and such a brand of paper would be a wise investment or a particular brush might help even just a little, you could guarantee that the next week she'd return with every conceivable size of sketchpad and not one but each and every brush available.

And as for that chap he'd seen Alperton talking with. A little chunky around the midriff, in need of a shave and definitely not his type, but with a certain dishevelled strength detectable above the crumpled cowhide jacket and the unpolished shoes. He wondered if Valerie knew what her husband was up to. After his encounter the previous day and now with the certainty of his true identity, Clive Somerset had reappraised the situation and arrived at a quite startling conclusion.

'Shall we?' Alperton held open the door and they disappeared inside, where they were met almost immediately by a frenetic little Parisian woman sporting a chef's apron, a head of unruly dark hair and an explosively short temper. Clive noticed the warm smile of recognition she flashed his host and was relieved to hear Alperton burst into fluent French.

The interior of Le Felteu, if one had been feeling generous, might best have been described as shabby chic. Gravity defying wallpaper bulged from the plaster, threatening to dislodge the desultory collection of reproductions clinging there and which briefly caught Somerset's eye but were quickly dismissed. Alperton had long been of the belief that the ancient wallpaper was the only thing holding the place up. Simple tables and benches stood in two short parallel lines accommodating the thirty or so covers. At one end, an open door led through to a noisy kitchen into which the frantic little Parisian woman disappeared amid a flurry of barked instructions and agitated gesticulations. Alperton and Somerset were left to find their own table, where Alperton, clearly very much at home and happy to play the host, began casually examining a small chalkboard displaying the dishes of the day.

'The *navarin* looks good, although the *confit* here is really excellent,' he said, as the owner reappeared to place a couple of portions on a neighbouring table.

'Not ideal, on my diet.'

'Ah, yes,' Alperton said, remembering Somerset's condition.

'But I suppose I could make an exception,' he continued, seemingly pleased with his decision.

'I shan't tell anyone,' Alperton said. 'Soul of discretion,' he added, unnecessarily tapping his nose.

'Our little secret?' Somerset put in, polishing his spectacles on his cardigan.

'If you like,' Alperton replied laughing easily, relieved to find his dining companion so at ease.

'Initially, when I became sick, well I put it down to losing Daniel of course.'

The owner returned and Alperton ordered two portions of the duck and a demi-carafe of the house red which he knew to be acceptable but whose price tag wouldn't alarm his guest.

'Sorry, you were saying.'

'I thought I was unwell because, well, you know? Anyway, after some tests they said I was a bit over-weight and beginning to exhibit all the warning signs of diabetes. All controllable, provided I lose some weight and I'm careful with what I eat.' Somerset laughed, thinking about the leg of duck he'd just ordered. 'I just have to try and look after myself a little better.'

'That's terrific news,' Alperton replied, raising his glass. 'Val told me you'd packed in the teaching. What are you doing in Paris? Bit of a holiday?'

'Something like that. A bucket list. I think that's what people call it. What about you? What brings you to Paris, John?'

'Oh, nothing nearly so exciting, I'm afraid.'

Somerset was about to ask again when their food arrived.

'When do you head back home?' Alperton enquired between mouthfuls.

'I'm not, well not straight away at any rate. I'm going to Florence at the end of the month.'

'Goodness,' Alperton said, aware that he was secretly more than a little jealous.

'I should have been there by now, but I decided to spend a little more time in Paris.'

'Well,' Alperton continued after both men had eaten in silence, 'what do you think, about the food?'

There was no doubt in Clive Somerset's mind. It was one of the finest meals he had ever tasted. 'But do you know what I love almost more than the food?' he asked. Alperton shook his head, uncertain as to exactly what the other man was driving at. 'I think places like this are fantastic,' Somerset concluded, looking about him. 'I love watching other people, don't you?' Alperton nodded slowly, not at all confident he'd understood. 'Take this pair here,' Somerset whispered, pushing his spectacles up his nose whilst indicating a young couple two tables away. 'A first date, I think you'd probably agree? Look at the way he tries to dominate the table, although I'm not convinced he's usually as smartly dressed as that. He looks a little awkward, don't you think? She, on the other hand, she's assured in her beauty, happy to have a suitor to toy with. She'll let him try everything in his repertoire to impress her, safe in the knowledge there are countless more just like him. Look at how she sits back,' Somerset said warming to the subject and pausing only to skewer another forkful of duck. 'And look now, see how her eyes flit around the room. She's already boring of him and searching for her next distraction.'

'And you can tell all of that simply by looking at them out of the corner of your eye?' Alperton asked.

Somerset laughed heartily and took another enthusiastic gulp of wine. 'I have been known to be wrong,' he said. 'It's such a wonderful hobby though. I can take it with me anywhere and it requires no equipment or investment. It's also a little of what I do, do you see? To capture the essence of the individual, even if that isn't quite how we actually *see* them. Picasso, with his confident bold brush strokes was bullish, frighteningly direct and often objectionably overconfident in life. Turner, by contrast, was a shy man, deeply ill at ease and racked with self-doubt, ever anxious that his gift would never be quite enough. His paintings are fragile and delicate, just as he was I suspect. Each are magnificent in their own way, of course, and far beyond my humble abilities, but it's Turner's brittleness of character that lends his work real greatness, I would submit.'

'Really?'

'An artist's work almost always reflects some aspect of their character. Surely that can't come as any great surprise. It's much the same as a person's body language.' Alperton glanced back at the young couple. 'Or their choice of clothing,' Somerset continued, causing Alperton to involuntarily draw a hand down his tie and check his cuffs. 'Some wish to be noticed in life, to be taken seriously, and they often make this statement with the clothes they wear. Others, myself for one clearly, prefer not to walk in the limelight and dress and behave accordingly. Then there are the clowns and exhibitionists.'

'And what do they wear?' Alperton enquired wearily, starting to tire of Somerset's theorizing.

'They dress to deceive,' Somerset smiled. 'They would not have us glean their nature and choose instead to disguise their true selves in fabrics and fripperies, tassels and affectations.'

'How fascinating,' Alperton concluded, adjusting the napkin on his lap and stifling a yawn.

'But I can see I'm boring you. Daniel was just the same. He never understood my fascination with the appearance of a perfect stranger. You'll have to forgive me, an artist's obsession with the world around him,' Somerset said shaking his head. 'And you still haven't told me what *you're* doing here. Where are you staying?'

'The other side of the river,' Alperton replied, lazily raising a hand. 'Latin quarter.'

'Very nice,' Somerset said, wondering why he was being lied to. 'Handy for Saint-Chappelle.'

'Exactly.'

'And you're managing to fit in some time for business between trips to the Île de la Cité?'

'What is this Clive, twenty questions?' Alperton laughed, helping himself to another fork of potatoes *sarladaises*. 'Have some more wine.'

Somerset held out his glass.

'What about you?' Alperton was asking. 'I'm not going to lie, I'm more than a little envious of your plans to tour Europe. Not cheap though, I'd imagine?'

Somerset chuckled to himself. The Alpertons certainly didn't have any money worries. 'When Daniel died, I sold everything and came out here. You might be surprised just how little there was to show for it, a lifetime of painting and teaching. Barely enough for me to pay for the course in Florence, some life drawing classes here and my train tickets. I've been living on my wits for the last few months.'

'What about Daniel, when he died, his estate?'

'His sister got the lot. I never saw a penny.'

'Well that's simply terrible,' Alperton said, surprised by how much he absolutely meant it.

Somerset nodded his agreement and let Alperton replenish his glass. 'Listen John, as we're on the subject, and I hate to do this, I mean we barely know one another and believe me, as soon as I get back from Florence I'll make sure I square up with you, but you couldn't see fit to lend me, and I absolutely mean lend me, some money could you? I hate to ask, I really do, but I had no idea how expensive Paris was going to be and it's eating through my savings at a rate. Once I get to Italy every-thing'll settle down I'm sure. You never know, I might even sell some paintings, and then the first thing I'll do of course is find a way to wire you the money.'

'How much do you need?'

'A couple of hundred? Maybe three. That should tide me over.'

'I'm sorry Clive, I simply don't carry that sort of cash around with me.'

'No, no, of course you don't.'

Somerset thought the price of Alperton's umbrella alone would have paid not only for his train ticket south but also the bulk of his accommodation.

Alperton took another sip of wine and regarded the man opposite. So, Clive Somerset was trying to tap him for cash, was he? Bit rich. He hardly knew the man and, if this was his way of getting out of paying for lunch, it was a pretty damned unorthodox one.

'I suppose you could always take out the money from a bank here though,' Somerset suggested.

Good Lord. He wasn't giving up either, Alperton thought. He might have considered it a minute ago, but not like this. Bloody cheek.

'I'm sorry Clive, bit awkward with my bank at the moment too. Expensive children to maintain, if you follow me?' he replied pushing away his half-finished confit, suddenly eager for their meal to be at an end.

'No. Of course. Quite understand,' his dining companion nodded.

Well that was something of a relief, Alperton thought. Perhaps now he might be permitted to enjoy his dessert?

'Maybe I should ask your friend?' Somerset said, deliberately placing his knife and fork on the clean plate in front of him.

'I beg your pardon?'

'Perhaps I should ask the man you met in Saint-Chappelle yesterday?'

'I'm sorry Clive, you've completely lost me,' Alperton replied, trying to laugh it off.

'Thick set. Eastern European was my first impression, and I wasn't far off, as it turned out. Nasty looking birthmark down one side of his face. You said that you'd never met him before.'

'That's right,' Alperton replied.

'But that's not quite true, is it?'

'What are you talking about?'

'And I'm sure you couldn't forget a face like that, especially as you had lunch with him a few days ago in a restaurant on the Avenue de l'Opera. Not to mention a cosy little tête-à-tête in the Musée de l'Orangerie the day before that.'

'Have you been following me, Clive?' Alperton asked, looking closely at the man opposite him.

'I was bored, and I thought I recognised you. Not sure what made me do it really. Nothing better to do I suppose. Looking for a spot of excitement.'

Alperton took a decent gulp of wine, shifted his cutlery around uneasily and decided to go on the offensive.

'Do you make a habit of following people?'

'My initial instinct was to wonder if you weren't having some sort of Caravaggio-esque mid-life crisis,' Somerset said, smiling at the very idea.

'This is outrageous!' Alperton hissed, taking the napkin from his knee, balling it up and looking to their bustling Parisian hostess for the bill.

'Just before you go, I wonder if you'd care to know exactly where your friend works, John?'

'And how the hell would you know that?'

'Because, after lunch the other day I decided to follow *him* instead of you. What a fascinating individual.'

'Keep your voice down you bloody fool.'

'Ah, I see, you already know.'

'Shouldn't you be in Florence by now?' Alperton said to himself.

'John, are you threatening me?'

'I wouldn't say so. How many people know you've elected to stay put rather than go south?'

'John! You are threatening me.'

A tiny porcelain saucer arrived at Alperton's elbow baring a handful of mints and a folded piece of paper which he hurriedly picked up. Somerset seized the opportunity and rose from his seat, found his coat and made for the door. Alperton took a bundle of notes from his wallet and with only a cursory glance and without counting them, left them on the table next to his unfinished meal. Clive Somerset was already halfway out of the tiny bistro.

***

Hunter licked his fingers and was about to turn over another Russian police report on Yuri Sklepov when Fairchild spoke up.

'I think you're going to want to see this,' she began. 'Evgeny Tikhonov, Dmitry Patzuk's Mr Fix It and general go to guy in a crisis...'

'Yeah,' Hunter said, 'what about him?'

'He wasn't in the army.'

'No?'

'No,' she said, shaking her head. 'He's FSB.'

'He's what?'

'He works for the Russian Secret Service, Scott, and has been doing for considerably longer than he's been working for Patzuk.'

'Really? He's a spook?' Hunter said. 'I take it Patzuk's never found out?'

'He's still alive isn't he, so I'm guessing not? He did do a spell in prison though,' Fairchild said flicking back through the file and finding a copy of his record. 'It might be worth getting this properly translated but that date,' she pointed to a series of numbers, 'that predates the first record we have of him working for Patzuk, doesn't it?'

'Hold on.' Hunter began leafing through the file in front of him. 'Sklepov, the driver, he was in prison from '95. Look, three years for stealing a motorbike. I'm prepared to bet it's the same prison Evgeny Tikhonov wound up in. They set him up. The FSB recruited Tikhonov, sent him to the South of France for a bit, probably so that everyone would forget about him, then brought him back to Russia only to have him arrested and banged up in prison with orders to chat up Patzuk's driver and infiltrate his crew,' Hunter said.

'It's certainly a theory. Probably shared a cell,' Fairchild added archly.

'So the Russians are every bit as interested in Patzuk and Lobanov as we are,' Hunter said.

'And then there's this?' Fairchild continued, holding up a sheet of bank transactions showing a series of payments made from a GDLC Holdings in Harley Street to a private account in Nevis in the Caribbean over a six-month period.

'I have no idea,' Hunter replied. 'Who the hell are GDLC Holdings? They'll be registered at Companies House I guess, whoever they are. Wait a minute.' He tapped away at the iMac. 'There's not a lot to go on. They're a limited company dealing primarily in stocks and shares.'

'But with offices just up the road?'

'I expect Harley Street's just a PO Box. An accommodation address. Lends them that veneer of respectability.'

Fairchild raised her eyes to the ceiling.

'Tikhonov's been paid for something,' Hunter continued 'but we've no way of finding out what that something is or who was really paying him. What do we know about him? Where's he from?'

'Kamchatka.'

'Never heard of it,' Hunter said, shaking his head.

'It's a peninsular in the east. Brown bears, lakes and volcanoes. Pretty wild.'

Hunter smiled. 'Let's see his picture?'

'That's the other thing,' Fairchild replied, almost embarrassed. 'There isn't one.'

'Let me see,' Hunter said, taking the folder from her. A quick flick through the flimsy file was enough to confirm that Fairchild was right. Hunter picked up The Service's modest findings on Yuri Sklepov. There were photographs of him at various stages of his life, as a teenager, a young man, then his police mug shot, an Interpol bulletin with a passport photo stapled in its corner and even surveillance photographs taken of him by The Service itself. He opened Dmitry Patzuk's file, which was similar. There were even *some* photographs of the famously camera-shy Oleg Lobanov. Admittedly many were of the back of his head as he raced to get into a car but Hunter had a reasonable idea of what he looked like. Not so Evgeny Tikhonov. He went through the file again, from front to back, twice. There wasn't a single picture. He found the bulletin Interpol had issued when he'd first left Russia, alerting their European counterparts that he was now moving freely across the continent and potentially working there too. The small square photograph which should have been stapled into the top righthand corner had been removed, leaving two tiny puncture marks and a barely perceptible shadow. This, Hunter reasoned, was deliberate and could only have been carried out since the file had been compiled, if not with Julian Palgrave's outright consent, then at least with his agreement to look the other way. Someone within The Service was quite determined that Evgeny Tikhonov not be identified.

He stared at Fairchild. 'What the hell's going on? Do we know where he was stationed in his time with the FSB?'

'Toulouse from '94 to '97. Then he was sent back to Russia. He goes to prison for six months where we now think he engineered a meeting with Sklepov. After prison he's based largely in Moscow, where he appears to have been working for Dmitry Patzuk until 2015. There's a brief spell in Paris, around the time he received those payments from GDLC, then he and Patzuk move everything to London from where he seems to have been operating ever since.'

'Then what?'

'Then nothing,' Fairchild said. 'There's no further mention of him in The Service's report.'

'We need to find out just what Evgeny Tikhonov was up to five years ago,' Hunter said.

'Clive, just hold up a minute,' Alperton called after him, trying to sound as reasonable as he could. But Somerset was already in the Bistro's somewhat austere entry vestibule, pulling on his jacket and heading for the door. 'Clive, come along, let's not be foolish about this.' And then the door was closing behind him and Alperton was cursing quietly under his breath and barging past diners and awkwardly positioned chairs. He watched in horror as the Bistro's door swung shut.

Fresh air and the wine he'd drunk hit Clive Somerset like a slap in the face. He shut his eyes against the rain and wondered what he'd done. Accused a man he hardly knew, of what? Consorting with a Russian oaf with a dark red birthmark and appalling tables manners? So what?

Somerset heard the door open behind him. John Alperton was moving toward him, arms outstretched. He stepped back. An unsteady foot, half-on, half-off the kerb. John Alperton's arms reaching for him. Slippery concrete, an imploring voice and then Clive Somerset was falling backwards. The screech of brakes. Cold tyres on wet tarmac. A dull, sickening thud and then nothing.

Clive Somerset lay in the road outside Le Felteu and quickly and quietly passed away before John Alperton or anyone else could help him. Alperton knelt by the body. He briefly contemplated retrieving Somerset's smashed and bent spectacles but didn't, felt moved to say something but couldn't. Aware that a crowd was gathering, he took his overcoat and laid it shroud-like over Somerset's body, pulling it up to cover his broken face. And then, quite suddenly, there were gendarmerie everywhere and people with cameras and John Alperton needed to be far away.

'I'll check the news outlets,' Fairchild suggested. 'Why don't you see what The Service was up to?'

She disappeared into the endless rows of box files and filing cabinets and Hunter approached Palgrave.

'If I wanted all The Service's records for a particular location...'

'I can look that up for you,' Palgrave told him. 'Let me know the relevant dates and off we go. Where is it you're after?'

'Paris, I guess, about five years ago?'

Palgrave tapped at his keyboard. 'Okay, there appear to have been two cells active in or around Paris at that time.'

Hunter thanked Palgrave and pulled up a chair at his computer just as Fairchild returned. 'Nothing very interesting that I could find for that week,' she said, 'just the usual collection of protests, strikes and RTAs.'

'Okay. Palgrave says there were two operatives working Paris and reporting back to London in March 2015.' Hunter typed and folders popped up on the screen. J Fraser and M Bayer.

He opened Fraser's file covering the time they believed Dmitry Patzuk had been there. Seven, one for each day of the week. He and Fairchild sat and read through her daily anti-terrorism reports. Concise, business like accounts of her time in Paris. Hunter could imagine her, enjoying the café culture, smartly dressed, walking by the Seine. Fraser's style was succinct, professional and to the point. She didn't smoke, Hunter thought, never walked on the cracks in the pavement, drank Badoit with her lunch, never took the nose off the cheese and was bloody good at her job. For her part, Fairchild was shocked by just how much had been going on in the city at a time when, if the national press were to be believed, everything had appeared peaceful and un-newsworthy. They opened her last report. She'd been busy working with the Counter Terrorism branch of the General Directorate for External Security at the time, chasing up joint operations into terrorist threats on both sides of the channel and mainly concerned with Algerian Jihadists entering France through the port of Marseille before travelling north to Paris, and so there was no reason for either of them to suppose that she had any connection with Dmitry Patzuk whatsoever. Hunter closed down her file.

'I suppose it's always possible that Dmitry just went on holiday?' Fairchild said. 'Did a spot of sightseeing. People do do that, you know?'

'I know, but most of them come back with the same passport they left on, or had you forgotten?'

'What about Fraser? Is there any point in talking to her?' Fairchild asked.

'Hard to say, isn't it? Why don't we put it in the report to Harper and see what he thinks?'

Hunter opened Marcus Bayer's folder. There was only one file. He clicked on the PDF and it opened instantly to display a standard report logged on the 4th April.

'So?' Fairchild said, looking at him expectantly.

'There's only a couple of paragraphs,' Hunter replied. 'Bayer flew in from Moscow, spent the day sightseeing, had a spot of lunch and then...'

Fairchild looked at him. 'And then what?'

'I don't know. The last two paragraphs of the report have been redacted.' Hunter turned the screen so Fairchild could see the blacked-out section of the report, yawned and shrugged his shoulders.

'It's all we've got,' Fairchild said. 'Better see if Julian can help.'

Hunter returned to Palgrave's counter.

'Any chance we could see this file please?'

Palgrave flicked through on his desktop.

'Isn't it on the shared drive? That's what it says here. One document which was scanned into the system on 4th April.'

'Yeah, that's the one. It's been altered though. Any chance we could take a look at the original?

'I'm not with you,' Palgrave replied, pushing his spectacles up his nose. 'What do you mean, it's been altered?'

'It's been quite heavily redacted,' Fairchild said, arriving at Hunter's shoulder. 'Any chance we could have a look at the file itself?'

'Fill in the form, I'll see what I can do.'

Hunter jotted the numbers into Palgrave's form, who took it from the pad, found the keys to the door behind him and disappeared.

Three minutes later he returned with the file Hunter had requested. A single sheet of heavily redacted A4, almost half of which was unreadable. Hunter held it up and he and Sam regarded it ruefully.

'No offence,' he said, 'but this is useless. It's the same as what's on the shared drive.' Palgrave smiled. 'And it's a copy.'

Palgrave's smile vanished as quickly as it had appeared.

'I beg your pardon?' he said.

'This was copied from the original before it was redacted. You can see there, where some dirt's got under the glass, but this,' Hunter pointed to the thick black lines which obscured much of the text, 'this has to have been done later. Look, the body text is that photocopier kind of grey, but these lines,' Hunter pointed to some of the redacted text, 'they've been done later, you can tell. Plus,' he tentatively felt at the corner of the page, 'this is photocopier paper. It's kind of thin and crappy.'

'Give that to me,' Palgrave said, taking the sheet from Hunter's hand.

'Is there any chance we could have a look at the original, please?' Fairchild put in for the umpteenth time.

'No,' Palgrave replied, abruptly cutting her short, 'there is not. I'm sorry Samantha, but this is all I have.'

Hunter turned to face her. 'Back to square one then.'

5

Sunday, 8th March 2020
The third death from coronavirus is announced.

'This is Frances Verity,' David Hunter said, smiling at the woman by his side. 'We've been seeing each other for just over a month now. It's all thanks to you, really,' he continued, laughing.

Scott was dumbstruck. And how, in any sense had this been anything to do with him? After a while his stunned silence became a question.

'You suggested I start going for walks, remember?'

'I said you should get a dog,' Scott replied indignantly. 'Jesus, Dad, when were you thinking of telling me?'

'We're telling you now,' Frances chimed in calmly.

'I met her on one of your walks. She was looking for her dog, as it happens.'

They smiled at one another. A private reminiscence and part of their briefly shared history.

One of *your* walks! So, this was it. This was the secret his father had been keeping from him. The reason for his abnormal *bonhomie* and, in Scott's mind at least, a very definitive betrayal of his mother's memory. Desperate to say something he found himself spluttering buts and half sentences, and then, finally, once his mind had cleared and his long dead mother receded into the depths of his memory, a fresh face filled his thoughts. What had his mentor Michael Healy always cautioned against? Don't trust anyone, even someone you think you know. *Especially* someone you think you know. Who was this woman? He looked at her now. She *seemed* genuine enough but how were you supposed to know? Scott knew how skilfully people in his line of work could engineer a meeting, how they could make it appear the most natural thing in the world. A dropped newspaper, a seemingly innocent request for directions or the anxious entreaties of a beautiful stranger who has lost her dog. He'd been completely taken in by Samantha Fairchild, hadn't he? The promise of a drink and a friendly smile. This woman could be anyone. Scott could see how attractive she was. His father would quite understandably have felt flattered.

And then, quite suddenly, he hated himself. What gave him the right to deny his father something he'd clearly been wanting for so long? Perhaps this woman was the happiness he'd been searching for? Wasn't that the most obvious explanation? And who was he to deny him that happiness?

'I'm sorry. This is all a bit of a shock. Really, Frances it's lovely to meet you. We should probably ...'

'Go for lunch, I'd like that, Scott. Your father's told me so much about you. I've children of my own you know, about your age?'

And then they were leaving the house behind, an awkward trio of unanswered questions, doubts and suspicions, walking down the lane to the closeted sanctuary of The Boot Public House.

That evening, once Frances had left, Scott found his father in the kitchen.

'Out with it then,' David Hunter had said.

'She seems really... pleasant.'

'Oh, Jesus. Pleasant?!' David laughed.

'Sorry. She's nice.' Nice wasn't a huge improvement on pleasant, David Hunter thought, but he'd take it. 'I mean it dad,' Scott continued, 'I'm happy for you.'

'But? Come on Scott, if there isn't a but, there bloody well ought to be.'

'Alright. What do you really know about her? You met her when? On a walk in Frogmore Meadows? You know as well as I do, she could be a bump.'

'Thank you very much,' David said, setting down a freshly dried wine glass with a little too much force. 'Has it ever occurred to you that she's simply attracted by my animal magnetism?'

'Oh God,' Scott said, aware that years of awkward social conventions were in danger of being turned on their heads. 'I'm going to try and pretend you didn't say that.'

'Okay, okay. Of course I've thought about it. But come on Scott, I left The Service years ago. Why on earth would anyone send somebody after me now? I've probably forgotten more than I ever knew. And at my age you'd have to agree there would be simpler and more effective methods. Isn't it conceivable that she likes me for me and that there's nothing more to it than that?'

'You're right of course, I know you are,' Scott replied. But as he spoke both men knew that the next day he would be beating a path to Julian Palgrave's office and asking for everything The Service had on Frances Verity. David Hunter didn't like to admit it to his own son, or even to himself, but secretly he was rather pleased. Pleased and relieved. It was, after all, exactly what he would have done.

***

The FTSE plunges more than 8%

Sandy Harper opened the manilla folder in front of him, licked the end of a crooked finger and pushed at the three sheets of paper.

'This looks a little more like it,' he said, slowly drawing one page towards him, 'which is good for you.' He tapped at a word, moistened his thin cracked lips like an antediluvian reptile and raised an approving eyebrow. 'Although it does raise some questions.' He squared up the sheets and closed the folder. 'Now,' he rasped, 'Get out!'

Hunter and Fairchild turned to leave, shocked by Harper's reaction but simultaneously thankful for their ordeal to be over so quickly.

'Not you, Mr Hunter. You may stay and entertain me.'

'I'm sorry?'

'Humour me,' Harper said, waiting for Fairchild to close the door behind her. 'Where did this unprecedented pile of detritus come from?'

'You told us to come back with more information. Put it a bit more succinctly, you said.'

'I remember,' Harper replied, interlacing his fingers and massaging his thumbs.

Hunter shrugged. 'There it is.'

'Indeed. What I should like to know is, *how* was this information obtained?'

'We did a search on floor four, to see if there'd been any Service activity which might have involved Dmitry Patzuk or Oleg Lobanov. I know there's not a great deal to go on. Decent photos are hard to come by and the Paris section's a bit sketchy, but it's all we could find.'

'And this name,' Harper said, reopening the folder and gently allowing his hand to settle over the page with exaggerated slowness. Hunter craned his neck to see which name he'd identified, but deep down he suspected he already knew. 'Marcus Bayer,' Harper almost whispered it. 'How is it that Marcus Bayer's name comes to be in your report? It is inconceivable to me that either you or the delicious Ms Fairchild could have stumbled upon it by accident. To think that the pair of you should have just discovered...' but Harper stopped himself short, '*this* name,' he reiterated awkwardly, 'It's difficult for me to believe. So, who told you?'

'No one. We went looking for service activity in Paris around the time Dmitry was there. There were only two of our agents working there when he visited. Bayer was one of them. We found a largely redacted file in his folder, pretty much just the time and date left on it.'

Harper looked back blankly. 'And you say there were irregularities with Patzuk's passport. Show me,' he said.

'I can't,' Hunter replied uneasily. 'Julian won't allow it to leave floor four.' Harper's roving tongue moved across his lips, his eyes flicked up to the ceiling, waiting for Hunter to continue. 'Patzuk took a break in Paris. Seems he left a Russian and came back a Brit.'

'Explain.'

'Different passports, which we thought was a bit odd, so we went back through all the records for Paris around about that time.'

'Alone?'

'No, Sam and I worked on it together,' which sounded as awkward as it felt, 'per your instructions.'

'What I meant was, from some of the content in this report,' Harper gave the documents covering his desk a contemptuous study, 'I can only assume the pair of you had help?'

Hunter laughed. Not outright, not in Sandy Harper's face, as he would have liked. A very private laugh.

'Something amused you, Mr Hunter?'

'The idea that we had help. We found a bunch of files logged by Fraser and Bayer in Paris from the time Dmitry's visa was due to expire. The only reason we found them at all was because we'd given up looking everywhere else. There are also payments to a man called Evgeny Tikhonov from a company called GDLC Holdings.'

'Yes, I noticed that,' Harper said.

'But nothing to say who GDLC are or what Tikhonov was being paid for. We were also wondering why such a substantial portion of the report has been redacted?'

'That, Mr Hunter, is the first intelligent question you've asked.'

'You don't know?'

'Difficult as this may be for you to imagine, I do not possess an encyclopaedic knowledge of the entire contents of floor four.'

'But you must know why something would be redacted?'

'I could hazard a guess, yes,' Harper replied, simultaneously closing the topic to further discussion. 'It appears that you and the delectable Ms Fairchild still have a considerable amount of work to do. If I am any judge, there will be an unblemished copy of this document floating around somewhere.'

'*Really?*' Hunter said.

'I expect so. You've spoken to Palgrave, I take it?'

'We have.'

'And he's looked?'

'Twice.'

'Much of the material on floor four has been scanned and copied. Some makes its way onto a disk or whatever contraption it is they're using these days,' Harper said, 'some remains in hard copy. The question you ought to be asking yourselves is, what became of the original?'

'Palgrave's at a loss.'

'Never mind Palgrave,' Harper snapped. 'Julian Palgrave is a liability. Unreliable and intransigent. Make sure he checks again, please.'

'Could it have been destroyed, shredded?' Hunter asked.

Sandy Harper looked up and away. 'Yes, yes, shredded,' he said, 'I'm sure you're right.' He paused for a moment, lost in the mists of time, and operations long dead. 'May I humbly suggest that you find Messrs

Fraser and Bayer and talk to them? They will almost certainly be able to shed some light on the redacted section of this report.'

'And GDLC?'

'The...?' Harper asked, waving a questioning hand in the air.

'Holding group.'

'Offshore is it?'

'St. Kitts.'

'Ah,' Harper nodded.

'Via a forwarding address in Harley Street,' Hunter added.

'I wouldn't waste too much time on it if I were you, Hunter. Concentrate on finding the file, please.'

'Fine,' Hunter replied, a little brusquely.

'I understand Yvonne Fraser is in the country. Palgrave should be able to supply you with her details.'

'And Bayer? Where's he?'

'Hmm, another excellent question. No one knows. After he...' a slight hesitation whilst Sandy Harper racked his brains for the correct word, 'after he retired from The Service, I'm ashamed to say we somewhat lost touch with Mr Marcus Bayer.'

'How do you expect me to find him then?'

Harper looked up slowly from the papers which occupied his desk. A long, lingering look of bored disappointment and contempt. 'You will find a way,' he said, quite deliberately. 'Perhaps I was wrong about you? Perhaps I should be conducting this conversation with Ms Fairchild. All you seem to have are questions, Mr Hunter. Questions and not much in the way of answers.'

'I'll find him,' Hunter said.

'Of course you will. Now, please close the door behind you,' Harper replied, returning to his paperwork.

✳✳✳

Hunter spun out of Harper's diminutive office and headed straight for floor four.

'Could you give me everything you have on Marcus Bayer, please?' he asked, taking the shameful rectangle of dirty grey card Palgrave offered him.

'You're number twelve today Mr Hunter,' Palgrave replied, placing

Hunter's phone in the dull blue metal box. 'Now what was that name again?'

'Bayer, Marcus Bayer.'

'Bayer?' Palgrave repeated, closing his eyes. 'Marcus Bayer?'

'He was a spook. I need to find him.'

Palgrave's eyes flashed behind his spectacles and his expression changed. 'Not really the done thing around here, handing out files on employees.'

'Ex-employees,' Hunter added hopefully.

'Even so, I think I ought to phone Davenport first and see what she has to say.'

Hunter waited patiently whilst Palgrave made the call. 'Well,' he said, sounding more than a little put out, 'you appear to have made some very influential friends in the short while you've been working here. I shall go and find Mr Bayer's file for you right away.'

Palgrave returned several minutes later carrying a thick manilla folder bound together with an ancient rubber band. 'I don't know what you're up to Mr Hunter, but I would urge you to behave as respectfully as possible when it comes to retired members of The Service,' Palgrave said, handing him the file.

'I will,' Hunter replied, a little baffled.

He went to his table. There were dozens of pictures, case files and reports, running in chronological order. There were passport sized photographs and a progress evaluation of a man who looked only a little older than himself. Bayer had studied languages at university and might very well, Hunter supposed, had The Service not got their hands on him first, have gone on to become a translator. His particular field of expertise, Russia.

Hunter skimmed through his training until he came to Bayer's first operation overseas. Whilst he continued to peruse Bayer's file, looking for clues as to his current whereabouts, odd names leapt out at him. Sandy Harper had sent Bayer to Tashkent to babysit a British trade delegation looking to strengthen ties with some of Uzbekistan's major gas and oil exporters. There followed more work in the region with Bayer reporting this time to Tobias Gray. Then Hunter noticed that he'd been sent to Turkmenistan as part of a two-man team with Tom Fratton. A photograph of the pair horsing around in the nation's traditional headdress, each with a shot glass in their hand. Then Bayer and

Fratton had been sent to Moscow by John Alperton as part of a much larger surveillance operation. Hunter's blood ran cold when he read the name of the man they had been sent to spy on. Aleksei Kadnikov, the man who had turned Tobias Gray and the man Hunter suspected he'd briefly glimpsed outside George Wiseman's flat in Kensington all those months ago. The Service had put together a significant team to keep an eye on Kadnikov throughout 2015. There had been twenty-four-hour surveillance details and a budget to match. And then, with the op presumably still ongoing, Marcus Bayer's file came to an abrupt and decidedly unceremonious end followed by his almost immediate departure from The Service on 1st April, 2015.

'Is there anything else I can get for you?' Palgrave asked.

'Thomas Fratton's file, please?' Hunter said, soberly.

Palgrave nodded, as if to acknowledge that that would be the next logical step. Something was still bothering Hunter. Something didn't quite add up, although just what that something was, for the time being at least, he was struggling to understand. Perhaps Fratton's file would provide some answers. He thought for a moment, anxious that his next step not be a missed one, his mind clouding with dropped comments and chunky keyrings, then added as casually as he felt able, 'and Samantha Fairchild's?'

Again Palgrave nodded, but this time more hesitantly. 'If you think that's wise, Mr Hunter.'

Hunter spent the next thirty minutes examining Thomas Fratton's file up to its shocking conclusion, concentrating on his time operating with Bayer. None of it proved much help in locating the Russian analyst and so Hunter closed the file and reluctantly slid Sam's significantly thinner folder in front of him. K for what, he wondered, or whom? Kate? Katherine? Karl? Kiev? Kadnikov? For the briefest moment he considered what he was about to do, then, with real certainty, Hunter no longer needed nor wanted to know. He collected up all three files and returned them to Julian Palgrave.

'Find everything you were looking for, Mr Hunter?'

Hunter nodded. 'Yes, thanks.'

They listened as the lift arrived and the doors swished open. Hunter had lost track of time and so when Fairchild walked in he was relieved he'd returned her file unopened when he had.

'What's so important?' she asked.

'We've got to find Bayer. I've just finished going through his file and there's nothing. Any ideas?'

'What about his family?' Fairchild asked.

'There isn't one. He's an only child. Both his parents died within six months of one another just as he was preparing to graduate from university.'

'Bloody hell.'

'Right. He dropped out for a couple of terms, did a spot of travelling to discover himself, then re-sat the following year. Perfect for The Service. Strong in languages, an expert in Russian politics, no family. He was probably skint and at a loss after his parents died,' Hunter said, thinking back on his own chaotic recruitment. 'Service bides its time, steps in, providing him with a reason to carry on and a ready-made family, of sorts.'

'None of which gets us any closer to finding him.'

'I guess I'll have to go and see Margaret Fratton then,' Hunter said.

'Who's she?'

'Long story. Her son used to work with Bayer.'

'Oh.' Sam seemed about to say something, then hesitated.

'What?' Hunter asked.

'Do you think that's wise?'

'What do you mean, wise? Have you got any better ideas?'

Fairchild looked at him, in his desert boots, skinny black jeans and Dead Kennedys T-shirt. Hunter looked like he hadn't slept for a week, his eyes were dark and sunken, he stank of cigarettes and stale alcohol and there wasn't a hair on his shaven head.

'I'm not being funny, Scott. But if you go round there looking like that, you'll...'

'I'll what?'

'You'll scare the crap out of her. And in any case, I've a feeling you'd much rather go meet Yvonne Fraser.'

'And what does *that* mean?'

'It means you'd better tell me where poor old Mrs Fratton lives,' Fairchild continued, not missing a beat. 'Anyway, you haven't told me why she would know where Bayer is?'

'Because he killed her son. So, I'd read his file before you go.'

Fairchild stopped smiling.

'Yeah, perhaps you're right,' Hunter said, 'perhaps I shouldn't see the old girl. I'll text you her address.'

'And what are you going to be doing while I'm off with Mrs Fratton?' Fairchild asked.

'I'm going to go and see Yvonne Fraser.' Fairchild shot him a look. 'Like *you* told me to.'

✳✳✳

The woman Hunter met on Wandsworth Common was older and more jaded than her photograph suggested. Yvonne Fraser was world weary and defiantly cynical, not to mention harassed and exhausted.

'You work for Sandy Harper?' she asked by way of an introduction.

'At the moment, yes,' Hunter said, as they walked through open parkland.

'You poor bastard.'

'Tell me about it,' Hunter said, smiling.

'Go on then,' Fraser said, a little impatiently, 'he hasn't sent you out here for the weather. What do you want to know, about Paris?'

'Evgeny Tikhonov.'

Fraser thought briefly. 'Russian traitor. What about him?'

'Traitor?'

'I just assumed, because you're here and we're talking about him.'

'Did you work with him?'

'A little, yes.'

'On what?'

'Nothing specific. Cat and mouse stuff, mostly. They like to know what we're up to, we like to think we know what they're up to. It's a game, Hunter, it's a bloody game.'

'Right.'

'Sorry. I'm very tired. The short answer is, I didn't have a lot to do with Tikhonov. Didn't like what I saw.'

'No?'

Fraser shook her head. 'His motives always struck me as somewhat questionable for a start.'

'Ever read his file?' Hunter asked.

'Never felt the need to.'

'So, you can't think of any good reason why Tikhonov's photograph's been removed?'

Fraser stopped in her tracks.

'As in taken out?'

Hunter nodded. 'I'm guessing it was a passport sized photograph about the same as...'

'The same as mine?' Fraser said, smiling for the first time. 'It's alright Scott, so you checked me out. I'd have down the same, especially if I had that prick Harper breathing down my neck. So, his photo's gone?'

'Yeah, all of them.'

'*All* of them?' Fraser said, sounding genuinely surprised. 'Well, he certainly was an ugly bastard. But then if we removed all the pictures of ugly men from The Service's records, there wouldn't be many of you left, would there Scott?'

'I guess not,' Hunter said, feeling himself colour.

Fraser shook her head again. 'Sorry, I've no idea what anyone would want with Evgeny Tikhonov's mugshot. Probably in Blackmore's locker,' she said, laughing to herself. 'Have you spoken to Palgrave?'

Hunter nodded. 'We've got one more person to talk to and then we're all out of ideas.'

'I don't think so,' Fraser said, a little uncertainly. 'I was the only one working Paris at the time.'

'Marcus Bayer?'

'Oh, him.' Fraser seemed surprised. 'Well good luck tracking him down, bloody waste of space, he vanished years ago. I don't even think Sandy Harper knows where he is.'

Hunter thanked Fraser for her time. He was just about to return to Central London, all the while praying that Fairchild's journey was proving more productive than his own. 'I don't suppose GDLC Holdings means anything to you, does it?' he asked as an afterthought.

'Sorry, Scott, I really have to go,' Fraser replied, already halfway out of the park.

'GDLC, you don't know them?' he called after her as she made off.

'Take care of yourself Hunter.' And then Fraser was gone.

***

Tuesday, 10th March 2020
Risk levels rise to high and the FTSE loses another 10%

'Mrs Fratton?'

'May I help you?'

Margaret Fratton chose not to hide behind net curtains and chains, but instead stepped out confidently onto the front step of her post-war bungalow and regarded Samantha Fairchild with a healthy mixture of curiosity and suspicion. Sprightly for her age, her mind undimmed, her wits as sharp as the pleats in her skirt. It was rare that anyone she didn't know called on her these days, particularly now, when the news was almost exclusively one health scare story from a Chinese wet market after another. But there was something in the open honest face smiling back at her which Fratton warmed to.

'I'd like to talk to you about your son, if you wouldn't mind?'

Fairchild had had the whole train journey to come up with a ploy to gain admittance to the old girl's house but after much deliberation had decided she was, on this occasion at least, going to be truthful. The nature of his death had shocked her and Fairchild felt she owed Margaret Fratton her honesty.

Fratton smiled a sad smile and moved back to the open door behind her. 'You'd better come in then, and please call me Margaret. I should offer you a cup of tea and biscuits, but I don't expect you'll be staying long, will you dear, what with this virus I mean?'

Fairchild followed her into a front room of heavy furnishings, third-rate valances and tired chintz. Hanging above a much loved but now neglected recliner, a sampler of the twenty-third psalm and next to that a three-year-old golf calendar featuring an artificially exceptional fairway, basking complacently under a faraway sun.

Fairchild nodded. 'We're trying to find Marcus Bayer.'

'Ah. So, you're not here to talk about Thomas at all, are you? You're here about Marcus.' She shook her head, already disappointed in her guest. 'You'd better take a seat,' Mrs Fratton said, gesturing to a lumpy looking sofa, 'although you'll have to forgive me, but I have very little to say about that young man, in no small part because of that retched D notice of yours. I'm right, aren't I, you do work for the same people Thomas did and not some newspaper?'

Fairchild nodded. 'That's right, but if there was a D notice served on your son there's no record of it that I've ever seen.'

'Not Thomas, dear. Marcus.'

'I'm sorry, I'm not sure I understand,' Fairchild said, settling into the settee and wondering if she would ever be able to get up again.

'One of your lot,' Mrs Fratton said, bitterly. She seemed about to launch into a full-blown attack on The Service, but stopped herself, perhaps aware of the futility of the gesture. 'They sent someone out here to reason with me. Smart chap, rather dishy actually. Talked a whole load of hogwash about duty and sacrifice. Told me Thomas had been indispensable, that sort of guff. Then, once he'd buttered me up and down a bit, he suggested I sign an affidavit swearing I'd never talk to anyone about Marcus Bayer.'

'The trouble is, Margaret, that now it's really important we find him and he seems to have completely disappeared.'

'Ashamed. That's what he is. Ashamed of what he did,' the old lady said, hovering in the space between Fairchild and the kitchen.

'I know how your son died Margaret and I'm truly sorry, really I am, but it was an accident, wasn't it?'

'Yes, it was,' Fratton said. 'I'm not talking about that. He left my son's body over there, do you see? We were never given the opportunity to bury him, properly say goodbye. He's still in Russia, in some muddy field no doubt.' She reached for the tissues she kept on the mantelpiece and wiped her eye. 'That's why I can never forgive Marcus Bayer.' She dabbed at the end of her nose. 'Do you have anyone?' Fairchild felt herself blush. 'Thomas, he had Marcus. I think, when you do the sort of work you do,' Mrs Fratton continued unapologetically, 'then you need someone you can turn to when everything goes wrong. Someone in whom you can really trust.'

Fairchild was a little taken aback by the old girl's choice of words. *When everything goes wrong*, she'd said with real certainty. Not if, but when.

'Is there someone you trust above all others? Someone who will make sure you're alright?'

Fairchild thought for a moment, then shook her head.

'No. No there isn't really. Oh, I don't know.' She'd been caught off guard by the directness of the question. 'It's complicated.'

Mrs Fratton laughed. 'Look at me, dear.' She brushed some imaginary crumbs from her thick plaid skirt. 'I'm seventy-nine. But I'm not so old that I don't remember complicated!'

They both laughed and then, with a little effort, Mrs Fratton moved back towards the kitchen. 'I'd offer you that cup of tea now, dear, but I have a feeling you have more pressing matters to attend to?' She pointed to the mantelpiece which ran above an old and unreliable electric fire. It was covered in souvenirs and *objet d'art*. Ornaments collected from far flung corners. A flamenco dancer, rudely carved and painted, thin and naked without her voluminous serviette skirt, standing in stark juxtaposition to a parade of shining babushka dolls. The largest, Boris Yeltsin, shoulder to shoulder with Mikhail Gorbachev. In their shadow Brezhnev and Nikita Khruschev huddled conspiratorially. Stalin, alone, observing the old woman's sitting room from a different angle. But between him and Czar Nicholas II there was a small yet irksome space. Large enough for another piece, but currently home to nothing but dust. Fairchild supposed that somewhere, under a chair perhaps or behind a sofa and quite out of the reach of elderly widows, Vladimir Ilyich Lenin lay patiently, waiting to be found. 'He writes to me, quite regularly as a matter of fact, Christmas cards and the like and always when it would have been Thomas's birthday. I can't bring myself to open them of course, but if they're of any use to you, please, be my guest.'

Fairchild saw, tucked behind an ornamental wooden bowl, a thick collection of envelopes, some as Mrs Fratton had said, clearly containing Christmas cards, but others letters. She took them down, but even as she held them in her hands, Fairchild knew she would never open them. As she turned each envelope over, she began constructing a picture of Marcus Bayer, the man who had taken Margaret Fratton's son from her. Perhaps she was right, perhaps he was ashamed, but here, judging by the sheer volume of letters he had written over the course of the intervening five years, was a man desperate to make amends and in any way possible. Bayer's hand was small and unwavering and as Fairchild felt the thickness of each letter she could imagine the pages of emotional outpourings within.

She turned over envelope after envelope, hoping for some clue as to his whereabouts, praying he had written a return address on the back, or that there might at least be a postmark. The envelopes were broken at regular intervals by Christmas cards wearing seasonal stamps. The first few correspondences Fairchild examined were thin, insubstantial pleadings, containing little more than a single sheet of paper. Then, as she travelled back through time, the envelopes grew thicker as Marcus Bayer unburdened himself of his guilt, until finally she arrived at his first communication. It took her a moment to realise, but then she saw. This letter was not like the others. Mrs Fratton, still reeling with grief no doubt and probably unaware of the sender's identity, had opened this first letter.

Before she slid out the envelope's contents, Samantha Fairchild promised Margaret Fratton, Marcus Bayer and herself one thing. She would not read the contents of this letter. It would not be right. She would see if there was an address and that would be enough.

Four pages of tightly spaced, neatly written text slipped from the envelope and there, at the top right corner of the page, an address in Lancashire. Guilt, she reflected as she prepared to record the information, true guilt, that would live with someone for the remainder of their life, was a dreadful thing. An ugly emotional handicap few could bear, as she understood all too well.

Fairchild took a picture on her phone and sent it straight to Hunter's before replacing the envelopes on Mrs Fratton's mantelpiece. She'd just sat back down when the old girl returned from the kitchen. She looked down at Fairchild. 'So dear, did you get everything you came for?'

'I did Margaret, and a bit more too actually,' Fairchild said, smiling. 'What about you?'

'What about me, dear?'

'Do you have anyone?'

Margaret Fratton shook her head slowly. 'Not now, no. My husband passed away not long after Thomas,' she said, before turning away suddenly.

Worried she'd upset her, Fairchild collected her belongings and prepared to leave. 'Thank you for your time. Would you mind if I were to call on you again, perhaps when this,' she raised her hand, identifying the invisible and potentially deadly virus, 'when this is all over. Just for a chat?'

'I should like that very much, dear,' Margaret Fratton said.

6

Evgeny Tikhonov stepped out onto Blomfield Road. A forty-five year old Russian from the Sea of Okhotsk and the land of volcanoes, who at five eleven and 175 pounds no longer made the weight. He was rich for a poor man and honest for a thief. Tikhonov was a killer, although never with his own hands. He'd been to prison but only as a means to an end. He'd been a spy too, when it had suited him, and now he was all of these whilst simultaneously being none.

Tikhonov gave a gentle wave farewell to Valentina as he walked down Warwick Avenue ignoring the busy spill off to Paddington Station. Normally he would have taken the underground. It was one of the rare perks of living where he did. But today he was running late and so would flag down a cab and subject himself to the horrors of the Westway instead.

Tikhonov hadn't slipped into his life of crime, he'd dived in head-first, as though it had been a cool swimming pool on a hot summer's day. He'd been lured by the financial rewards a life of espionage simply couldn't provide. Working for the KGB, the FSB and then anyone who'd pay him had been as glamorous as it had been stimulating and, initially, he'd been pleased to satisfy a latent sense of moral obligation to the country he reluctantly called his home. But then greed had over-taken honour. Spying was hard, financially unrewarding and danger-ous. Working for Dmitry Patzuk was just dangerous. And, providing the two revenue streams never intermingled, Tikhonov's life would remain both exciting and profitable which was just as he liked it. There had been a regrettable incident a few years ago when he'd crossed that line, used his contacts in the one world to aid his employers in the other, but he'd learnt from the experience. It had not ended cleanly, although Tikhonov had got what he'd wanted from the affair, as he always did. Yes, it was better to compartmentalise his two lives and make quite certain that they, like wives and lovers, never met.

Recently there had been rumours that the intelligence services in the city he now called home were undergoing some sort of a renaissance. He would have preferred this not to have been the case. Evgeny Tikhonov was a great believer in the status quo. It was always good to know at which tables his enemies and allies dined. It made for more peaceable mealtimes and convivial after dinner conversation.

Today he was on his way to meet a business consultant from the City. Patzuk still had many friends in Russia, one of whom had decided, or more likely Tikhonov thought, allowing himself a knowing grin, been persuaded, to make the break and move to Londongrad. *Would he be able to hang on to his lucrative drugs business in Russia whilst laundering money through London and live, as Dmitry Patzuk appeared to, an untroubled life of almost tax-free luxury?* Tikhonov already knew the answer to that. It would involve the purchase of expensive real estate and the transferring of funds offshore but he suspected, even despite recent tightening of financial regulations, it would only be a matter of time before Patzuk's friend was joining them. Tikhonov unenthusiastically recalled the fuss there'd been shepherding Patzuk into the country and prepared himself for more of the same.

There had been an uneasy truce between Westminster and Whitechapel. The British Government was generally more accommodating if their boys in the City were happy and could be relied upon to dutifully turn a blind eye to any financial impropriety. The boys in the City, for their part, weren't any trouble as long as the money kept flowing roughly in their direction, remaining steadfastly indifferent as to its source or provenance. The system, such as it was, was essentially the same the world over, fundamentally flawed and in need of help, like a functioning alcoholic, gratefully dependent, whilst simultaneously self-harming. Tikhonov enjoyed an expression the English liked to use.

The tail was wagging the dog, they said. But then this particular dog seemed perfectly content, provided he remained well fed and his greedy belly was rubbed regularly. Tikhonov was just happy for the whole shameless exercise to tick over remorselessly. He didn't care as long as he was never called upon to clean up the resultant and inevitable mess.

Seeing his raised arm, a black cab slowed, slewing up at the kerb next to him and Tikhonov gratefully jumped in. If he were able to help ease this latest arrival from the motherland, that would make everyone happy, the guys in the City with their expensive coke habits and penchant for extravagant lunches, his employer, everyone. Everyone had their noses in the trough, not least Evgeny Tikhonov. He'd make sure he was rewarded for brokering the deal, probably sell some coke along the way and hopefully buy a large portion of good favour from Dmitry Patzuk.

✳✳✳

Sam Fairchild was waiting for Hunter outside Harper's office.

'So,' Hunter said, 'how was Peterborough?'

'He wants *you* to go and see Bayer.'

'Why can't you go?'

Fairchild glanced anxiously at Harper's office.

'Oh,' Hunter said. 'In which case, before I go, I'm going to need a copy of that file to show him.'

'Why?'

'I don't know, there's just something not quite right about it,' Hunter said.

'Well half of it's missing for a start.'

'No, it's not just that. There's something else,' Hunter said. 'I get this feeling Bayer'll know, once he's seen it.'

Fairchild let out a derisive snort. 'There's not much chance of that though, is there? Palgrave's *never* going to allow it. I suppose you could ask Harper to secure it for you but...'

Hunter shook his head. 'They're not really in the habit of doing each other favours, are they? Then there's Quick of course. We'll have to take a copy.'

'How? Ask Palgrave if we can borrow his photocopier? I don't think so.'

'I've got an idea,' Hunter said, taking Fairchild by the elbow and steering her toward the lift, 'but you're going to have to play along.'

***

'Good afternoon, Miss Fairchild, Mr Hunter,' Julian Palgrave said. 'Your phones, please.'

'Could I have a quick look at the redacted file from yesterday?' Hunter asked, as Palgrave passed him a grubby rectangle of cardboard with the number 12 printed on it.

'Certainly. Let me sign in Samantha's phone first and I'll be right with you.' Palgrave shot Fairchild a friendly smile and the number 8, then retreated to the locked room behind him to find the Bayer file.

In no time he was back waving the redacted copy triumphantly above his head. 'Knew just where to look,' he said, as Hunter filled in the requisite slip. Hunter was about to thank Palgrave when Fairchild returned clutching a scrappy piece of paper.

'Sorry, Julian,' she said, flashing him a winning smile, 'I'm going to need to see all of these, I'm afraid.' She put the note on his counter. Hunter was amused to see a list of a dozen or so different documents.

'Good heavens, Samantha, and I've just locked up,' Palgrave groaned, struggling not to admonish her. 'I do wish that perhaps the pair of you might coordinate your requests a little better in future?' he continued, pushing the requisition slip towards an apologetic Fairchild.

Palgrave took the completed slip from her, cast an eye down it and smiled wryly to himself. 'I'll see what I can do, Sam.' He turned, unlocked the door behind him and disappeared. The door swung awkwardly shut on its heavy spring. Fairchild and Hunter watched through frosted glass as Palgrave locked it behind him, then Hunter leapt over the counter and Fairchild took Bayer's heavily redacted file and began flattening out any creases. Hunter found the scruffy rectangle of card in his jeans pocket and put it on the table, then began a frantic search for the matching box whilst Fairchild kept one eye on the door behind him.

'Come on, Scott, for Christ's sake.'

'I'm going as fast as I can,' he hissed back through gritted teeth.

'I reckon you've got about three minutes.'

'I said, I'm going as fast as I can, but all these boxes look the bloody same.' Hunter looked at Fairchild and forced himself to remember they were supposed to be on the same side.

'Number 12.'

'Thanks Sam. I can read,' Hunter said, holding up the rectangle of card.

'Then come on, he'll be on his way back.'

Hunter pulled one of the small metal boxes from its storage place. 'Got it.' And put it on the counter between them. 'Where's the key?'

'What key?'

'The key,' Hunter said, very deliberately 'to the fucking box, Samantha. Where is it?'

'I don't know, it's your plan. Have you tried his desk?'

Hunter opened the top drawer and went through it as quickly as he could whilst trying not to disturb its contents too obviously. No luck. Then the middle one until finally in the bottom drawer he found a small bunch of silver keys. He held them up to Fairchild.

'Great,' she said. 'Now get on with it.'

There were a dozen keys of varying shapes and sizes circling one thick metal ring. Hunter quickly discounted two of them as being far too large. Next was a group of six keys, identical in size and each with the name of the filing cabinet manufacturer on them and that left four small dented and burnished keys, one of which must surely open the box in front of him containing his phone. The first he tried wouldn't fit the lock at all, nor the second. The third slid easily into place but would not turn and Hunter thought might snap if he forced it. Fairchild was looking from him to the door and back again. 'Scott!'

'I know. It has to be this one.'

Hunter held up the last key on its thick metal ring. It was obviously too large. He looked at Fairchild, his hands open in speechless exasperation.

'Give them here,' she snapped impatiently, examining the makers name on each one. 'These are for the bloody filing cabinets.'

'I know that! So where's the key for *this*?' Hunter said, pointing at the small metal box between them.

'How would I know? Maybe he took it with him?'

'Great.'

Hunter began frantically scouring Palgrave's desk again, then looked back at Fairchild.

'What?' she said, realising he was staring at her.

'Hairpin.'

'Why?'

'You're going to have to pick it. Hair... Pin!'

Fairchild ran a hand through her short blond bob.

'I haven't got one.'

'What do you mean you haven't got one?' Hunter said, struggling to keep his voice down, 'You've always got one. About there,' he said, pointing at his own head. 'Yesterday it was a bloody ladybird or something?'

'Not today.'

'Christ. What about the fastener on the file?'

'I can try.'

Fairchild took the paperclip holding the sheet of A4 in place and did her best to straighten it before looking at Hunter.

'What!? Get on with it,' he said.

'I need two,' Fairchild replied remarkably calmly.

'You're kidding, right?'

'A torque wrench and a pick,' she continued, as if about to launch into a lecture on the subject.

Hunter opened the top drawer again, convinced he'd seen something suitable there. 'They always manage it with one in the movies,' he said to himself, finding another paperclip.

'Well, I need two,' Fairchild replied, snatching it from him.

'How long have we got?' Hunter whispered.

'I don't know. That was quite a list I gave him but he can't be long now,' Fairchild said, fiddling with the lock. One hand pushed gently but firmly with the clip, the other twisted quickly once and there was a satisfying click as the box opened and she handed Hunter his phone. He tapped in his pin, slid his finger across the menu screen and found the camera. Fairchild held the file straight whilst Hunter photographed it.

'Right, come on, before he gets back,' she hissed.

'The bank statement.'

'The what?'

'The statement from GDLC, Sam.'

'I really don't believe you sometimes. Where is it?' Fairchild said.

'There,' Hunter said, pointing at Tikhonov's file. 'There!'

Fairchild held it up and Hunter took another photograph.

'Got it. Ready to see if you can lock that back up?'

Half a dozen rapid movements later and Hunter had attached and sent the pictures to one of the many mobiles in his flat. He flicked the phone off, carefully replaced it in the metal box and hoped that Fairchild would be able to lock it, then watched as she expertly manipulated the two clips. They listened to Palgrave's returning footsteps. 'Come on, Sam.'

'I'm going as fast as I can, but you're *really* not helping.'

The light from the adjoining room flickered off and immediately the long thin rectangle of tempered glass set in the door began to darken with Palgrave's approaching figure.

'Come on, Sam!'

'Will you shut up! I'm nearly there.' Another click and Fairchild let out a hushed sigh of relief. 'Done.'

She shoved the box at Hunter, who rammed it under the desk as the key twisted on the other side of the door and the handle began to turn.

Hunter leapt back over the counter. Sam pushed her hands through her short blond hair and threw on her sweetest smile.

'Julian, you are a superstar,' she beamed, as Hunter fought to regain his breath, 'thank you so much.'

'You're welcome, Sam,' Palgrave said, adjusting his cardigan, 'although I'm struggling to see just how all these files are related.'

Hunter moved away from the counter, leaving Fairchild to flirt with Julian Palgrave. He was just about to take his seat in front of the Mac.

'Excuse me, Mr Hunter.' Palgrave held up a single sheet of paper. 'What is this?'

Hunter stared at the redacted copy of Bayer's report in Palgrave's hand.

'That's mine,' he said, quickly.

'I know it's yours. What is it doing here?'

'I'm sorry,' Hunter stammered, 'I must have forgotten it.'

'And why is it not in its folder?'

Hunter stared at the floor whilst Palgrave shook his head. 'This will not do, Mr Hunter. Once a file is signed out to you it becomes your personal responsibility. It cannot be left lying around, willy-nilly. You must learn to think a little more of the burden of our shared security. I'm afraid I shall have to inform Sandy Harper of this.'

Samantha Fairchild stood clutching her huge collection of files and shaking her head at Hunter. 'Come on, Scott. Julian's just trying to do his job. You might be a little bit more careful,' she finished, smiling at Palgrave.

'Thanks, Sam,' Hunter said, picking up a pen and gratefully signing back the Bayer file. 'I'll try and remember that. Anyway, you'll be pleased to hear I think I've got all I need.'

'Julian,' Fairchild called sweetly.

'Samantha.'

'Seems I may have been mistaken. I won't be needing these after all.' She placed the stack of manilla folders on Palgrave's counter. 'Thanks anyway.'

Palgrave stopped in his tracks. 'I beg your pardon?'

'Sorry' Fairchild said, trying to mask her embarrassment.

Palgrave looked at them, impatience rising. 'But the files... you've signed them out?'

'My fault,' Hunter said, detecting Palgrave's growing exasperation.

'I do wish the pair of you would make up your minds. Goodness me. Your cards then please.'

Fairchild and Hunter placed them on the counter, retrieved their phones and headed for the lift.

Three floors later and Quick welcomed them as they entered the reception area. They were in the no man's land between the lift and Quick's collection of security devices when Hunter suddenly remembered. 'Sam,' he whispered as they approached the walk-through metal detector, 'I forgot to delete the bloody text.'

She fixed him with a look. 'Well, it's too late now,' she said. 'Next time we do *my* plan and not something you just dreamt up between floors.'

'If you wouldn't mind placing any electrical items on the tray for me, sir?' Quick was saying.

There was nothing for it. Hunter emptied the contents of his pockets into the shallow plastic tray and watched as they vanished into Quick's x-ray machine. Then he and Fairchild walked through the metal detector and stood waiting patiently for their possessions to be returned to them on the other side.

'Whose is the,' Quick held up a mobile phone to the light to get a better look at the maker's name, 'whose is the Samsung?'

'That's mine,' Fairchild replied, trying to mask her relief.

'If you wouldn't mind, Miss?'

'Of course not,' she said, keying in her pin number whilst Hunter slipped his mobile into a back pocket.

Quick's finger slid across the screen a few times and then he was returning the phone to her. 'Thank you, Miss.'

Hunter stood by the doors to the outside world, holding one open as she approached.

'Now all we have to do,' Hunter said, 'is find Marcus Bayer.'

'Mr Hunter,' Quick's voice cut across the entry hall, rooting him to the spot. 'It is Mr Hunter, I am right, aren't I?'

Hunter let Fairchild brush past him and turned to face Quick.

'Yes, yes that's me.'

'I thought so. I knew your father, back in the day. Lovely man, I hope he's well? Please send him my regards, will you?'

'I'll make sure I do,' Hunter said, before turning and gratefully leaving the building.

✱✱✱

Evgeny Tikhonov told his taxi driver to pull over.

'Really? Here?' the man asked, surprised that the smartly dressed foreigner with the swirling birthmark should want to be dropped off in the middle of nowhere.

'Here,' Tikhonov confirmed, whilst pushing a couple of notes at the man. He took them, grunted and began looking for change but Tikhonov raised a flat shovel-like hand.

'Really? Thanks,' the driver said, smiling. 'Thanks very much.'

Tikhonov hauled himself out of the cab and waited for it to drive off. He understood why Cabral had picked this spot. It was neutral ground, free from unwanted guests. He looked out over the wide-open piece of wasteland and then down to the Thames as a lighter barge chugged its way towards the Estuary. The area was in a peculiar transitional phase, halfway between whatever it had once been - housing estate, swimming pool or warehouse - and what it was to become. Tikhonov knew all about the money to be made from slippery waterside property developments, he'd helped Patzuk broker enough of them. But currently this was a blank canvas, an open piece of bumpy concrete wasteland, riddled with potholes, fractured rebar and standing water. Some enterprising soul, Tikhonov was pleased to see, had erected a kiosk and was charging people eight pounds a day to park their cars there. Smart move, he thought. Old school. Easy walking distance to both The Square Mile and The Shard on the opposite side of the river. Handy for the water taxis too. He liked the guy in the kiosk. It was just the kind of stunt he might have pulled.

He trudged a couple of lonely circles, kicking at stones and broken concrete, then watched Sebastian Cabral arrive. When he'd been Cabral's age Tikhonov had been edging onto the boxing circuit, spending the bulk of his life in and out of the gym preparing for the next big fight, skirting round the fringes of the criminal underworld which ran them and waiting for the payday which would change his life forever. That day had never come and it appeared to everyone, including his mother, that if Evgeny Tikhonov didn't get a decent fight and a reasonable paycheque soon, he'd probably wind up in prison. Tikhonov had just resigned himself to such a fate when the KGB stepped in, trained him up and set him on his path. Ironically, less than four years later, his saviours had ordered he be arrested and take a short prison sentence. That still made Tikhonov smile. He watched Cabral slow by the temporary kiosk, wind the window of his Porsche Carrera down and flick the man inside the middle finger. Then Cabral spotted him. He revved the little black sports car, throwing up clouds of dust and loose chippings.

Tikhonov shook his head. Twenty-five years ago he'd have dragged the arrogant son of a bitch from his car and beaten him to a pulp. But now he'd been summoned here to explain himself.

'I'm worried we may have a problem,' Cabral drawled in estuary English as Tikhonov slid into the passenger seat beside him. Tikhonov didn't bother to reply, just wondering if there had ever been a time when there hadn't been a problem. 'I understand from an interested party, concerned his stock portfolio is about to disappear down the khazi, that we are to become the focus of some unwanted attention from Her Majesty's Government.'

'Sorry to hear,' Tikhonov said. 'What has this to do with me?' Whilst, after extended periods in both Paris and Marseilles, his French was more than passable, Evgeny Tikhonov's English was still rudimentary. Picked up along the way.

'My understanding,' the wideboy to his right continued, 'is they're looking for anything which will connect us with... well with you, actually.'

'Me? And who are *they*, Inland Revenue?' the Russian laughed. 'They already try.'

'No. This time the Secret Service will be conducting its own investigation.'

Tikhonov nodded slowly, chewing over Cabral's pronouncement. 'I'm interested to know,' he asked slowly, 'who told you?' After all, it hadn't been that long since he'd been on good terms with some pretty influential members of Britain's political elite, not to mention its Secret Service community.

'Like I said,' Cabral continued, a little cockily for Tikhonov's tastes, 'I have a client. He's well connected, if you know what I mean? Financially insecure and concerned about his failing investments. Coronavirus is kicking the crap out of the FTSE and he's anxious he's gonna lose the roof over his head.'

'Does this well connected, financially insecure spy have a name?'

The lad in the Jermyn Street shirt laughed nervously at the Russian's choice of words and shook his head. 'Let's just say, he ought to know what he's talking about.'

'I see.' It appeared, Tikhonov thought, that the British Secret Service could be every bit as mercenary and unscrupulous as the Russian one when it came to lining their own pockets.

'So, if we're going to assist your friend from Vladivostok, I need to be reassured there's nothing which is going to rise up and bite me in the arse six months from now, if you know what I mean?'

Tikhonov nodded, bored by their conversation. 'I assure you, my employer will vouch for him.'

'Why does he want to come over here anyway?' Cabral asked, rolling the back of his hand under his nose and sniffing a distinctively trading floor sniff.

Tikhonov smiled. 'English Premier League. He love your Manchester United and Arsenal.'

The lad snorted a laugh, a laugh which said he didn't believe a word of it but that it would do. It was just enough of a lie to hang something on.

'Will he need a passport?' Cabral asked.

'In hand.'

'And what about you and your employer? How can we be certain there isn't anything in *your* past which is going to come back to haunt us?' Cabral asked.

'I think you would do well to remember who you are talking to,' Tikhonov replied coldly. 'We can always move our business interests elsewhere.'

'Okay, okay,' the lad replied, lighting a cigarette, 'keep your fucking hair on.' Tikhonov looked at him. He'd forgotten quite how much he hated working with these arrogant shits from the City. 'All I'm saying is, neither of us wants the Old Bill at the door in the middle of the night, agreed?'

'Agreed.'

'So, let's make certain any loose ends are tied up and tidied away, that's all I'm saying.'

Tikhonov nodded. Perhaps Cabral was right. 'When can we make arrangements?' he wanted to know. 'Provided house is in order,' he added as a sarcastic afterthought.

'Soon.'

'Good.'

'When's he expected over then, this mate of yours?'

Tikhonov eased himself out of the passenger seat and looked at the enterprising man in the ramshackle kiosk who was living on his wits. He considered the young financial whizz in the £90,000 Porsche and wondered which was the more deserving.

'The less you know, the better you sleep,' he said, looking back towards the water. He liked this part of London. It was everything Moscow would never be. And there was The Thames. A busy waterway of pleasure cruisers, water taxis and house boats. A Thames river bus slowly cruised into the nearby quay, a pretty little girl, her nose pressed up against a steamy window, waving gaily to anyone who would return her self-effacing salutation. And, as he watched her, Tikhonov came to a decision. 'I think we're done here,' he concluded abruptly.

'Okay, but just keep in mind, I think they'll be closing the borders soon, so if your guy's coming, he needs to get on with it.'

Tikhonov tried not to slam the car's door. Was it really possible, he wondered, after all the trials and tribulations of the Cold War, that a nation could be brought to its knees by an invisible bug? 'I must be getting back to Valentina,' he said, as Sebastian Cabral sped away.

✳✳✳

The man in the broad-brimmed hat took the binoculars from his eyes and reached for a cigarette. He watched Evgeny Tikhonov get out of the small black sports car, prepared to follow him. But the heavyset man in the all-weather jacket, turned up jeans and tan boating shoes was making for Tower Bridge Quay and a waiting water bus. Kadnikov lit the fresh Parliament. He could wait. He knew how dissatisfied Ivanov was with his current life. How he was telling anyone who'd listen his intentions to leave the motherland and head for London, the land of milk and honey, where the streets were paved with gold. He knew how dissatisfied Ivanov was because he had helped orchestrate the whole affair. Ivanov was Siberian through and through and would never leave, even with all his money. Christ, he even had a house on Lake Baikal. *He* would never have left, Kadnikov reflected, if he'd had a house on Lake Baikal.

It had been his idea to float Ivanov past Dmitry Patzuk. Kadnikov had always known he was a greedy bastard, so he'd gambled, and he'd been right. Just the merest sniff that another wealthy countryman was potentially going to be his neighbour and Patzuk had wasted no great time getting Tikhonov to start preparing the ground for his arrival. Patzuk would have been at the airport as Ivanov stepped off his private jet, ready to smooth out the red carpet and introduce him to his hedge fund managers. If, that was, Ivanov had ever had the slightest intention of leaving Russia.

Getting the information into Patzuk's hands had been the real challenge. It couldn't have been seen to have come from him, naturally, particularly as he was supposed to be on the other side of the globe dipping his toes in the Pacific. But Aleksei Kadnikov still had a marker or two of his own to call in and only a fool walked away from the table completely empty handed. None of it mattered. The only person

Kadnikov was interested in was the man who was walking away from him and down to the river. The man who had betrayed him, twice.

He took a tiny notepad from his jacket pocket, found a stubby pencil and quickly jotted down the Porsche's registration number. He watched as it left the makeshift carpark, kicking up dust as it went and prayed he would be able to keep up.

7

Wednesday, 11th March 2020
The Bank of England cuts baseline interest rates to
0.25%

Hunter turned off the M6 just north of Lancaster and followed signs to Arnside. He'd spent half of the journey with one eye on his mirrors but without knowing why. The five-hour drive from Sarratt, where he'd picked up his father's Volvo, to Silverdale in Lancashire had been tiring and uncomfortable but it had given him time to think. Tracking down Marcus Bayer in a sleepy little village like Shalfleet ought to be easier than finding him in London. There were probably fewer than a hundred houses in the village. Hunter saw the Post Office from where Bayer had sent his letters. Next to that, a greengrocer's and mini-mart. At one end of the tiny high street stood a Norman church, although from everything he'd read in Bayer's dossier it seemed unlikely Hunter would find him there. At the other end of the village, a small tear shaped green, a bench and a pub. After so long sitting in his father's car, with its failing air conditioning and sagging suspension, Hunter would take liquid refreshment over moral platitudes any day. He parked up and headed for The Coronet.

Even for lunchtime on a weekday Hunter supposed the pub was quiet. He drew up a leather covered barstool and ordered a pint. The barman offered him a menu. 'If you're quick,' he said, glancing at the clock over his shoulder, 'we could probably rustle you up something to eat. Otherwise,' he continued, casting a scant eye around the deserted pub, 'I think we're probably going to shut up for the day.'

The landlord caught Hunter looking at the clock behind him.

'I know,' he said. 'We're just counting the days until we have to shut up for good, so...'

Hunter stared back at him blankly.

'You been living under a rock, son? I think we've got a week at best before government shuts us down completely. Bloody coronavirus!'

'I heard that!' a woman's voice echoed from the kitchen. 'You know what to do.'

The landlord of The Coronet screwed up his face, reached into his trouser pocket, found a pound coin and put it in an old jam jar on the bar. 'Costing me a bloody fortune, this is. You trying to get home before we go into lockdown?' he asked.

'No, actually. I'm looking for someone. Marcus Bayer. Does he ever come in here?'

The landlord of The Coronet thought for a moment before shaking his head.

'Sorry son, never heard of him, and I know most folk in the village. You got an address?'

'Not really. He's lived here for about five years. Early thirties? Marcus Bayer, you're quite sure?'

'Aye, and I'm surprised if he's been here that long and I don't know him. It's not a big place, as you can see.'

The landlord's wife and custodian of the booming voice, emerged from the kitchens, cutlery in one hand, a plate of fish and chips in the other. 'How do. Did he do the jar then?'

Hunter nodded.

'That had better have come out of your own pocket and not the till,' she continued, smiling at Hunter whilst addressing her husband.

'He's looking for someone called Bayer,' her husband said, shaking his head. 'I told him, no one round here called Bayer that I know. Have you tried Silverdale?'

Hunter shook his head.

'Top of Hill Street,' his wife said over her shoulder as she brushed past Hunter. 'You'll find him at top of Hill Street. The pottery, about halfway along, although I think they're probably shut right now.'

'Oh! You mean the butcher of Shalfleet!' her husband put in, realising.

'I do wish you wouldn't call him that,' his wife said. 'If he's not there,' she placed some cutlery in front of the only other customer and shot her husband a warning glance, 'you'll find him at the old Forestry Commission, Shalfleet Woods.'

'I'm sorry,' Hunter said, genuinely confused, '*where* does he live?'

The barman nodded apologetically, 'She's right of course. When you said...'

'Bayer.'

'Aye. I'm not sure I've ever known his name,' he said, shaking his head, 'we just call him the butcher. He moved out here about three years ago.'

'Four,' his partner corrected him, 'I remember, I was pregnant with Lucy. He came in here a couple of times. Odd man.'

'You can say that again,' her husband said, now sure they were talking about the same person. 'No sooner had he moved out here than he buggered off to live in a tent in the woods. He's one of them bloody tree hugger types.'

'No he's not and he doesn't live in a tent neither. He's built a house,' his wife corrected him.

'And how would you know?'

'I've seen it, with Lucy.'

'You took our Lucy out there to see the butcher?'

'It's quite cosy actually,' his wife continued, ignoring him.

'He's a bloody weirdo if you ask me.'

'Then it's just as well for all of us that nobody is asking you,' she continued, her voice starting to rise. 'He's rather sweet actually. Well spoken, polite, which is more than I can say for some folk round here. And he was lovely with Lucy.'

'So,' Hunter said, eager not to be the cause of an escalating domestic dispute, 'if he's not at the pottery, he'll be in the woods? And they are?'

The landlady took a scrap of paper from the pad by the phone and drew him a rudimentary map.

'We're here, pottery's here and there's the track that leads to Woods. It runs down side of houses here,' she said, pointing and smiling broadly at Hunter. 'I do hope you find him. I don't expect he gets many visitors.'

No, Hunter thought, I bet he doesn't. He seems to be going to extraordinary lengths to avoid seeing anyone.

'How do you know one another anyway?' she asked as Hunter was about to leave.

'Same professor at uni.'

'Aye, that figures,' the barman muttered.

'He said I should look him up, if I was ever round this way.'

'Know him well then, I expect?'

Hunter shook his head. 'Never met him.' He thanked the pair for their help, left the pub and followed their map up Hill Street. Beneath a grotesque sign depicting a cow's head sandwiched between a pair of meat cleavers was Shalfleet's pottery, purveyors of quality meats and poultry and the source, Hunter realised, of Marcus Bayer's rather unpleasant moniker. However long Bayer had owned the establishment, he still hadn't found the time to change its livery.

As the landlady of The Coronet had predicted, and despite a sign to the contrary, the pottery was shut. Hunter pressed his nose to the glass, squinting hard. Below vacant black carcass rails, lonely creations inhabited dusty shelves. A salvaged whisky barrel dominated the centre of the room displaying local business cards and pamphlets for nearby attractions. In the rear a serving hatch, which once would have transported cuts of beef, led through to a back room and, Hunter imagined, a kiln and workshop. He tried the handle again. Hunter assumed the pottery was just another victim of the virus. A narrow passage ran down one side of the shop. At the rear Hunter found another door with a long, thin window running across it. This too was locked, so he dragged over an old plastic garden chair.

The inside of Bayer's workshop was a creative jumble of finished and half-finished projects. Bags of white slip lined one wall. In the centre of the room, a large casting bench stood shadowing half a dozen grubby buckets. An old Victorian mangle sat discarded in one corner. Along the other wall, the wall backing onto the passageway, ceiling high shelves stacked with every imaginable silicon mould, from ashtrays to dog bowls. The whole room suffused with an ethereal porcelain-pink hue. But not a sign of Marcus Bayer.

Hunter retraced his steps. At the main street he consulted his map and turned right. Over the brow of the hill was another short row of cottages and then he was at the edge of the village standing next to a green signpost pointing down a footpath and away.

As he took the stile and began down the path, the temptation to compare Bayer with his father was overwhelming. Both men had been in The Service, although at very different times. Both had left abruptly and then retreated from life. His father had found a sleepy little village in Hertfordshire. Bayer appeared to have taken things one step further.

Gradually the simple stone path he'd been walking on petered out and Hunter was left with grass, trampled flat by ramblers. In the distance, a wisp of pale smoke broke the treeline. As he drew nearer to the source of the smoke Hunter saw more signs of human occupancy. To his left a large area of coppiced hazel. Looking up there were bird boxes and squirrel runs. Abruptly the wind changed and the smoke, which had been rising vertically into a grey cloud filled sky, began streaming horizontally toward him, triggering memories of bonfire nights and undercooked potatoes. He continued to follow the trail, through a wooded section where the undergrowth thickened suddenly and the plume of smoke he'd been following briefly disappeared. And then the woods which encompassed him were thinning and broadening, welcoming Hunter into a larger clearing.

Ashamed he'd expected a hippy inspired chaos, Hunter found a neat, functional site. To his left an open sided construction. Tall wooden A-frames lashed together and covered with a huge swathe of tarpaulin and roughly the size of a small bicycle shed housed hundreds of carefully split and stacked logs. Adjacent to that, a small wooden hut on stilts, which Hunter took to be a composting toilet. To the right of that Bayer's house, for it was indeed a house and not a tent or a hut he had built. Off to the other side, a row of solar panels and a well maintained polytunnel and behind them, beneath a solid line of pale beech trees and disguised under a thin coat of moss, and momentarily transporting Hunter back to Shenzhen in China, a large and uncompromising steel shipping container sporting a shiny new padlock.

Bayer had lovingly constructed a huge log cabin. A single storey structure with two sets of reclaimed windows at the front, an open porch and a beautifully fashioned roof covered in carefully split wood shingle. At the roof's apex, the source of the smoke and the only metallic object Hunter could see, a tall, thin silver chimney stack. The whole scene wouldn't have looked out of place on a Swiss postcard. As Hunter stared more closely he noticed odd signs of human embellishment, an animal's skull mounted above the door, beautifully planted boxes of flowers beneath each window. On the decking, propped up next to a well-used shave horse, a pair of collapsible buck saws and a drawknife for removing unwanted bark. Behind them, hanging from a line of crudely protruding nails, a snow shovel and a couple of chainsaws. And everywhere, competing with the smell of the cabin's wood burning stove, the delicate scent of spruce resin. Bayer's abode wasn't one of necessity but of great pride. Hunter strode up the path to the front door, fascinated to meet the creator of such a home.

He knocked and waited, examining the craftmanship which had gone into each stacked timber.

'Who are you?'

A firm, cultured voice from behind him. Hunter spun round.

The man stood deliberately at arm's length. Tall, thin and clean shaven, his skin darkened from the outdoors. He was dressed from head to toe in green and brown camouflage fatigues. He wore sturdy boots, their toecaps flecked with spots of off-white slip. Gripped tightly in both hands, a three-foot felling bar with a vicious looking hook at one end. By his side, a panting German Shepherd.

'Who are you?' he reiterated.

'I'm looking for Marcus Bayer.'

'Not what I asked. Who are you? This is private property,' the man replied, raising the felling bar, 'and *you* are trespassing.'

'Simon Frost,' Hunter said quickly resurrecting his alias from Hong Kong, 'and if you're Marcus Bayer I need to talk to you. It's important.'

The man advanced on him, the hooked bar still clutched firmly at his chest, the dog never far from his side.

'I don't like strangers. Who did you say you were?'

'Frost,' Hunter said again, raising his voice above the barking Alsatian.

'Never heard of you and clearly Anushka here doesn't like you much either.'

'Uncle Archie sends his regards,' Hunter said, desperately wondering how he was ever going to convince the man to speak to him. 'Are you Marcus Bayer or not?'

'Uncle Archie? This is bullshit. I don't have an Uncle Archie.'

'Sure you do,' Hunter said. 'You remember Uncle Archie, right?'

Bayer swore loudly and at the world. 'I don't like strangers and I particularly don't like Sandy Harper,' he said barging past Hunter, the bar now reassuringly by his side. He let Anushka in then closed the cabin's door firmly behind him. For several long minutes Hunter stood by the window watching Bayer go about his daily routine, until eventually he returned.

'Listen,' he growled, 'I have nothing to say you or to any friend of Uncle Archie or Sandy Harper or anybody else, so you can stand there as long as you like, it won't make a scrap of difference. My advice, bugger off and bother somebody else before I lose my patience and let Anushka out.'

'I'm not a *friend* of Harpers,' Hunter said desperately, 'I work for him. Subtle difference, but one I thought you might have understood.'

Bayer hesitated. 'I see,' he continued unsurely. 'You *work* with Sandy Harper?'

'Yes,' Hunter replied, anxious he'd broken with protocol but relieved he was finally getting somewhere.

Bayer nodded and disappeared momentarily. Then he was flinging the cabin door open wide, a double-barrelled shotgun in his hands.

'In which case, you have exactly 10 seconds to get off my property before I shoot you,' he shouted, before counting slowly and pushing a deep red and brass shotgun shell into the gun's chamber.

Hunter turned and ran.

✳✳✳

That evening, he sat in the driver's seat of his father's Volvo.

Yvonne Fraser had left him no reason to suppose she was hiding any information about her time in Paris. She'd been open and honest with him. Bayer, on the other hand, seemed so determined not to talk to him, he'd drawn a gun. There was great hurt there. Hunter had read the file and could see how Fratton's death still haunted him. But there was more, he was certain of it.

The idea of driving all the way back to London only to have to return the following morning and finish the job seemed utterly pointless. He would wander down to The Coronet, have enough to drink to numb him against the night ahead and sleep in the back of his father's car.

The following morning, after a bitterly cold and uncomfortable night, Hunter was forced to watch the sun rise, heralding an early start to the day. He checked his phone for messages then took a short walk around the village to stretch his aching limbs. At the other end of the village was a garage. He bought fresh cigarettes and a coffee from the machine. His father's car had become Hunter's private torture chamber but there was nowhere else for him to go and so, reluctantly, he returned to it to doze and smoke and plan his next move. He remembered sitting watching Bennett and Healy in a similar position in South Ken. This, he supposed, was as much a part of the job as anything else. He was about to light another cigarette when his phone pinged with a message from Samantha Fairchild. How should she proceed and when was he planning on coming back? He sent a brief text suggesting she return to floor four to make sure they hadn't missed anything and had just finished explaining he'd elected to stay the night when Marcus Bayer strode out of the woods, Anushka by his side, and walked up to the pottery. Hunter threw back the last of his coffee, removed his gun from the glove compartment and followed.

'I've told you, I want nothing to do with you, Sandy Harper or The Service. I don't care how important it is. Get out!' Bayer barked at him across the old oak whisky cask.

'I can't, as you should remember if everything I've been told about you is true.' Hunter reached behind him into the band of his trousers and slowly withdrew his Glock. Bayer eyed the gun as Hunter turned it over in his hand before noisily laying it on the counter between them.

They stared at it, black and uncompromising.

'That doesn't change a thing,' Bayer said, gesturing at the weapon. 'I still have nothing to say.'

There was the slightest flicker from the man facing him and then Hunter was having to react, already he understood, too slowly. Bayer held the gun at arm's length, pointing it directly at Hunter's head.

'I told you, I've nothing to say. You'd better leave and you'd better leave now.'

Hunter shook his head and stared squarely down the muzzle of his own gun.

'No. You should understand better than anyone. If I go back empty handed,' Hunter said glancing at the gun, 'for whatever reason, they'll only send someone else and I'm not convinced you want that? The girl they'll send has a particular fascination for explosives. I'd imagine she'd relish the opportunity to turn your beautiful little house into matchsticks.'

'Don't threaten me.'

'You're the one holding the gun,' Hunter replied.

'Yes, I am aren't I?' Bayer said quickly racking the Glock.

'You're not going to shoot me,' Hunter continued, 'Just like you weren't going to shoot me yesterday. I've read your file.'

Bayer put the Glock down on the table between them and turned his back on Hunter. 'There's nothing more to say. You're wasting my time. Just leave me alone will you?'

Up until that point, Marcus Bayer had been uncompromising and confrontational, but now there was something in his voice which Hunter hadn't heard before and he knew there was no point in pushing him any further. Bayer was defeated. Weary and exhausted from the fight. He wasn't going to talk to Hunter, but now the fire had gone from him. Hunter remembered how he'd felt when Amy had died. Sometimes the grief, the loss, was so overwhelming that all forms of communication stopped. He suspected, even after so many years, this was exactly what Marcus Bayer was experiencing. Hunter could have pressed the muzzle of the Glock against the man's temple and threatened to blow his brains out, but Marcus Bayer simply had nothing more to give.

'I'll come back tomorrow,' he said, as Bayer went to lock himself away with his precious pots and porcelain.

'Do what you like,' Bayer replied without a backward glance.

Hunter picked up his gun and left. He spent the remainder of the day wandering the village and the surrounding countryside, always conscious to give the pottery and Marcus Bayer a wide berth. He heard from Fairchild, who was cooped up on floor four with Julian Palgrave and clearly not enjoying the experience. She too had concluded The Service's archives had more to give up. Hunter found the village shop and bought fresh supplies, then took himself back to the pub for a meal.

That evening, as he knelt in the back of his father's car trying to create a bed for himself, Hunter saw Bayer's camouflaged figure emerge from the footpath which led to the woods. He looked up and down Hill Street and, not seeing Hunter, strode off in the direction of the pub. Hunter slipped out of his car and followed at a discreet distance.

Opposite the pottery stood an old red telephone box. Bayer rummaged through his pockets, found some small change and tapped in a number. A brief wait and then he pushed in a coin followed by an even briefer conversation. Then he was striding back down the road toward the woods and Anushka, leaving Hunter with more questions than answers and the prospect of another bitterly cold night ahead.

Friday, 13th March 2020
The Premier League is suspended.

The following morning, Hunter stood with his back to Marcus Bayer's cabin and watched the sun rise. From Bayer's hideaway in the woods it was difficult to believe Shalfleet had ever existed. Hunter couldn't even hear the bells from the old Norman church. He craned his neck, peering up into the purple-blue Lancashire dawn. Not one of the hundreds of contrails which criss-crossed London's busy skies. He folded his arms and fought off the overwhelming urge to close his eyes and fall asleep where he stood. He was used to sleepless nights but there was something about spending the night in a car which was debilitating, both physically and mentally. His neck and shoulders ached, his backside was numb. Hunter turned as a face appeared at one of the windows and a hand wiped away the morning's condensation. Then Marcus Bayer was standing at his open door restraining a growling Anushka.

'I've brought you something,' Hunter said.

'I don't want anything of yours,' Bayer replied.

'I wasn't talking to you.' Hunter delved into his jacket pocket and produced a paper bag. 'Come on girl,' he continued, holding out the treat.

The Alsatian's growling subsided and Bayer allowed her to take the morsel from Hunter's outstretched hand. 'Thanks,' he said. Hunter smiled and nodded back, pleased the ice had finally been broken. 'This doesn't change a thing though. I don't want anything to do with you or the people you represent. I know who you are and I know what you stand for and I don't like it. She's just a dog.' They looked down at Anushka who was busily licking Hunter's hand and nosing at his pockets. 'Although it does seem she's taken a bit of shine to you,' Bayer added, a trifle disappointedly. He took a long slow breath then closed his eyes and exhaled noisily through his nose. 'You're not going to leave us alone, are you Mr Frost?'

Hunter shook his head. 'I can't.'

Bayer looked at the dog sitting obediently next to Hunter and panting happily, her tongue lolling indifferently from the side of her mouth.

'You better come in then,' Bayer said, standing to one side. 'But before you do, where's the gun?'

Hunter patted his back.

'Lose it, or we don't talk.'

Hunter removed the Glock and put it in a steel fire bucket by Bayer's front door.

The interior of Marcus Bayer's cabin was considerably more homely than Hunter had imagined. Rugs had been thrown over wooden floorboards and there was a rudimentary kitchen with a plumbed-in sink and waste disposal. In one corner, Anushka's basket, which Hunter thought looked a hell of a sight more comfortable than his father's Volvo. A set of roughly made ladders extended into a small loft space in the cabin's rafters and where Hunter supposed Bayer slept. There were also signs of someone who worked the land. Along one wall an array of protective clothing and helmets hung from a line of handcrafted wooden hooks. Bayer knelt by the wood burning stove and coaxed a fire into existence. He threw in a handful of kindling from a wicker basket positioned under the ladders. A quick re-arrange and a small fire crackled contentedly.

'First off,' Bayer said, suddenly all business, 'why are you here, should anyone decide to ask?'

'Same university. I'm looking to follow in your illustrious footsteps. Professor suggested I look you up. You're a bit older, obviously so...'

'Professor have a name?'

Still the tradecraft then, Hunter thought, even if he has left.

'Dieter Müller.'

'Subject?'

'German. And before you ask, there's a car parked up the road.'

'Fine,' Bayer said, nodding his understanding. 'And my connection to the good professor?'

'Never taught you, but heard you were the brightest star to emerge from the languages department in many a year.'

'I'm flattered.'

'Suggested I look you up for some pointers.'

Both men knew it was a flimsy cover, never designed to withstand rigid scrutiny. Hunter was banking on the remoteness of their location being enough.

'One last thing,' Bayer said over his shoulder as he continued to fuss the fire. 'Would you have shot me, back at the shop?'

'No. Firstly, I'd probably have missed.'

'At that range?'

'Even at that range,' Hunter said smiling.

'And secondly?'

'Oh, the gun. It wasn't loaded.'

Bayer spun around.

'But then you're about as fond of guns as I am, otherwise I'm guessing you might have clocked that?'

'Is it loaded now?' There was a brief moment when Hunter worried the man opposite him was about to reach for an axe or a shotgun but then Marcus Bayer burst out laughing. 'Oh, never mind. Tea?'

'If you've nothing else,' Hunter said, not really meaning it.

Bayer went to a long handmade set of drawers covered in slip-ware and shrink pots which ran beneath one of the windows and returned with a handful of fresh pine shoots. A large blackened kettle was slowly coming to the boil on top of the stove and Hunter was horrified to see Bayer scrunch the needles in his hand before tipping them into the waiting water. 'Pine needle tea. High in vitamin A and C. Very good for you. Reduces free radicals, keeps your blood pressure down and helps you think straight.'

'I'll take your word for it,' Hunter replied.

'What makes you think I can help you, Frost?'

'I was doing some snooping around...'

'Of course you were,' Bayer said, who'd been waiting for an opportunity to voice his disapproval.

'On floor four.'

'Ah, that kind of snooping around.'

'And I came across your name.'

'I don't know what you're talking about.'

Hunter sighed, weary of Bayer's act. 'I found your files.'

With a slight movement of his head, Bayer silently acknowledged that he would play along. 'Why the interest in me? I was...'

'I know, a low-level analyst.'

'Not that low,' Bayer replied quickly.

'So you *were* in The Service then?' Hunter said, trying to hide the triumph in his voice.

'*You* say you saw my name in a file,' Bayer all but conceded.

'Not in. On.'

'I don't follow you?' Bayer said, pushing a steaming mug of tea in Hunter's direction.

'You'll understand better if I show you the file,' Hunter replied, ignoring the offer.

Bayer screwed up his face and shook his head.

'I don't think so. That would involve a trip to Bedford Place, and I'm not quite ready for that. I'm sorry, Frost, I'm sure you've come a long way and everything but... Anyway, who'd look after Anushka?'

'None of that'll be necessary,' Hunter continued, reaching into his bag and producing a crumpled sheet of paper.

'Where did you get that?' Bayer asked.

'I told you.'

'Does Julian Palgrave still work there?'

'Yes.'

'Does he know you've got that?'

'No.'

'Have you *any* idea the shit you'll be in when he finds out, because he will? You'll be lucky if you don't lose your job too.'

'Relax,' Hunter said absently passing the page to Bayer. 'It's a copy, of a copy. The original must've been shredded.'

'Nevertheless, how the hell did you get this past Palgrave, not to mention Quick?'

'Long story. This was scanned into the system on the 4th April. Look, your name's at the top,' Hunter replied, ignoring Bayer's question.

Bayer held the page in his hand but didn't look at it, a curious expression on his face.

'Did you say this was filed on the 4th?'

'You can see,' Hunter said, pointing at the date.

'In my name?'

'That's what it says... Three days...'

'*After* I left The Service,' Bayer said, finishing Hunter's sentence for him.

'I *knew* it!' Hunter said, frustrated Bayer had inadvertently beaten him to it.

'I left The Service on the 1st April. April Fool's day,' Bayer continued with a rueful smile. 'Not a date I shall ever forget.'

'I need to know what's in that report that was so incendiary that almost half of it's been redacted,' Hunter put in, anxious that Bayer didn't quietly drift off down memory lane.

Bayer now gave the file his full attention. 'It says it was sent after a stint at Paris station. It's true, I was in Paris at about that time, briefly after Moscow, but only on my way home. The Service wasn't able to get me on a direct flight to London, and even if they had, the feeling was, what with one thing and another, it was a bit on the nose, so they stuck me on a plane to Paris. I had twenty-four hours to kill and then the Eurostar back to St Pancras, followed by a two-day bollocking dressed up as a debrief somewhere in South London after which I was handed my p45. And I never went anywhere near Paris station.'

'When did you file this though?' Hunter said, pointing at the report.

'I didn't,' Bayer replied adamantly. 'That's what I'm trying to tell you. I didn't write a word of it. I've never seen it before and that's the honest truth. I'm not arguing with the chain of events, it's all correct, but if you've really read my file, you'll know I wasn't exactly hired for my secretarial skills. If I'd written this it would probably have been at least a week late, typed under pain of death with Sandy Harper stood breathing down my neck. As it was, I never got the chance. They sacked me on the 1st.'

'What happened in those twenty-four hours in Paris?' Hunter asked.

'The idea was a short layover then the first train home the following morning. I stayed in a hotel near the Gare du Nord. Can't remember its name before you ask. This stuff,' Bayer said gesturing at the half of the report which remained un-redacted, 'this is all correct. I stepped off the Moscow flight, took myself out to lunch and that was that.'

'So what's in the bottom half of the report?'

'Couldn't tell you because, like I said, I didn't write any of it, either half.'

'Ever come across a man called Evgeny Tikhonov?' Hunter asked, trying a different tack.

Bayer shook his head. 'Never heard of him. France wasn't my thing, remember, I was just passing through. Who does he work for? Russian, I presume?'

'And you didn't redact this document?

'No.'

'And you didn't scan it into the system?'

'No! I've never seen it before. Anybody could have done that, I guess. Drag and drop,' Bayer said demonstrating the action for Hunter.

'But what would be the point? Half the document's already been so heavily redacted as to make it illegible.'

'Couldn't tell you,' Bayer said with a shrug, 'although I agree with you, it does seem someone is quite anxious that it disappear, or at least remain well hidden.'

'Is it possible the original still exists somewhere?'

Bayer's face turned upside down and he shrugged again. 'Shredded, like you said. That's the most obvious explanation.'

'I'm stuffed then?'

'Looks a bit that way. Listen,' Bayer said, suddenly embarrassed, 'are you hungry? I've some eggs and sausages and you can tell me what you're really working on?'

Hunter thought on the offer. Harper had said that his discretion was paramount, but then Harper wasn't there and he was starving. He might just choose to be a little selective with exactly what he shared with Marcus Bayer.

'That would be great, thanks.'

Bayer thrust a blackened metal tripod at him. 'Follow me. You can't beat eating outdoors. I love it.'

'What do you do for power?' Hunter asked.

'There are solar panels around the back. I don't need a lot. Fresh water from the stream. If we're quiet you can hear it.' Hunter indulged his host. In the background, behind the sounds of trees breathing in the wind and the occasional songbird there was the happy burbling of a pastoral stream. 'I came here to get away. The pots, the clay, it all helps me forget.'

Hunter understood better than he should have what Bayer was saying. When his mother had killed herself, and feeling betrayed by his father, he too had retreated to a faraway place. A world in which he shaped his surroundings, holding ultimate control. Hunter had found his solace in codes and numbers, Bayer in the gentle art of pottery, a manic Alsatian and the great outdoors.

'But it can't ever really work, can it?' Hunter asked, as much to himself as to Marcus Bayer. 'It can't make the events of the past truly disappear, can it?'

Bayer smiled at him and Hunter felt momentarily ashamed. 'What?' he asked.

'I know what you're going through.'

'I doubt it,' Hunter replied.

'I think I do. I know *you*, Simon Frost' Bayer continued undeterred, 'better perhaps than you might imagine.'

Hunter gave a derisive snort and pretended to examine a charred log from the previous day's fire.

'Indulge me for a moment. You're clever. Probably off most people's charts.' Hunter smiled modestly. 'But you're a loner, am I right? You find it preferable not to form close personal bonds. The reason...,' Bayer paused, Hunter's story perhaps too close to his own. 'I don't know the reason, but you choose your own company because in the past others have let you down? Disappointed you perhaps? Even betrayed you?'

Hunter shook his head. 'You're wrong.'

'Perhaps. Or perhaps you're the one who's let *them* down. Is that it?'

'No.'

'You seem very sure of that.'

'Well, not intentionally,' Hunter replied, letting his guard slip.

'Ah, I think I understand,' Bayer nodded. 'You're an orphan,' he continued, happy not to explain himself further.

'No,' Hunter said quickly, eager to correct him.

'Perhaps not literally, but spiritually,' Bayer replied sanctimoniously. He considered Hunter again. 'There is something though, isn't there? I'm right, aren't I? A hole in your life. A void The Service has tried yet failed to make its own.' Hunter was surprised to see Bayer produce a packet of firelighters and a box of matches. 'What? Were you expecting a handful of birch bark and a ferro rod?' he said, bringing the fire to life.

Bayer briefly left Hunter and returned with a frying pan and an armful of well-seasoned logs. He handed one to Hunter, allowing him the satisfaction of throwing it onto the already sparking kindling whilst Anushka ran round and round in excited and dizzying circles. Once the smoke died down and the fire was white hot, Bayer slid the pan over the tripod and produced a grease proof package, a knob of butter and half a dozen sausages.

'I'll save you the psychobabble, Frost. Can you tell me what you're investigating or not?' Bayer asked as the butter hit the pan and sizzled merrily.

'A little, yes,' Hunter replied. He'd been thinking whilst they'd waited for the fire to settle. His brief, he'd realised, had in fact been rather vague. Look into wealthy Russians settling in Britain, just don't mention any of The Service's previous investigations. The man to his right had been a specialist in all things Russian, so who better to confide in. He would just be certain not to mention The Service's involvement in any way. Surely Bayer would understand that better than anyone?

The sausages slid into the pan eliciting fresh yelps of pleasure from Anushka, whilst Hunter explained the basics of his brief and Bayer nodded silently to himself.

'I can see why they're anxious,' he said. 'When you look at the mess these guys left behind. The worry in Westminster must be that, now they're here buying up houses on Eaton Square and leaving them empty just to minimise their tax liabilities, there's very little in place to stop them behaving just as appallingly as they did in Russia. Once the money's crossed that border it becomes incredibly difficult to trace. Just ask the banks in St. Vincent or Jersey. Once it's gone, it's damned near impossible to track down. The man you're after?'

'Patzuk.'

'He wasn't always so successful, you know.'

'Started out flogging vodka made from cleaning products.'

Bayer laughed. 'Amongst other things. But do you know how he went from that to owning half of Chelsea? Trucks,' Bayer said laughing. 'Trucks,' he said again, as if unable to believe it himself. 'There was a factory, Perm I think, on the Kama River near the Urals. Patzuk managed to get one or two of his cronies into lowly paid jobs and before too long they were robbing the place blind. Slowly he got more and more of his men into the plant, initially just stealing parts which he resold on the black market, but then after about six months, Patzuk had so many of his men at the factory that at the end of the day they just drove off in a brand-new truck.'

Hunter smiled at the sheer audacity of it.

'A brand-new truck, full of brand-new parts,' Bayer continued. 'Then he found a way to make the fleet disappear altogether. He got one of his men into middle management. Then this guy could just wipe any record of the vehicles from the company's database. It was like they ceased to exist. Very popular with the local gangs too,' Bayer laughed. 'Completely untraceable, and perfect for robberies and bank jobs.

'When the police did finally manage to get into Permsky AZ, they discovered that most of the original management team had "disappeared" only to be replaced by Patzuk's men.'

'Weren't they arrested?'

'All the company's employment records, paper of course, were kept off site in corporate buildings on the other side of town. The same night as the police raid, those offices mysteriously burnt down.'

'Don't tell me,' Hunter said. 'It was an accident.'

'How did you guess?' Bayer smiled. 'Dodgy wiring in a faulty electrical socket on the top floor, according to the police report, even though passers-by distinctly recalled the fire starting at street level. The police didn't ever really pursue the investigation but when the local mayor decided to get involved and push things along, he was quickly arrested on trumped up rape charges.'

Hunter shot Bayer a dubious look but Bayer shook his head.

'The guy was well into his seventies. Anyway, it's all academic. They found his body less than forty-eight hours later in the local park, beaten to death.'

'Jesus,' Hunter muttered, recalling the black and white photographs Fairchild had shown him.

'With the death of the mayor it was only a matter of time before there was a second investigation into the running of PAZ. Even the local police couldn't overlook such a brutal murder. But Patzuk was way ahead of them. He already had all the key players on his payroll. The real owner of the plant, well, he's still after answers. He decided to exert what little pressure he could at a higher level, hoping to bypass much of the criminal elements basically running the place out from under him.'

Bayer absently pushed a darkened sausage around the pan and struggled to control Anushka.

'It's important to remember that if there's one thing Russian low-ranking political figures who are themselves on the take do not appreciate, it's unnecessary meddling. So, before you know it, the truck plant's real boss is being investigated for non-payment of taxes. The police shoved all their findings under the noses of the FTS who were themselves desperate to draw a line under the whole bloody affair, and that's the last anyone heard of him. He vanished, leaving a nice vacancy for one of Oleg Lobanov's more respectable employees. And that, my dear Mr Frost, is how you steal an entire company out from under the nose of the state.'

'Bloody hell!'

'I'm afraid that's only the tip of the iceberg,' Bayer continued, having given up trying to control his dog. 'Truck companies, car plants, it's all quite small beer really compared to some of the enterprises Lobanov's involved in.

Professor Marcus Bayer paused and helped himself to a sausage.

'1992 was the ideal time for men like Patzuk and Lobanov. Hyper-inflation, prices rising twenty, thirty times, unregulated banking. In October the government rolled out a voucher scheme. I know you've been told not to bother with Lobanov, but this is how he made his fortune. Everyone in Russia was presented with 10,000 roubles worth of government vouchers.'

Hunter shot Bayer a disbelieving look.

'I know it sounds like a lot, but it's actually only about a month's salary.'

'Still sounds okay to *me*,' Hunter said.

'Yeah, but money's only ever really handy when you can spend it. These vouchers weren't much use to anyone, a little like a Russian Bitcoin. Lobanov's masterstroke was buying them up in bulk, then collectively they became worth having.'

'He *bought* people's vouchers?'

'Sometimes for as little as the price of a bottle of vodka. He collected up as many vouchers as he could and waited for a nod from a friend in the government. Finally he gets a tip-off that the government are about to auction off hundreds of the country's most valuable assets. This causes, as any economist could have predicted,' Bayer said rather smugly, 'a colossal slump in the value of those companies. Lobanov's eyeing up a particularly juicy looking copper exporter which should have been worth tens of millions of dollars. He watched its value hit rock bottom, cashed in thousands of dubiously obtained vouchers and pounced. There was only one other competing bidder, and that was Dmitry Patzuk, who put his name in to try and give proceedings just a hint of credibility, so essentially the whole sorry exercise was a one-horse race. Lobanov picked up the company at a fraction of its true worth and so began, one by one, the wholescale sell off of Russia's assets.

'Once he'd acquired the copper works, the first thing Lobanov did was withhold his workers' wages. They tried to complain but, because the trade unions were so weak Lobanov simply chose not to listen. He took each month's withheld wages to the local bank. The factory was enormous and so the bank's completely dependent on it for its survival and didn't kick up a fuss. Lobanov turned up with millions in roubles and invested them at a high rate of return. Once he'd made a quick buck out of his own workforce he creamed off a healthy profit which he split with the bank's owners. Then all he has to do is decide when or if he's ever going to backpay his employees.'

Bayer broke off to throw Anushka a carelessly cremated offering.

'Perhaps wary that the government was about to take an unhealthy interest in his activities, most, if not all of the money Lobanov's gener-ating at this time quietly disappeared offshore before any investigation was ever launched.'

'What about Patzuk? Surely he couldn't have become as wealthy as he did running a truck company and acting as Lobanov's heavy?'

'No, you're right. He played a very important role in Lobanov's next venture. Kama-Invest. They opened offices right across Russia, one in each major city and several in Moscow. Patzuk wrote ads which appeared in all the national press and on the television. Don't forget, people were desperate. They applied in droves, eager to invest what little money they could spare, sometimes more, in the hope that they might make a quick buck at a time when hyperinflation was kicking the arse out of Russia's economy.'

'Sounds like a Ponzi scheme,' Hunter said.

'Yeah,' Bayer nodded. 'Oleg was offering an incredible return on their investment and initially a few lucky individuals, just enough to spread the word, did in fact make a sizeable return. But then, once the public had begun to wonder how the company might ever be able to deliver on its promises, people decided it was time to take back their shares. Patzuk, as Lobanov's muscle, was less than sympathetic. Things came to a head when one of their investors, having tried to see someone for days, took her own life in the lobby of one of his buildings. Word quickly spread that Kama-Invest was not about to honour its shareholders. The next day, when there was the very real possibility of a run on its stocks and when hundreds of investors showed up to withdraw their hard-earned roubles, Lobanov shut up shop. They were greeted with closed doors and boarded up premises.'

'He'd done a runner.'

'Vanished overnight,' Bayer nodded. 'The whole concern was one elaborate shell company. The only genuine thing about it, the stationery and the very real misery it caused thousands of ordinary people. They lost everything, their lives' savings, everything. Lobanov moved all his assets to a third party, probably his wife, and from her to a series of offshore accounts, never to be seen again.

'Your average Russian, after a lifetime of communism, simply wasn't ready for the sudden lurch to capitalism, poor bastards. They were systematically and comprehensively shafted, thousands of them, and by their own countrymen, too. They never questioned what was sold to them in print or on the television for the simple reason that that was how the system had always been. You never question the state.

'Lobanov and his team of vultures were pretty clever, but they couldn't have pulled it off without Dmitry Patzuk's help.'

'And no one questioned where or how their money was being invested?' Hunter asked.

'Would you? Imagine, you've had a lifetime of financial hardship. Barely enough to get by on. Then someone's offering you the moon and the stars. Would you have questioned it? It was a shared delusion which fed on a nation's need for fiscal good news. An attractive, but highly unstable house of cards.'

'What about taxes? Weren't the government after Lobanov for income tax?'

'Why else do you think he's here?' Bayer chuckled.

'The investors, were any of them able to recoup their money?'

'Kama-Invest went bankrupt. That should have meant they could reclaim at least a small percentage of their initial investment, but by this point Lobanov had disappeared.'

'And these are people our government's happy to do business with?'

'They're happy to take their money, if that's what you mean? Or they were up to a point. Lobanov wouldn't have turned up here unannounced. During his meteoric rise, he ingratiated himself with any number of high-ranking political figures, members of the Russian military and even some of the KGB's top men. He was in a position both to help them and, when it suited him naturally, receive help from them. No one was too rich or too powerful that he wouldn't approach them. And in turn, they all understood, the men he did approach, that as soon as his name was even whispered, they were in danger, no matter who they were. With Dmitry Patzuk backing him up, Oleg's ability to intimidate was without equal.'

'But what finally got him was the tax?' Hunter said.

'Yeah, sort of. But not before one last spectacular deal with the Federal Assembly. You have to understand that at the time, crime was rampant. The Duma turned to the one person they feared more than anyone, Oleg Lobanov, and offered him total control over any business of his choosing; banks, natural resources, oil, steel, aluminium, *anything*, provided he root out all of the criminal elements involved in the running of those companies. And they gave him carte blanche. He was to use any and all means at his disposal. So he went to his enforcer, Dmitry Patzuk.'

Bayer threw another half log on the fire and watched it spit and crackle.

'There were summary executions right across Russia. Leaders of criminal syndicates were shot in their beds, taking their kids to school, anywhere. No one was safe.'

'And he couldn't be stopped?'

'They tried,' Bayer replied grimly, prodding at the fire with a crooked stick, 'but how do you stop the very thing you've helped to create? There was a powerful boss in Norilsk. He ran an aluminium plant. Sensing that Patzuk would come for him, and thinking he could do something about it, the owner decided to strike first. He put out a contract on Lobanov.

'Eventually two men came forward. They would kill Lobanov, for the right fee, which was said to be enormous.

'It took them months to track him down, but through their underworld connections they made contact with one of his men. A counteroffer was put to them, through this third party, that they stop looking, go back to their boss, and kill him instead. Lobanov would pay over twice what they were being offered.

'The following day they showed up at one of the factory owner's houses and shot him dead in front of his family.'

'So that was why Lobanov left?'

'No, no. He would never have allowed the killings to be traced back to him. No, he had a holding company based in Moscow. After everything he'd done for the Russian government,' Bayer paused, wondering if his student would react, but Hunter just nodded solemnly and continued to stare into the flames. 'After everything Lobanov had done for them, the holding company was raided by the Moscow tax police. Men sent from the Interior Ministry forced their way into his building and started demanding to see paperwork and generally throwing their weight around. Some of his staff were imprisoned and badly beaten. The upshot of it all, overnight Lobanov is staring down the barrel of a 170-million-dollar tax bill. He packed his bags and left the next day.'

'What about Patzuk?'

'Dmitry Patzuk had not inconsiderable business interests of his own by this time. Nothing on Lobanov's scale, but businesses all the same. The big difference was he wasn't under any threat from the state. He stayed.'

'And looked after Lobanov's concerns?'

'Possibly. He left for the UK just before I left The Service, by which time I'd lost much of my interest in Russia's criminal underbelly. I'm guessing, because of the timing of his departure and the fact that Patzuk was originally from Kiev, from about the middle of 2014 onwards he became increasingly disillusioned with the way Russia's foreign policy was being handled. First there was the state sanctioned assassination of Boris Nemtsov and then, later in 2015, Putin attacked the Crimea. I should imagine that was the beginning of the end for Patzuk. But by then he had no need to stay anyway.

'Don't get me wrong, I'm not saying the UK is perfect, in fact the pay gap between rich and poor seems to be widening daily, but despite its hundreds of years of varied history, and thanks to the overnight change in the political climate, Russia was left, to all intents and purposes, a virgin state, lacking any of the institutions or traditions to curb the excesses of new money. The irony is of course that the bedrock of Communism became, in no short order, the Wild West.

'In each new territory he overtook, Lobanov made sure to spend a decent percentage of his profits establishing new schools, funding hospitals and hospices. He owns a football team and opened an opera theatre. Although very few if any of the public know who he really is, they are all both simultaneously grateful and terrified of him.'

Hunter could see why Sandy Harper had dissuaded them from even opening a file on the man.

'But there was one,' Bayer continued, content to hold court. 'We never had a name, a photograph, not even a description, just an account from a former employee of Lobanov's who's no longer with us. Legend has it Lobanov and this man met only once and then behind closed doors. He arrived and left unseen but, after their meeting, which was brief our source said Lobanov was visibly shaken. His aides were expressly forbidden from having him followed. They asked if the man was susceptible to blackmail or extortion. Again, Lobanov told them his visitor was to be left alone.'

'Do you know who it was?' Hunter asked.

'Don't you?' Bayer said.

Hunter thought back to the files he'd read on floor four and the names which had caught his attention. There was one name, wasn't there? A name which had appeared regularly. Hunter's own godfather had referred to him as Landslide. Landslide, he'd said, held all the answers.

Hunter shrugged his shoulders and laughed it off. He wasn't there to rake over ancient history. Harper had sent him to get answers from Marcus Bayer. Answers he hoped would put him closer to understanding what had happened in Paris five years before and what, if anything, Dmitry Patzuk and his boss had had to do with it. 'You mentioned a holding corporation.'

'Uh huh.'

'It wasn't GDLC Holdings, by any chance?'

'Sorry,' Bayer said shaking his head. 'There were dozens of faceless corporations which sprung up around that time.'

'They're mentioned in Evgeny Tikhonov's file,' Hunter continued, hoping to jog Bayer's memory. 'It shows a bunch of payments from them to a private account in Nevis.'

'Like I said, it doesn't ring any bells and I've never heard of Tikhonov. GDLC's probably just another shell company.'

'Could it be worth going after them anyway, to see where the payments were coming from?'

'Not unless you've got an extremely good lawyer,' Bayer said. 'Show me the document again.'

Hunter found the printout of the bank transactions and handed it to him.

'No, not this, the other one. The redacted one.' He took it from Hunter. 'This is where you should be looking. Forget the money trail. You could be old and grey before you get anywhere in Nevis. That place is sewn up tighter than a drum.'

Sandy Harper had been of a similar opinion. Thanks to Bayer, Hunter now had a much deeper understanding of the system which had led to the creation of both Dmitry Patzuk and Oleg Lobanov. But despite having plenty to say about Patzuk, Marcus Bayer hadn't known any of the smaller players in his team. He'd never even heard of Evgeny Tikhonov and knew nothing helpful about the report which had been filed on 4th April in his own name. Hunter was rapidly running out of options. It was perhaps time for him to play his final card.

'Who did you call last night, after my visit?'

Bayer didn't speak. He rose quietly from his place by the fire, handed Hunter back the sheet he'd been examining and took Anushka by her collar. 'Goodbye, Mr Frost.'

8

Monday, 30th March 2015 Paris.

John Alperton did not hurry back to London. There was business with the Russian to conclude. He'd arrange a time and place for their sordid little transaction and then, and only then would he head for home. He would pay up for Russia's treasures at 11 o'clock the following evening on Pont des Arts.

It only took the French Police a couple of days to trace the owner of the expensive Italian overcoat he had left at the scene of the accident. They'd found a receipt for a silk scarf he'd bought Valerie in a charming little boutique on Boulevard Saint Germain. Simple detective work had turned up the name Henry Lazarus, a British citizen who took a flat off the rue Saint-Honoré. Alperton had just finished breakfast when the buzzer sounded. Two stern, young policemen stood on the landing outside his apartment. He ushered them in, offered them coffee and thanked them profusely. The gracious Englishman abroad, eager to please and sorry to have troubled.

Thank you for dropping by, and how may I help you? Yes, it certainly sounded like his coat. He had wondered where it had been. He'd assumed someone at the restaurant had probably picked it up by mistake. Yes, it had been raining, but then he had had his trusty brolly. When might he be permitted to have his overcoat back? Oh, and what about the poor soul who had perished, did they have any idea who he was?

132

Yes, they knew. Another Brit, they said, eliciting a wild array of astonished and incredulous reactions from Henry Lazarus.

'That's why we assumed you must have known one another?'

'I'm afraid not,' Alperton replied. 'Quite a coincidence though,' he'd mused to himself before picking his way awkwardly through some broken schoolboy French. Had either of the two gendarmes present been a little more observant they might well have realised that Mr Lazarus's bookcases were bulging with Dumas, Proust and Balzac with not a scratch of English to be found.

He had been spotted, they said. A witness remembered two men exiting the restaurant together. One the deceased, the other matching his description.

'They said you appeared deep in conversation.'

'Really? I don't recall.'

'There were raised voices,' the other said.

'I don't believe so,' Alperton replied, shaking his head. 'Perhaps I'd stopped to ask him for a light? I'm a smoker, you see?' he continued, guiltily producing a pack of Marlboro to corroborate his credentials. 'I'm sorry but when will I be allowed to have my overcoat back?'

He wouldn't, they'd said. He must come with them to the station, bring his passport and any other supporting documents he felt might be pertinent. And he should be prepared to be there for some time. This had been when John Alperton had inquired if he might first make a quick but necessary phone call. He should have been heading out to a meeting. People would be wondering where he was. If he could just let them know not to expect him? The officers conferred and Alperton had asked, just to be absolutely certain, that he was not being placed under arrest. They had agreed and reluctantly let him retreat to the sanctity of his bedroom, where he placed two short telephone calls.

Alperton found a stone-coloured, single breasted raincoat which lived permanently at the flat, and with a grim solidarity agreed they should probably get a move on, as though that had been his intention from the beginning. A ten-minute car journey later and he was being led into a police station near the Place de la Concorde. Inside, rows of cheap plastic seats accommodated the battered and abused of Paris's 8th *arrondissement*. The two men escorted him to the counter and Henry Lazarus was just about to present the first of a stultifying collection of papers when he felt a reassuring hand on his shoulder.

There followed a brief conversation between the owner of the hand and the increasingly perplexed policewoman on the other side of the counter. Mr Lazarus, it appeared, was free to go. All he would require would be his overcoat, *s'il vous plaît*. There was another fleeting protest. The gentleman with the reassuring hand and the calm demeanour produced a tightly folded sheet of paper from the depths of his jacket, showed the holy relic to the desk sergeant and then, two minutes later and reunited with his overcoat, Henry Lazarus was walking from the building, free as a bird and not a question answered.

The next day, having reluctantly disposed of the offending garment in the hopper of a passing refuse truck, he made his way to Gard du Nord carrying the passport of a man named Baker, boarded a train for London and waved farewell to France's capital for what he supposed could be the last time.

✳✳✳

As Hunter drove back to London that evening and still kicking himself for the manner in which his meeting with Bayer had ended, he received another text from Samantha Fairchild. He was to get over to Bedford Place first thing in the morning, there was something she needed to show him. Hunter had always intended on paying number 20 a visit. He had reasons of his own for seeing Palgrave. He parked up in the grubby courtyard at the rear of his flat in Harrow and went to buy something strong and wet. Although exhausted from two nights' lost sleep in the back of his father's clapped-out Volvo and more driving than he'd undertaken in years, Hunter was under no illusions. He didn't expect to sleep well. The world around him still felt in motion and he was struggling to process Marcus Bayer's lengthy lecture on Russian social science.

There could be no getting away from it, Bayer had been helpful. Perhaps even a little too helpful, Hunter thought. He'd painted a working picture of the systemic corruption which had beleaguered Russia at the end of the previous century. But, when Hunter had asked after specific people, Bayer claimed not to have known any of them. Then there had been the matter of his mysterious phone conversation. On the drive home he'd drawn up a list of possible candidates. Was it conceivable that Bayer still had contacts in The Service, or even in

Russia? Perhaps he was feeling threatened by Hunter's promise of an investigation? Could Bayer know Oleg Lobanov? Hard for Hunter to imagine, especially after hearing him talk about the millionaire. He decided, for the time being at least, to put it from his mind and try to concentrate on something else. His father. His father and his father's new girlfriend. Yes, Hunter thought, as he handed a twenty to the man in the corner shop opposite his flat, it was all adding up to another terrible night's sleep. Once back at the flat he found a book. A well-loved copy of The Great Gatsby his father had lent him. Hunter carefully placed the airline ticket he used as a bookmark, but knew he shouldn't, by his side and read until his eyes watered, and tears, which he made no effort to prevent, rolled down his cheeks in warm damp tracts.

Thursday, 16ᵗʰ July 2015.

Valerie Alperton attended a small service at Saint Bride's off Fleet Street, little aware of the role she was about to play in the ongoing tragedy of Clive Somerset. She went alone, John Alperton having, necessarily, been otherwise engaged.

At the church Somerset's watercolours lined the aisles. The mourners were forced to agree it had been a terrible shame, after Daniel and with every indication that finally Clive seemed about to be getting his life back on track.

The service concluded, the Reverend invited the congregation to take a moment and quietly admire Somerset's work. Valerie Alperton found herself introduced to Pamela Landry, Daniel Landry's sister. Her first impressions however, were not favourable. The other woman was blunt, forthright and, given the circumstances, bordering on the disrespectful. But gradually Landry calmed down and Valerie began to understand that her rather aggressive exterior was in fact a mixture of social awkwardness and anxiety. The two women fell into hushed conversation as they walked up and down the aisles of Saint Bride's, examining Somerset's draughtsmanship. Then, at the end of a row of landscapes and perhaps anxious that her new ally was about to make her excuses and leave, Landry blurted something out. She confided in

Valerie Alperton that there had been more to Somerset's death than anyone present was aware. Valerie had raised a shocked hand and shaken her head in disbelief. Landry reassured her that she intended to get to the bottom of it. A pro-bono lawyer specialising in human rights cases, she was already looking into a story one of the papers was about to publish. It was the least she could do, she said, to honour the memory of her dead brother and his partner.

'He was on anti-depressants, wasn't he?' Valerie Alperton said, as Landry suggested they take a seat in the back row of the pews.

'Who told you that?' Landry asked.

'I'm sorry,' Valerie said, 'I didn't mean anything by it, it's just, that's what I'd heard.'

'Did he really strike you as the sort of man who would kill himself?'

'No,' Valerie said after a little thought, 'but then, after he lost your brother, he must have been awfully lonely?'

'I expect he was,' Landry said.

'And his health was pretty poor,' Valerie Alperton added confidently.

'All true,' Landry admitted, 'but suicide? Not the Clive I knew. Think about it. Why go to the bother of making all those plans to study, to travel, if ultimately you intended to end it all. It doesn't make sense.'

Valerie Alperton had to concede that she agreed. 'I expect it was just a horrible accident then. I gather it had been raining, the pavements were wet. He slipped?'

'There was another man,' Landry said with her now customary lack of tact.

'No, no,' Valerie Alperton shot back, shaking her head and jumping to Somerset's defence. 'I'm sure not. Clive was totally devoted to...'

'There was another man,' Landry reiterated firmly. 'They left the restaurant together. He laid his coat over Clive's body.'

'Oh,' Valerie replied weakly. She had been unaware of that. Privately however she did wonder if Pamela Landry wasn't in danger of over dramatizing what was surely already a tragic situation. Some people, she thought to herself, did love a crisis when often the most obvious and potentially mundane explanation was the correct one. 'Were they, you know, lovers?' she asked, inexplicably flustered.

Landry shrugged. 'I don't know, but the other man was English.'

'You're sure?'

'Quite sure, yes. Someone heard them talking outside the restaurant and the owner of the place was able to identify him.'

'So,' Valerie Alperton said, 'who was he?'

'That,' Landry replied, gazing up at the barrel-vaulted ceiling, 'is exactly what I intend to find out.'

That evening Valerie Alperton returned home eager to share every last lurid detail with her husband. Hearing the news of an impending newspaper article, John Alperton wasted no time in contacting Tobias Gray, who in turn didn't hesitate in slapping a D-notice on the whole affair, thereby drawing a thick, ugly line under the incident.

***

Saturday, 14th March 2020
The number of confirmed cases rises to 1,140.

When Hunter entered the lobby of 20 Bedford Place he was surprised to find he was not alone. Until today he had only ever arrived with Samantha Fairchild, as though their comings and goings were being carefully orchestrated so as never to coincide with any of The Service's other employees. But now there was the same smartly dressed young man he had seen leaving floor four when they had first been introduced to Julian Palgrave. He appeared to be caught up in a heated conversation with Quick, who was scrupulously turning out a well-loved leather shoulder bag.

'Come on Quick,' the man in the suit and military Oxfords was saying, 'you're going to make me late.'

'Sorry, Mr Enderby. Orders from on high. I'm to be more vigilant from now on,' Quick replied, resentfully raising a heavy pair of eyebrows to their unseen masters above and shaking his head.

'How long have you known me, Quick? This is ridiculous.'

'Sorry, sir. New broom. People have been getting a little lax of late, taking things home with them,' Quick replied, re-clipping the leather bag and giving it an approving tap. 'Sorry to have held you up, just trying to do my job. You're all good to go now.'

Hunter took the lift up to floor four. How could they possibly have found out? The only person other than Sam Fairchild who knew of the redacted file was Marcus Bayer who hated The Service from top to bottom. Hard then to imagine that he was somehow responsible, although it might go some way to explain the recipient of his mysterious phone call. Who had he called? Certainly not Sandy Harper. Everyone else he'd worked for had resigned, defected or died.

The lift doors opened and Hunter found Julian Palgrave peering eagerly at him over his spectacles.

'Well?' Hunter wanted to know.

'Well, she checks out,' Palgrave said, looking thoroughly pleased with himself.

'Really?'

'Really. National Insurance, bank accounts, tax returns, the lot. I can even tell you where she gets her roots done.' Hunter waited in silence whilst Palgrave adjusted his glasses. 'Verity's her maiden name. She was married to a Mr Peter Gilmore until six years ago. Divorced, which seems to have been as painless as any divorce,' Palgrave said with what Hunter took to be a pang of regret. 'I suppose you could put that down to her being a lawyer, I don't know. She got the house, the kids, the lot. Everything down to the doormats and the family pet. He seemed happy to walk away from the whole enterprise, and yes, I checked him out thoroughly too, before you ask. Squeaky clean.'

'What are you two talking about?' Fairchild put in, arriving at Hunter's shoulder.

'I'll tell you later,' Hunter replied before returning to Palgrave. 'Too clean?'

'Really. There's no pleasing some people,' Palgrave sighed. 'He's just an ordinary Joe. Plays it by the book right down to sticking to the speed limit. He probably doesn't stop in box junctions or break wind in public either. Can't blame a chap for being square, Scott,' Palgrave said, barely believing his own rhetoric.

'Political affiliations?'

'Nothing out of the ordinary. She gives money to a few charities every month, Save the Whale, Amnesty that kind of thing. The woman's practically a saint.'

'Money problems?'

'You did hear me when I said she was a lawyer? Added to which she came into some money a while back. Paid off a sizeable lump of their mortgage just before they split. All above board.' Palgrave put down the notes he'd been reading and removed his spectacles. 'Why are you so desperate to find something on this woman, Scott?'

'I'm not, believe me,' Hunter said, meaning every word of it.

'Good, because I'm telling you, I've looked into every dirty little crevice and she's as clean as they come.'

'Are you done now?' Fairchild said, tugging at Hunter's elbow, 'because you're really going to want to see this,' she continued, holding up a crisp sheet of A4 and dragging him out of Palgrave's earshot. 'Fraser lied to you. After you told me she was so unhelpful the other day I took the liberty of going through her file with a fine toothcomb.' She waggled the page for Hunter to see. 'This look familiar?'

Five payments, identical in size to those made to Evgeny Tikhonov, from the same holding group and on the same dates, to Yvonne Fraser.

'She was up to more than she let on in Paris.'

Hunter took the page from her, angry and betrayed. He'd liked what he'd seen of the aggressive Fraser and now to discover that she'd not been honest with him was more than a little disappointing.

'Fantastic,' he said. 'Is it too much to ask that just one person around here is straight with me?'

Fairchild sighed. 'You're welcome, by the way.'

'I'll have to go back to Wandsworth and talk to her.'

'It certainly looks that way. Want some company?'

'Why not. This is going to be bloody awkward. It'll give you a chance to meet her, see what you think.'

The lift arrived and Sandy Harper emerged wearing a hangdog expression and somebody else's suit.

'Ms Fairchild, my office, now,' he grunted.

'Scott and I were just on our way to meet someone.'

'And now you are on your way to my office,' Harper shot back over his shoulder.

Hunter and Fairchild turned to follow Sandy Harper along the corridor.

'Not you, Mr Hunter,' Harper said, never looking back. 'You may go and conclude your social engagement.'

The shiny black Porsche led the Russian to a noisy cocktail bar in

Soho called Sham-pain, where the mark-up was two hundred per cent and cosy booths downstairs led to satin sheets and expensive lawsuits upstairs. The man in the broad-brimmed hat pushed at his sleeve and regarded his watch.

'Am I too late for drink?' he asked, his hand still at his wrist.

'Normally no,' the doorman replied, looking behind him into the crowded club, 'but tonight... Private party I'm afraid.'

'Oh, I see,' the other man said, sharing his pain.

'Sorry.'

'Quite alright,' the man in the hat said, replacing his cuff and turning as if to go.

'There's a pub around the corner...' the doorman suggested.

'Thank you.' The man reached inside his jacket. 'I don't suppose you have match, before I go?'

The doorman seemed only too pleased to have something to do and thumbed his lighter obligingly.

'Birthday, is it?' The man in the hat asked casually, drawing hard on his Parliament and appearing to stare deep into the noisy club.

'Couldn't tell you. Bunch of disrespectful arseholes though, between you and me. City types,' he added as a final clincher.

The man in the hat nodded his understanding. 'Bankers,' he said shaking his head.

The doorman laughed a throaty laugh. 'Yeah. Although I think technically this lot are something else.' He turned and found a clipboard which had been resting on a tall barstool hidden inside the door.

'Pegasus International Investments. I think that means they aren't bankers.'

'Of this I would not know,' the man said, pulling on his cigarette.

'They're all the same anyway. Nice to have the money though.'

The man in the hat smiled and nodded before throwing his half-finished cigarette to the kerb. 'Around the corner you say. A pub?'

'Take a right at the lights, past the deli,' the doorman nodded.

'Thank you for your help.'

9

Pegasus International Investments nestled comfortably in the heart of the City, one of many such institutions working out of the same glistening tower block.

'I wonder if you can help me, I'm looking for young man? I believe he works here.'

The girl behind the desk beamed back expectantly at the elderly gentleman with the unusual accent and the pervasive smell of tobacco as he removed his hat.

'I do not know his name, I'm afraid, but he drive black sports car, I think.'

The girl behind the desk, her interest already waning, continued to stare blankly at him. A short queue was developing behind the man. At its head, a distinguished looking businesswoman in an expensive grey trouser suit. 'Are you alright,' she enquired, eager to get on, 'can I help at all?'

'I had accident,' he continued, removing his glasses and polishing them nervously on his lapel. 'My eyesight is not so good you see, and the parking spaces are... too small. If you'll give me a moment,' he continued regarding the woman by his side. 'I'm sorry. I have here somewhere.' Awkwardly juggling hat and glasses he removed a notepad from his jacket pocket and laid it carefully on the desk facing the young receptionist. 'His registration number,' he continued, dabbing at the pad as he read out the personalized plate.

The receptionist shook her head, but the woman by his side stepped closer to the counter.

'May I?'

'Please,' the man replied, handing her the notepad.

'Do you remember, was it a black car?' she asked hesitantly.

'Yes. Very new. On parking meter, at corner.'

'I couldn't swear to it, but I think that's Seb's car. How bad did you say it was exactly?'

The man replaced his glasses and screwed up his face. 'A little scratched I'm afraid, along side,' he said, seeking to downplay the damage.

'Oh God.' The woman in the trouser suit glanced nervously at the receptionist then did her best to try and salvage the situation. 'I'd better go and get him, he'll want to take a look.'

'Would you mind not doing that?' the elderly gentleman asked quickly. 'I'm not trying to...,' he hesitated now, searching for the correct word, 'wriggle out of anything, but I am anxious and also late. My business card,' he said, starting the search, 'He could call me or send me email. I'm certain this can be resolved perfectly, but this young man... Seb?'

'Sebastian. Sebastian Cabral, yes.'

'Mr Cabral sounds, well a little...'

'Scary?' the woman suggested, forcing an uneasy smile.

'Yes,' he said, playing the venerable old gent beautifully and smiling back. He slid his card across the counter and she took it, the Good Samaritan. A name, not his own, a company, should anyone bother to check, which had never existed.

✳✳✳

Hunter took the Northern Line down to Clapham Common. The sun was starting to dip behind the long rows of terraced Victorian houses. He found Fraser's address easily enough. A house the same as all the others. From inside, the sounds of noisily happy domesticity. A television competing valiantly with at least two children and the first faint whiffs of that evening's meal. Hunter wondered how Fraser's neighbours would feel if they knew what she did for a living. If they knew the mother of two who kept strange hours and sometimes disappeared in a taxi unsociably early not to return for extended periods was in fact a spy, defending their way of life by sacrificing her own. Hunter heard the childish bickering of young voices but was too charged up to come back at another time. He strode up to the front door and rang the bell. The children's voices momentarily dropped below the level of the television and then he listened as a security chain was released. Yvonne Fraser stood in the doorway.

'Jesus fucking Christ, Hunter, what do you think you're doing?' she hissed. 'This is my home. What do you want?'

'You *do* know Evgeny Tikhonov.'

'I never said I didn't. We worked together, a bit, that's all, nothing memorable I can assure you.'

'I don't believe you.'

'*Plus ça change*. Right, this is over. Don't do it again or I'll go to Harper, understood?'

'You know more about Paris than you're saying. I'd go further. I think you know all about GDLC Holdings too.'

Fraser had been purposefully moving back inside her house, about to close the door on him, but turned.

'Go on,' she said.

'I don't know who they are, but they paid you and they paid Tikhonov. The exact same amount on the exact same day five years ago.'

'Wait there,' Fraser said, 'we're going for a walk.'

Two minutes later and Yvonne Fraser re-emerged, calling goodbye to her family whilst pulling on a long woollen jacket against the chill night air.

'Okay, so this is what I know,' she began 'and this is what I can tell you. Yes, I did know Tikhonov from my time in Paris, but I wasn't lying when I said I didn't know him well. I only met him a handful of times and even then, it was nothing special. He really gave me the creeps, Scott. The guy's a thug. Old school KGB. Highly unpleasant, and I'm not just talking about his appearance.'

'What about GDLC?'

'I'm getting to that. On 31st March I was sent a text message telling me to drop everything and go and meet Samphire that evening.'

'Samphire?'

'Tikhonov. I was to take him a package.'

'What was in it?'

'Slow down Scott. I got a text to say there was a package waiting for me at lost property, Gard du Nord. A size 1 jiffy bag addressed to Dominique Lagrène, with a *Fabriqué en France* sticker on the back. I was to go there immediately, take the package and meet Tikhonov that evening.'

'Where?'

'Pont des Arts. Eleven o'clock.' Fraser stopped and Hunter thought she might have changed her mind and be about to head home. 'Do you smoke, Scott Hunter?'

'Yeah.'

'Give us a fag will you? I'm not supposed to smoke in front of the kids.'

Hunter found a packet in the baggy pockets of his hoody and offered Fraser one, then took one for himself. He watched as she drew greedily.

'There was something about the whole op I didn't like. It didn't smell right. Too sudden, do you know what I mean?'

Hunter nodded.

'I texted back that it wasn't possible, which was almost true as it happens. I said I had to meet an asset that evening and that because of the speed at which the terrorist threat in Paris was moving at the time, it couldn't be put off. I got a text straight back to say that they would make alternative arrangements.'

'Who are "they"?'

Fraser stopped and stared at him. 'Come on, Scott. I was using a secure phone. A phone given to me by The Service.'

'*Who?*'

'Honestly,' Fraser said, shaking her head, 'I've no idea.'

'And what about the money?'

'That's as much a mystery to me as it is to you,' she said, flicking the ash from the end of her cigarette. 'It arrived in my account five days later.'

'And you never questioned it?' Hunter asked, trying to mask his incredulity.

'Have you ever received money unexpectedly, at a time when you've really needed it? I decided to say nothing and I challenge you or anyone else to say they'd have done differently.'

'Was the drop made?'

'How would I know?'

'Who made it?'

'Like I just said, I couldn't be sure whether it was made or not, Scott.'

'But assuming it was, then there was only one other person working in Paris at the same time as you.'

Fraser nodded. 'Marcus Bayer,' she said, confirming Hunter's worst suspicions.

'I bloody knew it.'

'But listen Scott, he wasn't working, not really. He was in transit, just passing through, on his way home.'

'He was there. And he was there long enough to meet Tikhonov on Pont des Arts.'

'Have you spoken to him?'

Hunter stifled a disappointed laugh. 'I've just spent the last couple of nights freezing my nuts off, sleeping in my car waiting to get some answers out of him. All he's done is lie to me and lead me up the garden path,' he replied as they turned back towards Fraser's house.

'Do you mind me asking? How did you discover I'd been paid by GDLC?'

'I didn't,' Hunter said quickly. 'I've got a partner, I mean she's not my... well anyway, you know what I mean. We're working together.' Fraser raised a rare smile. 'She dug it up in the files on floor four.'

'Okay, well, I'm not proud of it, but there it is,' Fraser said, throwing her cigarette to the gutter. 'It sounds to me as though all the answers you need are either there, or with Marcus Bayer.'

✳✳✳

'Are you the tosser that scratched my car?'

Kadnikov had been expecting the call.

'Mr Cabral.'

'You're going to pay to have that put right.'

'I understand, although you may feel differently once you've heard what I have to say.' There was a confused silence from the other end of the line allowing Kadnikov to press on. 'I wonder how your employers would feel if they discover you are dealing with Dmitry Patzuk?' he said, getting straight to the point.

'Who?'

Kadnikov fiddled with his smartphone and then, confident he had sent the photograph of Evgeny Tikhonov getting into Cabral's Porsche, returned it to his ear. 'The man in this photograph, he used to work for me. Now he buys and sells for a Russian mafia boss called Patzuk. Don't worry Mr Cabral, I don't want money. In fact, I'm not really interested in you at all. All I want to know is, where can I find the man in this photograph?'

Sebastian Cabral consulted his phone. 'I don't know.'

'That is unfortunate, for you at least. I can tell how much you love your car. Although it seems you may have to give it back, once your boss finds out who you've been dealing with.'

Cabral thought. He was by nature a risk taker, a gambler who played fast and loose with other people's money for a living and always without a safety net. Now he was going to have to gamble and hope that the man on the other end of the phone wasn't about to short sell him.

'He takes care of all of the arrangements, you've got to believe me. Everything's done by email. I've only ever met him a handful of times and never in the same place twice.'

'In which case Mr Cabral, I'm sorry for your car.'

'Hang on, hang on. There is someone who might know. I needed some gear for a party one time and he introduced me to this guy.'

'Where?'

'Do you know the South Bank Centre?'

'Yes.'

'There's a skatepark, under the QEH.'

Kadnikov made a brief note in his pad, consulted his watch, flicked his thumb across the phone and the line went dead.

***

Hunter returned to his flat in Harrow several hours later. He was tired. He slipped into the corner shop on the opposite side of the junction and bought some cigarettes, a small bottle of blended and a packet of cardboard which later he would rehydrate under boiling water to become noodles. He found his keys and inserted the Yale, giving it his habitual twist, whilst applying the slightest amount of pressure with his thumb, ensuring it would turn easily. The key stuck and so Hunter gave it a quick waggle and opened the door. He put the flimsy blue and white plastic bag from the corner shop on his kitchen counter and went to the cabinet to find a tumbler. The cabinet was just one of any number of things he'd been meaning to complain about, if he'd known how or who to complain to. It wouldn't shut properly. There was a knack to it. A tumbler in his hand he went to the freezer to fetch some ice, lit a cigarette and cracked the seal on the cheap bottle of whisky, then moved along the narrow corridor joining the rear of the flat to the lounge at the front. Looking out over North London, as the night began to settle and the streetlights flickered on, Hunter pushed at one of the futon's heavy rectangular feet, allowing it to settle back into the furrow it had left in the carpet. He retrieved an ashtray, stubbed out his cigarette, took a sip of whisky and, as the cheap liquor burnt a path to his stomach, watched the darkening night sky.

Someone had turned over his flat. The uncooperative front door, the open kitchen cabinet and finally the carelessly manhandled sofa. They had been so clumsy Hunter hadn't even bothered to check the tiny second bedroom housing his computer. From everything he'd read about Evgeny Tikhonov, recruited specifically by the FSB to join Patzuk's organisation, it was clear the Russians were every bit as interested in the respectable mobster as he was. He tried to think what, if anything, they might have discovered and was pleased to conclude, very little. He'd deleted the photographs on his phone and the hard copies had never left his person.

He took another sip and watched as the cubes of ice chased one another around the bottom of the tumbler. Harper had known his place would be empty. It was conceivable, wasn't it, that he'd assigned Samantha Fairchild specifically to keep an eye on him? The job they were working on was certainly easier with two heads, but it had already crossed Hunter's mind that he could probably manage equally as well without her. He thought back to their initial meeting at The Traitors Gate. Fairchild had already been there when he'd arrived, perhaps at a pre-meeting meeting. Then, just that afternoon, he'd witnessed Harper drag her off for a cosy little chat in his office. She certainly knew her way around his flat. A deliberately clumsy effort then?

10

The Foreign Office advises against all but essential travel to the United States

Bayer's lack of any phone meant that when Hunter woke the following morning he was left with no alternative than to navigate the roadworks of the M1 once more. He left early to avoid the traffic and, by lunchtime, having stopped at an unusually deserted service station for petrol, was in Shalfleet. He passed The Coronet and the butchers-cum-pottery, both shut. He parked up next to the signpost at the head of the path leading to the Forestry Commission site. Then he was following the now familiar track through a copse towards the sound of splitting wood. In the clearing outside his cabin, Bayer stood over a thick section of felled tree, swinging a heavy splitting maul whilst a pile of firewood grew about his feet. Anushka lay on the decking at the front of his cabin, panting in the midday sun.

'You did meet Evgeny Tikhonov in Paris on the evening of 31st March.'

Bayer looked up but didn't seem surprised to see him.

'I met a lot of people in my time with The Service. You'll have to remind me.'

'You met him on Pont des Arts and passed him a package. Ring any bells?'

The axe flew through the air and cleaved another log in two.

148

'No,' Bayer said, taking time to catch his breath.

'Are you saying you didn't go to Pont des Art on your night off in Paris?'

'No. Just that I don't remember a great deal about it and that the man I met I only knew as Samphire, that's all. I wasn't lying to you, I've never heard of Evgeny Tikhonov.'

'What was in the package, Marcus?'

'I don't know,' Bayer replied.

'I don't believe you.'

'I don't know, but I could hazard a guess if you'll just calm down?'

Dmitry Patzuk had left Britain on the 28th March a Russian citizen and less than a week later returned a British one. The package Bayer had passed to Patzuk's Mr Fixit, Evgeny Tikhonov otherwise known to The Service as Samphire, was a size 1 jiffy bag, Fraser had said. Hunter tried to visual the small mustard-yellow envelope. Probably about 6 by 10. The perfect size for a new identity.

'Why was The Service providing Russian hooligans with British passports?' Hunter asked, throwing the idea out to see if Bayer would bite.

'I don't think I said it was,' Bayer replied, his hands raised defensively in the air.

'You didn't have to. And if we were to re-examine your file a little more carefully, would we find a payment from GDLC Holdings to you on or about that date?'

'No,' Bayer replied bluntly, before balancing another log on its end and swinging the mighty axe over his shoulder.

'Really? Because everyone else seems to have been paid off. Why not you?'

'I was already on my way out, don't forget. In The Service's eyes I was finished, discredited. A blot on their already disgusting copy book.' Bayer's axe flew through the air. 'There was no need for them to pay me off,' he said bitterly.

'What do you mean?'

'Haven't you figured it out yet? GDLC Holdings, it's The Service's own private black fund, used for whenever they'd prefer not to be held accountable. The money's untraceable, probably dirty most of it, so I'd forget about trying to track it back through the banks on St Nevis if I were you. I was never paid by GDLC for anything. I was simply told where and when to be. They had me over barrel, so I did one last job for them.'

Hunter had always assumed the payments from GDLC had come from an external organisation. Why would The Service be paying its own agents to keep quiet and, more perplexingly still, keeping records of those payments, unless the activities carried out were in some way unlawful? Was The Service looking to cover its back by creating leverage over its own operatives?

'Who gave you the order?' He'd already tried and failed with Fraser but she, he reminded himself, was still an active field officer. Perhaps Bayer might be a little more cooperative.

But Bayer shook his head. 'I've no idea. It was all very last minute. My plane landed, I got the text whilst I was waiting for my luggage, caught a taxi into town, dumped my gear at the hotel, popped into Gard du Nord and then went out to meet Samphire that evening. The next morning I was on the first Eurostar to St Pancras and the end of my career.'

'And you never questioned it?'

'Why would I?' Bayer half-laughed. 'Would you, if your phone went right now and they asked you to move something from A to B? I doubt it.' Privately Hunter was forced to concede that Bayer was probably right.

'Who was *supposed* to make the Paris drop then?'

'Not me,' Bayer said quickly. 'I wasn't even meant to be in the country. Fraser?'

'She says not. Said the same as you, all very last minute.'

'Who else was working Paris at that time?' Bayer asked.

'No one, according to the records,' Hunter said.

Bayer thought for a moment. 'You're assuming this was all sanctioned of course?'

'What are you saying?'

'I'm not sure I'm saying anything, just that at the time there was a lot of movement between Britain and Moscow, which was seen by Whitehall at least as an extremely positive thing. Walls were coming down.'

'By movement,' Hunter said, 'I take it you mean people leaving Russia to come here?' Bayer nodded. 'But that still doesn't explain why

The Service was passing British passports to Dmitry Patzuk, a known criminal.'

'When did he come over from Russia?' Bayer asked.

'End of 2014.'

'Meaning Lobanov had already been here quite a while?'

'About fifteen years, yes,' Hunter said.

'And it doesn't bother you that *he's* living here on a British passport?'

Hunter had never really given it any thought.

Another log cracked in two.

'What do you know about the Golden Visa Scheme?' Bayer asked. Hunter shook his head and steadied himself for another lecture. 'In 1994 The British Government started a "high value investor" scheme dedicated to selling off UK visas and passports to anyone with enough cash. They were to buy shares in the Bank of England at a hundred thousand a pop. Small change to the likes of Lobanov. Ten million bought you permanent British citizenship after two years. They ran the scheme for a while and made a hell of a lot of money along the way, but then the Treasury stuck its nose in and, with an uncharacteristic attack of morality, decided it wasn't completely comfortable with the nature of the money the scheme was attracting and that they would, on this rare occasion, do what was right rather than what was easy. The Government had a re-think and decided to wind the scheme down in 2015.'

'Just as Patzuk was entering the country,' Hunter said.

'Exactly. As it turned out, the government's sudden burst of uncharacteristic integrity was pretty short-lived. Once they'd worked out how much money they stood to lose, they didn't scrap the scheme, just put up their prices. But Patzuk wasn't to know that. As far as he was concerned, he'd have had to go back to Russia to get his visa renewed.'

'Like Sklepov.' Bayer shrugged his shoulders. 'Patzuk's driver,' Hunter continued. 'He went back to Russia in February 2015 never to return.'

'Probably arrested as soon as he re-entered the country,' Bayer said.

'And if Patzuk thinks the only thing waiting for him at the airport is going to be a paddy wagon and a hot and cold running prison cell, he's going to try and do everything in his power to avoid ever setting foot in the place.'

Bayer nodded. 'At the time he thought he couldn't buy a passport from our government directly...'

'But Tikhonov was in a position to help him,' Hunter said. 'I've got to find out what's in the redacted section of that file. Someone in The Service has been selling British passports to Russian criminals, and I bet they were using GDLC Holdings to launder the money.'

'Don't forget, there's always the chance The Service doesn't have the original file at all.'

'Harper and I discussed that. I suggested it might have been shredded. He seemed to agree.'

Bayer let out an involuntary grunt. 'Unlikely though, don't you think?'

'Where is it then?'

'I don't know, but there are at least two people outside of Bedford Place with a vested interest in finding it before you do.'

'Evgeny Tikhonov and Dmitry Patzuk.'

Bayer nodded.

'I need to talk to one or both of them. Tikhonov's like a bloody ghost. We have *no* idea where he is, so I guess it'll have to be Patzuk.'

Bayer sighed and began taking off his gloves. 'Listen, if you do find Patzuk, you'll need to be extremely careful.'

'I know.'

'I'm not sure you do,' Bayer said, shaking his head. 'From what I've heard he's absolutely merciless. He won't hesitate to kill you if he finds out who you're working for.'

'I thought you said you'd never met him.'

'I haven't. But I hear things. Stories.'

'Go on.'

'People I met in Russia.' Bayer looked up toward the cloud filled sky and took a deep breath. 'They said that when he was a child, Patzuk, his mother would only ever bathe him in cold water. Even now, they said, he only ever takes an ice-cold bath.'

'Hardly makes him a mass murderer.'

'I haven't finished yet. Every night, before he goes to bed, he runs a bath for the following morning.' Hunter pulled a face. 'The idea is it's cold and still for the next day. Supposed to be invigorating.'

'Again, it doesn't mean anything, apart from he's a bit crazy.'

'Except that one night someone tried to break into Patzuk's house.

They'd identified his bathroom window as the best way in. Probably wasn't alarmed, that'd be my guess. Unfortunately they weren't aware of his rather unusual bath-time ritual. They came in through the bathroom window and fell straight into a tub of freezing ice-cold water. The commotion woke Patzuk and his entire family who stormed in to find the would-be assassin staring down the barrel of his own gun.'

'Patzuk shot him?'

'Oh no,' Bayer said, shaking his head slowly. 'No, he waited for one of his kids to fetch an extension cable and a portable electric heater. All the while he's asking the man who he works for. Patzuk gives him one last chance, then throws the heater into the bath.'

'Right. But the guy never gave up a name.'

'Oh yes he did,' Bayer said. 'Patzuk went after his entire family, one after another. The only one he left alive was the head, the man who'd ordered his execution. Now that's a cruel sadist. But do you know the worst of it? Patzuk forced his kids to watch the whole damn thing. Thought it would be a valuable life lesson.'

✳✳✳

Monday, 16th March 2020.
The Foreign Office advises against all non-essential travel.

Strange, the Russian thought, to be in a nation's capital, a city in which he had briefly operated on behalf of the motherland and yet not be able to call upon the extensive network of spies and informants he knew to be in play. But then again, in those intervening years, circumstances had changed and in ways he could never have predicted. Today, he hoped, would take him one small, yet distinctly unsavoury step closer to his goal. He put a handkerchief to his nose in an effort to mask the pungent odour of stale urine. And if the smell was objectionable, the relentless cacophony produced by the group of grown men on skateboards was intolerable. He'd taken the tube to Waterloo and from there walked along the river. The South Bank had changed immeasurably since his previous visits, but the impromptu skatepark beneath The Queen Elizabeth Hall was doing the re-generated area few favours. Each and every brutal concrete surface, aside from reflecting the deafening roar of tiny plastic wheels, was swathed in colossal and, to his eyes at least, ugly graffiti. Small pockets of men stood smoking and talking, their tender chariots clutched casually by their sides or waiting impatiently at their feet. Every now and then, one would break off and hurl himself up and down the ramped concrete which made this spot so appealing. It was rare for the Russian to feel quite so vulnerable and, when a fresh skateboarder shot towards him, he braced himself for the collision which never came.

After gingerly picking his way around the edges of the makeshift skatepark, Kadnikov believed he'd found what he'd been looking for. In one of the darker corners the South Bank had to offer, three young men talking quietly. The Russian was quick to note only two of them had boards. The third, spindly figure leading the conversation nodded quickly before deftly handing something to one of the other two, in a movement so casual it would have been missed by a less observant man. There was more nodding and then the two youths took off, away from the ramps and the graffiti. The Russian was now quite sure this was the man he was looking for.

'Paul Garin?'

Garin rearranged his head on his shoulders and peered down at Kadnikov.

'You police?'

'Do I sound like police?'

The dealer laughed. 'No! You sound like my fuckin' parents.'

'Very good, Paul. And how many friends of your parents can afford a coat or a hat like this? You're first-generation Londoner, I am right?' Kadnikov could picture his upbringing, see his parents, smell the *pelmeni* on the stove, hear the rough Georgian accent which Paul had struggled to shake off but couldn't. 'It says Pavel on your birth certificate, yes?' He didn't wait for an answer. 'Do your parents know what you do for living, Pavel?'

The cocky young man suddenly had nothing to say. No, I bet they don't, Kadnikov thought. The horror of discovering their only child was dealing sub-standard ecstasy and methamphetamines smuggled in from a basement lab in Liège would surely have killed them.

✳✳✳

'Haven't we got *any* photos?' Hunter asked, spreading out Evgeny Tikhonov's file to cover the one disreputable table floor four had to offer and which he'd very much made his own. He pushed the paperwork around for a bit, hoping it would somehow reveal something new and enlightening. 'It's no good, Sam, all this research. We just need to find two men, Patzuk and Tikhonov.'

'Has Harper said something to you?' Fairchild asked. Hunter looked at her. 'I mean, has he *ordered* you to approach them?'

'No,' Hunter replied, 'but it's obvious isn't it? There's more to this than Harper's letting on, I'm telling you. Let's start with Tikhonov. If we can find him, I'm sure we'll find Patzuk.'

Hunter picked up a selection of pages stripped from two glossy magazines. A reporter and photographer had been sent to document the excesses of a glitzy Mediterranean film festival and in so doing had captured Dmitry Patzuk and a couple of bikini-clad starlets enjoying cocktails on his yacht. 'This thing's bloody enormous,' Hunter said. 'Where did you say it's moored?'

'Pierre Canto Harbour on La Croisette.'

'Nice. And who's this guy here?' Hunter asked, indicating a shoulder leaving the corner of one frame. 'Is *this* Tikhonov? This could be the closest we have to a photograph of him.'

'I don't know,' Fairchild replied, struggling to hide her frustration. 'There's no address on any of our records, although it's safe to assume he's living under a false identity.'

'I wouldn't be so sure about that,' Hunter chipped in. 'After all, when he travels abroad, he uses his own passport and it's hard for me to imagine he couldn't organise a different one. I think we're just looking in the wrong places. Where's he from originally?'

'Kamchatka.'

'Which is a peninsular, right?' Hunter asked.

'That's right. Bears and boats.'

'Going to have to love the water then, isn't he?' Hunter continued.

'What's this got to do with anything, Scott?'

'I've got an idea where he might be, or at least what he might be living on. Let me see the boat show photos again.'

'We've been over this,' Fairchild said, handing Hunter the copy. 'He's never in shot. The best there is, is an arm or an elbow.'

'Does it show the date Patzuk bought his yacht?'

Fairchild pointed over Hunter's shoulder. '16th January. The day before the show closed.'

'Okay,' he said, hammering away at the iMac's keyboard. 'I need a list of all the companies at the boat show that year.'

'Why? I can tell you who he bought his yacht from.'

'I know, but I'm wondering if Patzuk wasn't the only one doing a spot of shopping that day?'

Hunter went to work compiling a list of over six hundred companies which had been at the boat show in 2016. He ruled out any of the firms selling add-ons and holidays, the ones hawking gadgets and insurance. With a list of all the companies who had made sales on the 16th January, he quickly found Dmitry Patzuk's name and began looking for Evgeny Tikhonov's. 'I don't get it,' he muttered, 'I was sure we'd find something.'

'What about the Sunday,' Fairchild suggested, 'the last day?'

'You think Tikhonov went back, maybe without his boss?'

'Worth a look, isn't it?'

'If he did, I don't see it,' he said to Fairchild. Hunter was just about to close the screen down when he spotted something. 'What about them?'

'Well,' Fairchild said dismissively, 'they're based in Holland for one thing.'

Hunter's fingers skated across the keyboard.

'And they renovate old barges,' she continued. 'Not really his style, is it?'

'Narrow boats,' Hunter said pointedly.

'What?'

'A barge is for moving cargo, a long boat is what the Vikings used and is long, and that,' he nodded towards the screen, 'is a narrow boat.'

'Alright, but I still can't see Tikhonov glugging champagne and chasing around after girls in bikinis on the back of one of those, can you?'

'But he's trying to disappear, Sam. He wouldn't buy the twin of Patzuk's boat, even if he could afford it,' Hunter said.

'Okay,' she conceded.

'And, on the 2nd June they flew over from Rotterdam to look at a sixty-five footer for sale in Northants called Summer Breeze.'

'And how could you *possibly* know that?' Fairchild asked.

'It's on their Twitter feed. There's even a picture of two of them enjoying a pint at The New Inn, Daventry. They were clearly quite excited to be working away from home for a change, which suggests it's something they don't do very often.'

'None of which proves it was Tikhonov who bought Summer Breeze,' Fairchild said.

'No,' Hunter replied, 'but I haven't finished yet. According to the marina's records, Summer Breeze was bought for cash.'

'So what?'

'And promptly disappeared.'

Fairchild shook her head then ran a hand through her short, blond bob. 'How do you disappear a narrow boat?'

'Not literally, Sam. It was removed from the Canal and River Trust's records.'

'Still doesn't mean it was Tikhonov.'

'Perhaps. But five-and-a-half months and many trips to The New Inn later, our friends from Holland are handing over a completely refitted boat.'

'Okay,' she said, clearly still sceptical, 'let's see what Evgeny got for his money?'

'That's the point. You can't. There aren't any photos, well not really. If you look through their Twitter and Facebook timelines they're backed up with pictures of the team handing over keys to happy customers.' Hunter scrolled up through the screen to prove his point. 'And there's a lot of happy chatter about Summer Breeze and what a great time they've had on their first business trip to England but hardly a shot of the boat and not a single mention of its new owner or the boat's name, which I'm guessing is no longer Summer Breeze. Look at the few pictures they did take.' Each photograph had been carefully framed to avoid the prow where the name might have appeared, only revealing a hull of freshly painted racing green and the occasional claret panel. 'The trouble is, if this is where Tikhonov is holed up, he could be anywhere. I reckon there are about twenty different marinas and moorings between Barking and Slough alone and that's even assuming he's in London. We haven't got time to search them all,' Hunter said, shaking his head.

'We won't have to,' Fairchild replied. 'What do you know about caviar?'

'Fish eggs? Sounds disgusting,' Hunter replied.

'Not if you're Russian. Black caviar's highly sort after and bloody expensive.'

'Bit of a leap from narrow boats. What's it got to do with Tikhonov?'

'Plenty,' Fairchild said, holding up a glossy sheet clipped from a Spanish celebrity news magazine and showing Patzuk standing on the prow of his gleaming new yacht.

Hunter shrugged. 'He paid eight mil and signed the cheque on the top of a box of Dom Perignon.'

'Héloïse Lloris and it was eight and a half.'

'Okay, but I still don't see what it's got to do with Tikhonov?'

'Look at the photograph,' Fairchild said, shaking the sheet at him. '*Look at the photograph.*'

Hunter squinted, trying hard to see what Fairchild had seen. 'There's Patzuk, he's on a yacht, the end.' Fairchild tapped her finger against the sheet and Hunter looked more closely at the bottom of the frame. 'I know, you said, he signed the cheque on a crate of champers.'

'Look at the crate, Scott.'

In the midst of a sea of half-finished glasses and empty champagne bottles was a tin, its lid at an angle, the handle of a white mother-of-pearl spoon poking out. 'That,' Fairchild said, trying to hide her triumph, 'is about a thousand pounds worth of finest Beluga caviar.'

'Bloody hell.'

'And the only place I know within a hundred miles of here you might buy one is Olivier's in Maida Vale and I bet Tikhonov's not far away.'

'You'd better pay them a visit then.'

Fairchild ran to Palgrave's desk.

'Julian, have you got a map of London?' she asked.

Palgrave made a derisory quip about the pope and Catholics and the next thing Fairchild knew she was staring at a pile of books and pamphlets a foot thick. 'There's topographical and thematic,' he began, removing the first six inches. 'And cadastral maps to most of the major landmarks, tube maps, train maps. I think there's even a couple of aeronautical charts.'

'What about an *A to Z*?'

Julian Palgrave drew a sharp intake of breath, closed his eyes and started to count, very slowly, to ten.

***

A tiny bell rang out announcing Samantha Fairchild's arrival as she entered Olivier's on Warwick Avenue. The first thing to strike her, the almost overpowering smell of the dozens of cured Polish sausages hanging from every available cabinet edge and rafter. Slowly, as she grew accustomed to the heady mix of garlic and marjoram, paprika and juniper berries, and seemingly with the place to herself, she began examining the store's shelves, running from floor to ceiling, stocked with everything from specially imported carbonated water from Georgia to row upon row of specialist vodkas. Two further long metal aisles cut down the middle of the shop to a line of refrigerated units and a door at the rear. Fairchild moved to the nearest display and idly picked up a stumpy yellow and red tin with a picture of a cow's head on its lid. Further along the shelf were jars of gherkins, pickled with borage and coriander and it was as she was trying to recall their bittersweet taste that the owner of Olivier's silently appeared at her elbow, catching her unawares. An ancient little man, a crop of untidy silver-grey hair sprouting defiantly from the top of his head. Beady little eyes peered up at her from beneath a pair of thick, black eyebrows.

'Good afternoon,' he said, in his thick Russian accent.

'Good afternoon. I wonder if you may be able to help me?' Fairchild replied, in fluent Russian.

He stared at her, the twinkling eyes unblinking and then, slowly, a broad Saratovian smile broke across his face.

'This *tushenka* is good, yes,' he said nodding enthusiastically whilst taking the tin from her, 'good quality beef, yes, yes, for English maybe? But for you,' he rummaged around on a lower shelf, '*this* I recommend.' He held up a smaller tin which Fairchild took out of politeness. 'Of course, I would be delighted to help you, young lady. But first you must tell me, where did you learn to speak such excellent Russian. Moscow?'

'St Petersberg.'

'Ah!' He nodded that that too would be an acceptable answer. 'What else can I interest you in I wonder? *Sushki?*' he continued gesturing toward a packet of the hard bagels. 'Or *kolbasa?* Ah, no no, something sweet for the pretty young lady?' He stepped back and pointed to the shop's huge selection of cookies. '*Pryaniki?*'

'No, thank you,' Fairchild said, replacing the tin he'd handed her. 'I'm looking for a man, actually.'

Olivier's owner's smile grew wider still and his eyes danced with delight. 'I think you do not have to look so often,' he said under his breath.

'He comes here to buy caviar.'

The man nodded again. 'A discerning gentleman, yes, yes. But many people come here for our caviar.' He swept a hand along a length of shelves groaning with tins of all shapes and sizes. '*Ossetra, Sevruga, Beluga?*'

'He has extremely expensive tastes.'

'Yes, yes,' the owner enthused, indicating the smaller tins commanding the higher prices. 'Any of these will make an excellent present for your friend.'

'This isn't a gift and he's not my friend,' Fairchild said flatly. 'You have, I believe, your own supplier?'

The owner nodded slowly. 'This is also true, yes, yes.'

'The man I'm interested in buys your own caviar.'

'Again, young lady, I don't wish to boast, but people come from across London for our caviar.'

'He buys only Royal Beluga from the Caspian. He's in the habit of buying 250 grams at a time.'

The owner of Olivier's raised his impressive black eyebrows. 'It is true, few of our customers can afford such quantities.' He looked up at Fairchild, still smiling. 'Can I ask the beautiful English girl with the excellent Russian she picked up in St Petersburg why I should help her find this wealthy customer of ours?'

'Because he works for Dmitry Patzuk,' Fairchild said, calmly running a hand through her blond bob and flicking the fringe from her eyes.

The owner's smile vanished and he turned quickly to the glass door behind him, locking it firmly and flipping over the closed sign. 'You should have said.'

11

Tuesday, 17th March 2020 Camden NW1.
Cinema chains announce they will close.

The young Georgian drug peddler had directed Kadnikov to a coffee shop in NW1. As he sat sipping an espresso and looking out over Camden Lock, Aleksei Kadnikov began to theorise about the man he was pursuing. The absence of any address, the thick waterproof jacket on a warm day and the tan coloured boating shoes worn without socks and displaying a white line of watery residue above the sole had all led him to the same conclusion. He devoted that afternoon to searching the canals of Camden but the Georgian had either been wrong, or his information had been out of date, because there was no sign of Evgeny Tikhonov. As afternoon had become evening and, convinced that he was on the right track but in the wrong location, he'd taken a cab to Warwick Avenue around the corner from what was laughingly called Little Venice. Only the English, he thought as he paid the cabby, could have taken something quite so run-down and miserable, with its scruffy bridges and shit smeared tow-paths, and named it after somewhere so magnificent.

A craggy faced man in his late fifties was unsuccessfully attempting to untie his dog, whilst cheerlessly whistling the same two bars of Carmen, round and around. The dog had been waiting patiently for him outside his barge but was now straining at the length of rope serving as a leash. Kadnikov lit a cigarette and watched whilst he dealt with the animal.

'Excuse me,' he said slowly, conscious of his accent.

The man stopped whistling and looked up as the dog threatened to yank the rope from his hand and streak off down the tow-path. 'You alright there?'

'I wonder if you could help me, please? I am looking for someone.'

'Oh yeah. I'll see what I can do. I know most people, if they're from round here.'

Kadnikov smiled and offered him a cigarette, which he politely declined.

'His name is Evgeny Tikhonov,' Kadnikov continued. 'He is Russian, like me,' he finished with a circumspect nod.

The other man thought for a moment whilst trying to control his dog, then shook his head. 'Sorry mate. We got all sorts round here, Poles mostly, few Slovaks, you name it, but no Evgenys, I don't think.'

'I understand,' Kadnikov said, and was about to move on but stopped himself. 'He has a... a birthmark, is this right? On his face.'

'Oh yeah, I know 'im. Ugly son-of-a-bitch,' the man said, holding a hand up to his cheek. 'Face like ten miles of bad road. No offence.'

'That sounds like him,' Kadnikov said, not really understanding.

'You've missed him though.' The man pointed to a vacant mooring on the opposite bank. 'He was there this morning. I didn't even hear him go. Went to take the dog for a walk and...'

Both men stared awkwardly at the uncomfortable space Evgeny Tikhonov's narrow boat had left and then at the overenthusiastic animal on its makeshift lead. A strange looking creature, the Russian thought. Was that a greyhound? The Americans had named a bus company after them. He'd used it once, a long time ago. This was not an animal you would find on the streets of Moscow. Too thin to survive the cold, its long, spindly legs made for sprinting. Ah, so the bus name made sense to him now. It would be excellent for coursing, Kadnikov could see that, briefly fast and agile. The dog turned its long, aquiline snout, looking directly at him as he sniffed the oil heavy air. The Russian adjusted his glasses, squinting into the light as it reflected off the water and cursed his luck.

'Where?' he asked.

The man opposite him smiled back honestly. 'Where what, mate?'

162

'Where did he go?'

'How the hell would I know? Who are you anyway, police?'

'No,' the Russian replied a touch too hastily. 'Not police. Old friend.'

'Really? That's funny, that's what the other guy said, although he didn't look so old to me.' He jerked on the dog's lead, bringing him to heel. 'I'll tell you one thing, for such an ugly sod he's suddenly got a hell of a lot of friends. Why do you want to speak to him anyway?'

'No reason.'

'Went on his barge once,' the dog owner continued undeterred. 'Not much to look at from the outside, but get inside and it was a regular little gin palace. Chrome and polished steel everywhere, and the wood, must have cost 'im a fortune. Walnut, I'd say, or something like that. Very nice, whatever it was. He's given it a fancy foreign name too. The Valentina something...' the man said.

'Tereshkova,' Kadnikov put in, suddenly quite sure.

'Yeah, yeah, that sounds like it. How'd you know that then? You been on his boat too, have you?'

'First woman in space,' Kadnikov replied. And a genuine Russian hero too, he thought. Perhaps Evgeny Tikhonov hadn't cut *all* his ties with the motherland?

Kadnikov drew long and hard on his Parliament then threw the half-finished cigarette into the canal below, where it hissed briefly. The animal was still looking at him, straining on its makeshift leash. Such trusting creatures, he thought, pushing his glasses further up his nose and blinking slowly in the light. Then, without another word, the short round man in the long trench coat and broad hat swivelled uneasily on his heels and set off back down the tow-path. He'd heard enough and he'd never liked dogs.

As the greyhound barked at his retreating figure he wondered where his fellow countryman might be headed. The fool with the dog had been right about one thing though. Tikhonov had either gone east, back towards Camden, or west heading out of London. Kadnikov smiled bitterly. The English had got to Tikhonov first. No matter, he thought, as long as the outcome was the same. He reached for another Parliament.

***

The Glastonbury Festival is cancelled and the United Kingdom's death toll exceeds 100 for the first time

Fairchild and Hunter took it in turns to keep an eye on Evgeny Tikhonov and pilot the Valentina Tereshkova west along The Grand Union Canal. They arrived at Batchworth Lock at dawn and Fairchild immediately pulled a blanket over herself and went to sleep, leaving Hunter to struggle with the narrow boat's heavy ropes. Tikhonov began meticulously preparing a pan of *kasha* for breakfast.

'I not going with you,' he muttered over his shoulder as Hunter stepped back into the cabin.

'I can't see why not,' Hunter replied. 'I've told you, you're not who we're interested in. We want Patzuk and *his* boss.'

'What makes you think I work for Dmitry Patzuk?' Tikhonov asked.

'We have a file,' Hunter continued, about, for better or worse, to nail his colours to the mast. 'It dates from your time in Paris and documents very clearly how you bought British passports.'

Tikhonov stopped stirring. 'Even if I believe you, so what?'

Hunter was going to have to take another leap of faith. If he was right, Tikhonov might be forced to back down. If he was wrong, it could be the last thing he would ever do.

'I'm guessing your superiors at the FSB weren't aware of this black-market operation?'

'You're lying. You don't know who I was working for in Paris.'

Hunter needed to find a way through the Russian's thick skull. He thought about the man he'd watched smoking in his car outside George Wiseman's flat in Kensington. He thought about the man who'd turned Tobias Gray and who had clearly been pulling everyone's strings until extremely recently. One man. One name. A name which had terrified Oleg Lobanov and he hoped would break Evgeny Tikhonov wide open. 'I know Aleksei Kadnikov's in town. I can only assume he's looking for you, too.'

Tikhonov swore under his breath. 'Kadnikov does not frighten me. I work for him, twenty years. I know Kadnikov. He try and try for ways to bring Lobanov down, but...' Tikhonov gave a shrug.

'And Patzuk?' Hunter asked.

Tikhonov just shook his head. 'Too dangerous. The man is... lunatic.'

'So why won't you come in? Let us protect you. Tell them what they want to know and let them take care of Patzuk?'

'Because,' Tikhonov said, offering Hunter a mug of steaming coffee, 'there are people who scare me more than Dmitry Patzuk.'

'And they are?'

Tikhonov shook his head again then took a long gulp of coffee.

'Has this person threatened you?' Hunter asked.

Tikhonov laughed. 'He would not do this. He is powerful. Can make Evgeny's life very... uncomfortable.'

'Is this someone who works for Patzuk? The FSB? Someone you used to work with in Paris?'

'I work for him a little, yes, but not Patzuk.' Tikhonov stared at Hunter, weighing him up. 'You work for Service, yes?'

Hunter nodded.

'Then I cannot trust you.'

'Looks to me as though you don't have much choice,' Hunter said.

'I cannot trust you because this man, this man work for Service also. This man, he call himself Lazarus. Henry Lazarus,' Tikhonov said to the canal. 'Tall and always well dressed. Very English, you understand me?'

Hunter did, because he knew Henry Lazarus too. Lazarus had recruited him, trained him, put him up in his disappointingly small flat in Harrow and sent him on his first true mission.

'You needn't worry about Lazarus,' he said, aiming to sound confident. 'He doesn't work for The Service anymore.'

'You're lying. You are full of lies, Scott Hunter.'

'No. He was my boss for a while. He resigned, recently.'

'Why?'

'He doesn't like change.'

'Who do you work for now, Mr Hunter?'

Hunter sighed. 'Come in, meet them for yourself,' he said, thinking of Sandy Harper and hoping Fairchild was asleep. 'Tell them *your* side of the story and be free of Patzuk.'

'No. I do not wish to continue this conversation,' Tikhonov said, slamming down his breakfast bowl and elbowing past Hunter to the boatman's cabin at the stern. Hunter followed him up the tiny set of steps to the open deck. The powerful Russian was looking out over the canal.

'I love water at this time of day,' he said. 'Very peaceful. No one here. Even enemies still in beds,' Tikhonov said, his gaze never leaving the water. 'So, you know I had other job?'

'Had or have?'

'Had,' Tikhonov replied with a single, emphatic nod of his solid, round head.

'You were planted in Patzuk's organisation by the FSB when you were just twenty.'

'Yes,' Tikhonov nodded again, looking out over the water as the wake of another boat slapped and rocked them. 'Two mistresses, one love,' he said, holding up a thick index finger to emphasise his point.

'I'm not sure I understand.'

'Five years ago, when Dmitry and I leave Russia, came here, I still work FSB. I report to Moscow, sometimes meet somebody here.' Tikhonov looked at Hunter, perhaps worried he'd said too much before shrugging an indecorous shrug. 'I was Cheka. You see?' Hunter nodded. 'But after I'm here a while, left Russia behind. I see what *could* be done...' Tikhonov faltered, his English deserting him.

'Your allegiances changed?' Hunter suggested.

'Da. I thought I leave my life with FSB behind. Maybe run business here. Legitimate business for Patzuk, and be happy. But your government not give him visa. He was furious. "My God, Evgeny, they give these *petuch* visa, why not me?" So, I go to one person I thought I knew here. Lazarus. Try not to look so shocked Mr Hunter. The English have saying, yes? "Small world. I scratch his back, you scratch mine." I say, Mr Lazarus, I get you many Russian secrets. Nasty, from FSB, from vaults of Russian Consulate, Boulevard Lannes.' Tikhonov permitted himself a chuckle. 'All I require return, one, single, clean, British passport, name Dmitry Patzuk.'

'And I take it,' Hunter said, 'that none of this was sanctioned by the FSB?'

'No,' Tikhonov said shaking his head vehemently, 'not sanctioned, no.'

'The secrets you bought Patzuk's passport with, were they...?'

'Genuine?' Tikhonov asked, lighting a cigarette. 'All genuine. I still had connections, my time in Marseilles. Not difficult for Evgeny to come and go in consulate. People remember me, so,' he smiled ruefully, holding up a hand to frame his blemished features.

'But I'm guessing they found out eventually?'

'Possibly,' Tikhonov nodded.

'And so now they're after you too?'

The Russian smiled, opened his powerful hands and shrugged.

'In which case,' Hunter said, trying not to let his rising exasperation get the better of him, 'I really don't understand why you won't let us help you?'

'Lazarus. That man he met, Saint Chapelle. A civilian. *Kill* him.' Tikhonov's hands chopped at the air, illustrating his point.

'Which man?' Fairchild asked from below, throwing off her blanket and yawning.

'When I work with him in Paris, a man. He recognise Lazarus. Very bad.'

Hunter cast his mind back to the reports he'd read. There'd only been two British agents active at that time, Yvonne Fraser and Marcus Bayer. He shook his head.

'I think you're wrong. It couldn't have been Lazarus.'

Tikhonov turned on him angrily. 'Do not suppose to tell me who I work with. Do you think I don't know who I eat lunch with, meet in gallery, under bridge, in train station? Will you tell me next I not meet Lazarus in Saint Chappelle? Are you? He *kill* a man. Englishman. Somerset was his name, like county.'

'How?'

'Push him, under wheels of bus,' Tikhonov said, demonstrating the action with one huge, open hand. 'In centre of Paris.'

Fairchild rushed up the steps, now wide awake. 'It was in the cuttings, on floor four! He was a retired teacher!'

'Da!' Tikhonov nodded enthusiastically. 'He was...' He held up the same enormous hand and waved it in front of his face. 'Artist?'

Hunter turned to Fairchild. 'Any chance you could look those cuttings out? Tomorrow maybe?'

The Service might not appear to have any record of Alperton's stay in Paris, but then perhaps that wasn't quite true. The redacted file, the missing photographs. None of that could have been done by Palgrave, not even by that shifty shit Sandy Harper. But Sir John Alperton, he could have done it, especially if he'd had something to hide.

'Did Lazarus ever say who *he* was working for?' Hunter asked.

Tikhonov slowly shook his giant head. 'Of course not. You ask

Evgeny, Lazarus only ever work for Lazarus. Now I have told you everything. Can I trust you?' he asked Hunter.

'I wouldn't,' Fairchild replied with a smile.

But Hunter was already descending the steps back inside the cabin. 'I need to make a call.'

***

'Sandy,' Miranda Davenport said, extending a cool hand before brushing at the back of her skirt and taking a seat next to him on the park bench. 'I'm intrigued. Just what did you consider so important it couldn't be put in an email?'

They'd agreed to meet in Russell Square, away from prying eyes and inquisitive ears.

'I've got it,' Sandy began. 'There was a connection between Alperton and the Russians, just as you said there'd be.'

Davenport coughed quietly into a delicately balled fist. 'I don't believe I said anything of the kind.'

'He was selling off British passports,' Harper continued undaunted, determined to air his grievance.

'Quite an allegation, Sandy. I take it you're prepared to back this up?'

'Fairchild. She found the Russian, ex-FSB and currently on Dmitry Patzuk's payroll. She's with him right now.'

'And he's willing to talk?'

'He's scared and looking for protection.'

'Scared of whom?'

'All sides, it would appear. He's convinced the Russians are after him, but he's worried that if he comes over to us, Alperton will try and keep him quiet too.'

'I presume you have conveyed to him that Sir John is no longer on our books?' Davenport asked. Harper nodded. 'And that if we were to extend this kindness, we shall be expecting him to bring to the table something more than misty-eyed reminiscences of his time in the FSB? He is retired, I believe you said?'

'There's a document, the girl found it in some old files. It's been heavily redacted, presumably by Alperton.'

Davenport watched as a badly deformed pigeon emptily scratched its way past.

'Again, quite a presumption, Sandy, and one I don't see furthering your Russian's case. Unless, of course, he were somehow able to produce the original?' She tilted her head towards Harper. As innocent a request as if she'd asked him to take her hand across the street.

'But...' Sandy began.

'Have you spoken to Julian?'

Harper stumbled again and Davenport saw to fill the awkward silence. 'What about the girl? See what else she can dig up? I've never been fond of blackmail, Sandy, so I would regard such a file as nothing more than a down payment. I feel that, if his safety is to be guaranteed, we shall have to reach a different arrangement, going forward.' And then Mrs Miranda Davenport was rising gracefully from the bench. 'I shall expect to hear from you, and soon Mr Harper,' she said, before walking south toward Bedford Place and the safety of her influence.

Harper padded down his Herringbone and found his mobile phone. 'Hunter? The Paris report. I want it. The original. No fucking about. That's the only way I'm prepared to entertain your Russian friend.'

✳✳✳

Evgeny Tikhonov looked expectantly at Hunter as he shut down his phone.

'Well? Are they interested? Will they help?'

Hunter shook his head. 'The problem is that as things stand it's your word against Alperton's, and even with his recent track record... They want proof. That's the only thing which'll buy your safe haven.'

'What proof? They talk to me, I was there. I tell them. This is proof.'

Hunter shook his head again. 'There's a report. They want it, the original. It's the only way.'

'And you have report?' Tikhonov asked, looking at Hunter suspiciously.

'Not the original, no.'

'And we don't know where it is either,' Samantha Fairchild said, stifling a yawn.

'We need to get you out of here quickly,' Hunter said. 'There'll be people after you and it won't take them long to work out where we are.'

'We need somewhere to hole up,' Fairchild added.

'And I know just the place,' Hunter replied, opening up his phone again.

As Fairchild and Hunter secured the boat, Tikhonov said goodbye to Valentina for the last time. Then the trio walked for fifteen minutes along the tow-path and into the centre of Rickmansworth. They hadn't long to wait at the busy roundabout before Hunter recognised a car and began waving frantically.

'Dad! Dad, over here!'

An ancient silver-grey Volvo swung off the roundabout and clattered to a halt just past them, a bemused David Hunter at its wheel.

'Scott?'

Hunter was already opening the car door and ushering the solid Russian inside.

'Scott?' his father asked again.

'Hello, Mr Hunter,' Samantha called from the back of the car. 'Nice to see you again.'

David looked at his son. 'Scott, what the hell is going on? Do I know her?'

'Kind of. I'll explain later.'

✲✲✲

Tuesday, 23rd May 2000 Royal Borough of Kensington and Chelsea.

George Wiseman flicked at the return on his Olivetti, slowly eased his shoulders back and craned awkwardly to peer down Landsdowne Terrace and eye the now familiar parade of cars parked up outside his apartment. In the years following his apparent retirement from The Service he'd carefully observed two shining stars of the global intelligence community; Bedford Place's *wunderkind* Tobias Gray and the FSB's very own Aleksei Kadnikov. Wiseman had watched that particular dance play out with considerable interest, always ready to step in and lay down the law. Kadnikov had certainly appeared as good as his word and so George had been content to watch both men marshal their troops across Europe and beyond. But then there had been the death of the girl, Kadnikov's stepdaughter, and Alperton's regrettable but all too predictable involvement. Wiseman hadn't approved of Gray's handling of the situation, and he'd been even less happy about events in Istanbul. Wiseman had only ever met Ewen Connolly on a handful of occasions but those had been enough for the truculent Scot to impress him. There had been mudslinging and recriminations. David Hunter had taken the fall, and in so doing had presented Wiseman with the solution to a conundrum which had plagued him for so many years. Wiseman liked Hunter, felt he could work with him. All of Alperton's intellect and guile but with none of the edges. He was as you found him. Clever, compassionate when the situation called for it but, above all, trustworthy. Yes, Hunter would make an excellent custodian.

***

David Hunter and his son watched as Fairchild led Evgeny Tikhonov around David's beautifully appointed garden.

'You brought a Russian spy into my house? Jesus, Scott, what were you thinking?' David said.

'He's not a spy.'

'*Really?*'

'Really. He's Vory now.'

'Oh, terrific,' David laughed. 'Even better. The Russian Mafia.'

'And I'm trying to protect him.

'From who?'

'Sir John Alperton, it seems, although I can't be completely sure.'

'Then you'd better make sure, Scott.'

'I can't. I can't do a thing until I find this bloody file.'

'I have no idea what you're talking about but may I politely suggest, you get on with finding it, whatever *it* is, and get *him* out of here?'

Scott smiled weakly and nodded to himself. 'I'd love to, Dad, believe me, I'd really love to.'

'Well then?'

'It's complicated.'

'It's a file isn't it? You've spoken to Julian Palgrave?'

'Several times.'

'And he won't let you see it?'

'It's not a simple as that. The file doesn't exist.'

David stared at his son. 'What do you mean it doesn't exist?'

'Just that. No one knows where it is, or if they do, they aren't saying.'

'Well, whilst I'm very sorry to hear that, I still want *him* out of here, and before Frances shows up, understood?

Hunter nodded.

'Now, what's so important about this file?'

'There was an op, in Paris, about five years ago. I'm pretty sure Tikhonov was involved.'

'Okay.'

'We found the file on flour four.'

'You just told me it doesn't exist.'

'Heavily redacted.'

'Ah, I see. So, without the redacted portion, you're stuck?'

'Still not that simple,' Scott replied. 'I don't think the key is what's *in* the file, redacted or otherwise, I think it's the fact that the file exists at all. Only two people were supposed to be working in Paris at the end of March 2015 and I've spoken to both of them. Yvonne Fraser, who claims to have been asked to help in the operation but refused, and Marcus Bayer, who shouldn't have been in the country at all had he not just accidentally shot and killed his best friend. If you take those two out of the equation, who's left?'

'I'm not sure I understand,' David Hunter said.

'Well, *someone* was supposed to meet Samphire on that bridge before either of them were involved.'

'And that's Samphire, I take it?' his father said, gesturing to Tikhonov.

'As far as I can make out, yes. He claims to have been working with John Alperton, but there's no record of Alperton being in Paris at that time.'

David Hunter's brow furrowed and he shook his head. 'Why don't you talk to the author of the report?'

'That's Bayer. Because he claims not to have written a word of it.'

'And you believe him?'

'Yes, it was filed three days after he left The Service.'

'Ah, now I think I'm beginning to understand.'

'Tikhonov claims he was dealing with John Alperton trading in dodgy British passports for Russian secrets. He says that Alperton pushed an innocent tourist under a bus, although he doesn't seem to know why. There's no evidence to back any of it up of course, apart from the redacted file, written by, well God knows who,' Hunter said, throwing his hands in the air. 'The only thing I do know with any real degree of certainty is, it wasn't Marcus Bayer. I'm running out of ideas Dad, and now Sandy Harper says the only way he'll even entertain talking to Tikhonov is if we can magically produce the original file out of thin bloody air.'

Hunter stopped and looked down the garden to where Samantha Fairchild had knelt to examine a small dark green succulent which was showing the first signs of delicate pink flowers.

'Dad? Who was Percy Blackmore?' he asked.

'Percival Blackmore!' His father laughed, relieved at the change in subject. 'The Prince, they used to call him. One of the founding fathers of The Service after World War One.' Scott's face crumpled. Surely whoever he was he would be a long time dead and no help to him now. 'Blackmore was a true eccentric I'm told,' his father continued, 'from a time when that was the norm. Whilst The Service you're a part of today is dramatically different from the one Blackmore helped to establish, none of it would have been possible without him.'

'I still don't understand,' Scott said. 'What's "Blackmore's bottom locker" then?'

David Hunter laughed again. 'You've encountered a rather charming aspect of The Service's lexicon. Blackmore's locker was where all the missing reports were said to have gone, and believe you me, there were plenty of them.' David smiled at the recollection. 'Report left on a train, must be in Blackmore's locker. File put in the wrong cabinet, lost forever, Blackmore's locker. Even I was known to file the odd bit of paperwork in Blackmore's bottom locker when things were particularly frantic.'

'So, Fraser's saying she thinks the original's simply been misplaced?' Scott said, enjoying the idea of his father being anything less than perfect.

'Sounds like it,' David said looking down the garden at the girl and the Russian. 'He can't stay here, you know that, don't you? You'll have to find somewhere else. I don't want to have to explain to Frances what a Russian mobster's doing in my house. Take him to Harrow.'

Scott shook his head. 'I'm not certain that's a good idea.'

'Why?'

'I've had visitors.'

David eyed his son anxiously.

'It's okay. I know a place,' Scott said. 'I'll take him for a drive.' He was going to need Fairchild to go back to Bedford Place and speak nicely to Sandy Harper.

'Alright,' his father said, handing him the keys, 'but before you go, how did you persuade a onetime member of the KGB who appears to work for the most dangerous Russian gangster in London to drop everything and sail out here?'

✳✳✳

Twenty-four hours earlier. Little Venice, W9.

Scott Hunter pulled the hoody tight over his head and flicked through the collection of photographs on his iPhone. The owner of Summer Breeze was being extremely careful not to give away the narrow boat's new identity, but there was still plenty for him to go on. He was looking for a wide-beamed boat with a semi-traditional stern and painted racing green with claret panels and gold trim. He'd shown the boat's picture to a few people before anyone had been able to help him. A man out walking his dog had recognised it immediately, helpfully pointing him in the right direction. Hunter swung round the bend in the tow-path and under the bridge carrying the A404.

'Evgeny Tikhonov?'

The man standing at the stern of the Valentina Tereshkova turned slowly to face Hunter.

'You are talking to me?'

'You're Tikhonov, aren't you?' Hunter called out casually, moving along the tow-path towards the impressive narrow boat, his phone held high in one hand, as if he were about to deliver a parcel.

'I do not know this name. My name is...' But Hunter stopped him. He shook his head and reached into the front pocket of his hoodie. The man facing him reacted immediately, like the athlete he might once have been, and Hunter found himself staring down the business end of a shiny silver pistol. 'Hands, where I can see them.' Hunter was already at the short metal gangplank, his head still shaking beneath his hood. The man holding the pistol repositioned the weapon in an attempt to cement his stance.

'You're known as Samphire, in certain circles,' Hunter continued, about to step onto the stern of the boat.

'Who are you? Get off!'

Hunter ignored the question, standing his ground and throwing an economical gesture towards the weapon. 'Throw it in the river,' he said dismissively, pointing at the gun.

'What?'

Hunter pulled down his hood, taking his time.

'Throw it... in the river. Now please, before we attract a crowd.'

'Are you out of your fucking mind? You walk on my boat, say these things? I give orders. I one with gun,' Tikhonov shouted back.

Hunter smiled and tapped his chest three times with his index finger, just below his sternum. 'Please put that away. I don't like guns, never have.' He produced a packet of cigarettes from the depths of his hoody and held them up for the man to scrutinise. 'In fact, I refuse to carry one, but I am told, by people that know, that a three thirty-eight, fired from an L1 Long, over the range of,' Hunter paused to consider, 'I'm not great with distances either as a matter of fact, so I'm going to say less than two hundred yards, yeah, that sounds about right, anyway, these people tell me that a round fired from that gun at that range will turn your brains to soup.' He tapped the index finger of his left hand on the flat of his chest again then looked at Evgeny Tikhonov, inviting him to do the same.

Tikhonov looked down. He watched as the tiny red dot of a sniper's laser sights danced across his chest. His head rose and he looked at the scruffy young Englishman who had boarded his boat. The red dot slowly slid up Tikhonov's chest, across his chin and nose and settled comfortably on his forehead.

'Like I said. Please throw that thing overboard so we can talk. I wouldn't want to make a mess of your lovely boat.'

Tikhonov thought back to his time in the ring. He'd always known when to throw in the towel. The gun spun and twisted through the air before splashing easily into The Regent's Canal.

Hunter reached behind him and produced his Glock. 'Thank you,

Mr Tikhonov.' He racked the pistol, putting a round in the chamber. 'If you wouldn't mind stepping inside?'

'You said you never carry gun?'

'I lied.' Hunter waggled the end of the pistol towards the cabin and then, when Tikhonov began to move towards the heavily varnished oak door leading inside, Hunter raised his hand. A second later and the red dot which had been following Tikhonov disappeared. Hunter stepped into the boat's cabin and invited the Russian to sit down.

Three hundred yards on the opposite side of the canal, and hidden by the tumbling branches of a weeping willow, Samantha Fairchild watched the man toss his gun into the water. She waited until Hunter had drawn his own weapon and ushered the other man inside. She waited for his signal, and then, just as Hunter had been about to enter the cabin, he'd turned and flashed a smile in her direction.

You, Scott Hunter, are one devious bastard, she thought, as she flicked off the tiny laser pointer. She spun the keyring around her finger before stuffing it back in her leather jacket and, trying not to laugh, made for the temporary footbridge and the Valentina Tereshkova.

12

Hunter sat in his father's car outside 19 Boden Road and listened to Tikhonov snore. He watched Fairchild make her way towards them. She was wearing skinny black jeans and a bright red leather jacket and taking, Hunter thought, an altogether different yet not entirely unattractive approach to keeping a low profile. Fairchild carried the previous day's Evening Standard tucked under her left arm, their pre-arranged signal that she had what he needed and all was right with the world. She never once looked his way but went straight up the short front path at number 19 and let herself in. Hunter glanced at his watch. He'd give it twenty minutes, have a cigarette, then rouse the Russian.

Hunter smiled to himself as he led Tikhonov up the path. Still the same crappy old front door, its paint faded and cracking, but he noticed a brand-new single-cylinder deadbolt lock, the cost of which, if Alperton had his way, was coming straight out of his pay packet.

Inside, little had changed. A spartanly appointed space used by The Service to keep people safe, not comfortable. Knowing the drill perhaps better than Hunter did himself, Evgeny Tikhonov wordlessly disappeared upstairs clutching his overnight bag. Hunter followed Fairchild into the kitchen and began searching through cabinets of tins and packets of pasta.

'Jesus, Sam, what took you so long?'

She didn't reply immediately, just thrust a mobile phone at him and

177

left a set of new yale keys on the kitchen table. 'You're welcome, by the way,' she said.

'Come on, I've been sat out there with him for bloody hours. We must have looked like the world's worst first date.' They listened as Tikhonov made his way back downstairs and the television went on in the next room.

'Make sure and have a nice evening,' Fairchild said, smiling sarcastically. 'I'll text you his new number once I'm out of here.'

'Okay, thanks Sam.'

Hunter put the kettle on and found a half-finished bottle of Scotch.

✳✳✳

The Bank of England cuts interest rates to 0.1%

Hunter's phone woke him early. There had been developments overnight and Davenport was asking him to deliver Tikhonov to Bedford Place immediately, then, once he'd done that, he was to go to a restaurant off the Strand for a meeting. Topic unspecified. He went to Tikhonov's room at the front of the house. The door was ajar, the room empty. His bag had gone too, Hunter noticed. He sprinted downstairs and nearly ran straight into the sturdy Russian.

'You have *kasha* for breakfast? Good start to day.'

✳✳✳

With Tikhonov safely in Sandy Harper's hands, Hunter arrived at the restaurant to find a red and white closed sign dangling lazily in the glass front door. He was wondering what to do next when it opened and a waitress breezed out.

'We're shut,' she said gloomily and contrary to the sounds and smells emanating from the kitchens below, 'and for the foreseeable future, I'm afraid.' She looked at Hunter in his broken shoes, jeans and hoody. 'Unless you're with that lot?' she suggested somewhat incredulously. Hunter nodded and she smiled at him. 'You'd better follow me then.' She led him through the main dining hall, through a desert of freshly polished tables and yawning empty chairs, to a tall thin staircase which ascended to the floor above.

At the top of the stairs an oak door opened into a modest private dining room. Three of the four walls wore a collection of characterless hunting prints. A large picture window dominated the far wall, looking out over The Thames. A grand old wooden table had been set for three, surrounded by six high backed chairs. In the centre of the table, a pair of elegant candelabra, their candles twinkling in the early evening light, keeping watch over a silver wine cooler brimming with ice and a fine bottle of champagne. At the far end of the table lay a single, embarrassed sheet of paper. A woman in her mid-thirties, wearing a business suit and sipping from a champagne flute was staring distractedly out over the river. Next to her, engaged in hushed yet convivial conversation, Sir John Alperton.

'Mr Hunter, good of you to join us,' the woman said cordially. 'Will you take a drink?'

'Who are you?'

'I'm the person offering you a drink,' she replied, her patience already wearing thin.

Hunter helped himself. 'You're Davenport, aren't you?'

The woman declined to answer. She took another sip of champagne and stared straight through him. 'After everything I've heard about his father, I never imagined he'd be quite so... uncouth,' she said to Alperton.

'Why am I here?' Hunter asked.

'We'd like to thank you,' the woman replied coldly.

'For what?'

'Dmitry Patzuk. And Evgeny Tikhonov of course.'

'You used me to get to Tikhonov,' Hunter spat.

'No actually,' she replied firmly, 'I employed you to do a job, and you've done that job remarkably well. Tikhonov, as it happens, was an unexpected bonus. Sandy has had a brief and,' she shot Alperton a knowing glance, 'I should imagine, rather blunt conversation with him but I understand now he's playing along quite nicely.'

'And Patzuk?' Hunter asked.

'Dmitry Patzuk,' Sir John Alperton said, looking at his watch and entering the conversation for the first time, 'is no longer any concern of yours.'

'He's dead, isn't he?'

Duncan Swindells

'Don't be so naïve, Hunter. We don't kill people. We may supply the bullets from time to time, but we don't kill people.'

'I shot the last person who accused me of being naïve,' Hunter said under his breath.

'My point exactly,' Alperton replied.

'You used Tikhonov,' Hunter said to himself and not expecting or receiving a reply.

'What interests me now,' Alperton continued, choosing neither to confirm nor deny Hunter's accusation and moving from his spot by the window, 'is how you came by this?' He held up the sheet of unredacted A4 which had been quietly stinking out the room. Hunter couldn't read its contents, but then he didn't have to.

'I've never seen it before,' he said.

'Is that so?' Alperton replied, advancing on him.

'John?' Davenport cut in, advising caution.

'Come now, Miranda. Aren't you in the slightest bit curious as to how young Hunter here and his rather incendiary accomplice came by this? I certainly am.'

'As I just told you, I've never seen it before,' Hunter said, knowing he was not being believed.

'And yet Palgrave tells me it appeared quite miraculously on his desk just this morning. You've been to Bedford Place already today, haven't you? Delivering Evgeny Tikhonov, if I'm not mistaken.'

'You know I have,' Hunter said, remembering his conversation with Julian Palgrave and the almost illegible signature he'd read in his tiny little black book. A signature left on Saturday 4th April, 2015. Illegible to most, but not to Scott Hunter. To Scott Hunter it was instantly recognisable. A signature he had his own long and often troubled relationship with. 'If you're trying to ascertain the prior whereabouts of that file,' he continued, the crabbed scrawl still fixed firmly in his mind's eye, 'how about trying Sandy Harper?'

'Don't be so ridiculous Hunter, it doesn't suit you,' Alperton barked.

'Because when he asked me to find the file, he requested quite explicitly that I find the *original* file. How did he know that the original file was not the redacted file on floor four? Even Palgrave didn't realise the file was a copy. But *you* knew,' Hunter said, looking at Davenport and groping for the last piece of the puzzle. 'How could you possibly have known?' he said, snatching it from thin air, 'unless,' he concluded,

180

turning to face his ex-boss and finally seeing the complete picture for the first time, '*you* told her?'

'What a fascinating exercise in deduction,' Alperton said listlessly and sounding anything but fascinated.

'I know all about Blackmore's bottom locker too,' Hunter marched on, determined the pair take him seriously.

'Really?' Davenport said. 'Do tell us what you think you know, Mr Hunter, but make it quick, please.'

'Lost files, discarded files, they all end up in Blackmore's locker. A sort of dumping ground to cover up careless agent's ineptitude.'

Alperton shook his head and forced a smile. 'I'm sorry to disappoint you Scott, but it's a myth, albeit a rather convenient one from time-to-time. A bedtime story told by drunken agents in The Traitors Gate after hours. An elaborate euphemism for the failings of inadequate operatives and nothing more.'

'But...'

'Thank you, Mr Hunter,' Alperton continued, withdrawing a cigarette lighter from his breast pocket, 'that will be all. And I take it you will forget anything you *may* have read,' he said, sparking the lighter and introducing it to the document's brittle edge. It didn't catch immediately, but coloured and scorched, giving Hunter his first and only glimpse of the text. And then it was gone, snuffed out as simply and easily as Clive Somerset had been. As Hunter watched the paper in Alperton's hand burn and crumble, disappearing before his eyes, so too, he realised, did some of the respect he'd had for the man in the expensive suit and true-blue-on-white silk tie.

'I've forgotten it already,' he said.

'Good. Then that will be all. We're expecting a dinner guest. If you'd be so good as to close the door on your way out.'

'One last thing,' Hunter said, knowing he was overstepping the mark. 'Patzuk?'

'What about him?' Alperton asked wearily.

'Were you ever *really* interested in him?'

'Oh, yes. You can't have filth like that wandering the streets of London unchecked.'

'But he wasn't your main objective, was he?'

Davenport swivelled to face John Alperton, interested to hear his reply.

'And neither was Lobanov,' Hunter persisted, struggling to turn the screw.

'How's the sleeping, Scott?' Alperton asked, noisily flicking his lighter shut.

'Better than yours, I should imagine,' Hunter replied, heading for the door.

Sir John Alperton turned away. He waited until Hunter had closed the door and then he and Miranda Davenport silently contemplated the flat-bottomed barges as they lumbered down The Thames.

Waiting for Hunter, at the bottom of the stairs, was a man in an open-necked shirt, smart casual trousers and a pair of black patent slip-ons, his features almost completely shrouded in a delicately patterned silk facemask. Around his neck, dangling from a gold chain, a trio of interwoven rings forming a Russian crown. On one wrist, and evidently the work of a child, three brightly coloured and tightly wound bracelets of cord. On his other wrist, the most expensive watch Hunter had ever seen.

He stepped back allowing Hunter to pass. Hunter's nodded thanks met only a pair of cold, unforgiving eyes.

All cafés, pubs and restaurants are to close

Hunter's phone woke him early the next morning with a text from an unknown number.

Daily Mail, page 6

He threw on some clothes and bought a copy of the paper and some milk from the corner shop opposite. The kettle clicked on and he rinsed out the old coffee grounds from the bottom of his cafetière before lighting a fresh cigarette and turning to page 6.

Gangland style execution of prominent Russian businessman sparks fresh calls for enquiry.

Dmitry Patzuk's body had been found the previous evening following an anonymous tip-off. He had been rudely crucified.

Hunter had just finished reading the report when a second text came through from the same unknown number.

Now you're appraised of recent events, I should very much like to buy you a drink. FitzRoy, The Mitre, W1

Hunter found the Mitre Pub down a quiet back alley away from Marylebone High Street. Ancient cobblestones in stark contradiction to double yellow lines and aggressive modern streetlights.

Whoever had sent the text, FitzRoy perhaps, had chosen the location with infinite care. The Mitre ought to have been shut but when Hunter tried the door, it opened easily. Inside, the interior split into two distinct halves. On Hunter's right, an open space with tall barstools and high circular tables misguidedly waiting on the day's menus and condiments. The other side of the pub was considerably older and completely different in style and character. Jutting from the bar, a series of wooden booths reaching up to the ceiling, each capable of seating five or six people and with their own door at the rear affording them total privacy and a private space at the bar. Hunter walked around the back of the booths. On each door, in worn gilt paint, the names of British Prime Ministers stretching all the way back to Robert Walpole. Now the text message made sense. Hunter opened the door marked FitzRoy uncertain who or what he would find but reassured by the heavy Glock in the waistband of his black jeans.

He breathed easy. The space was empty save for one high stool next to the bar. He checked his watch and then the clock on his phone. He was early, but only a little. He pulled up to the bar and wondered what the chances of getting a drink were. The location was perfect. Whoever joined him, he presumed Sandy Harper, although this was unusually clandestine even for him, so perhaps the recently returned John Alperton... Well, whoever it proved to be, they would be able to talk quietly in this very private space without the risk of being disturbed.

Hunter was checking the pub's clock against the one on his phone when the barman arrived. The clock was a little fast but his appointment was now definitely late. He negotiated himself a drink and continued to admire his surroundings. Yes, it would be impossible for anyone in the booth to his right to see him and likewise, he realised, equally impossible for him to see anyone else. A mirror ran the entire length of the bar and Hunter strained to see into any of the other compartments but, due to of the age of the glass and the sheer number of bottles lined up in front of it, any view had been conveniently obscured.

He consulted his watch again.

'If you keep doing that Mr Hunter, I'm worried you shall break it.' Thick, heavy words, correctly delivered behind an uncompromising Russian accent. 'Am I late? If so, I do apologise. This pandemic seems to have brought your country to its knees. Taxis are impossible to find.' The man coughed and Hunter heard a barstool scrape across the floor of the adjacent stall. 'I thought this would be a little more neutral than your Traitors Gate. I hope you don't mind, but I thought it was about time we met.' He coughed again. 'Although we have met once before, briefly. I wonder if you remember?'

'I do,' Hunter replied, struggling to recall the face which had examined him from a smoke-filled Mercedes parked outside a flat in W8.

'A shame about poor George,' the faceless Russian continued, as if reading his mind.

'I agree,' Hunter replied, squinting in the mirror behind the bar in an effort to catch even a fleeting glimpse of the man ordering himself a cognac.

'I shouldn't bother wasting your time, Mr Hunter.' There was a rustle of activity from the next booth and then Hunter saw the corner of a hat appear on the portion of bar between them. A gentleman's fedora, black and shiny with use and sporting a healthy band of silk. 'Are you aware of a man called Marcus Bayer?'

'I am.'

'Is Mr Bayer well?'

'As well as can be expected.'

'Good,' the man on the other side of the partition said, 'I am pleased to hear that. There is much to be learned from Mr Bayer's experiences. Now, I believe you have something for me?'

'I'm not sure I understand?'

'Come, come Mr Hunter. You know the whereabouts of Evgeny Tikhonov, do you not?'

'Yesterday I could have told you exactly where he was,' Hunter replied, determined the man on the other side of the partition not have it *all* his own way. 'Today however, he could be anywhere.'

'I see. In which case I shall settle for his mobile telephone number, please. I admire your attempts to protect Evgeny but I should tell you, you will not leave here until you have given me the information I require. I hope I make myself clear?'

'I don't have a number for him. Everything was done face-to-face.'

'Really, Mr Hunter? I would have assumed that once you had made yourselves comfortable in The Service's safehouse on Boden Road, the first thing would have been to provide Evgeny with a new burner phone, unless The Service has changed its procedure for walk-ins?'

His position untenable, Hunter scrolled through his address book and wrote the number on the back of a coaster before sliding it along the bar towards the black fedora.

'Thank you, Mr Hunter, that will spare me having to bother Ms Fairchild.'

'What promises do I have that he will go unharmed?'

'None, I'm afraid,' the Russian said, pocketing the coaster. 'And how is the lovely Mrs Davenport settling in, do you suppose?'

Another question which didn't really require an answer.

'You should know, Mr Hunter, I thank you. The previous employees of Perm AZ thank you, along with the thousands who invested in Kama-Invest. Anna Kuznetsov thanks you. Although I shouldn't get too excited about Oleg Lobanov. I have a feeling he may be beyond either of our reaches. However, I understand earlier this morning his jet was being readied, so perhaps, whilst he may escape both your government and mine, he is about to become someone else's problem and that may be the most we can hope for.' The Russian took another sip of his drink. 'Scott, may I call you Scott?' He didn't wait for an answer, the question nothing more than a habitual courtesy. 'Scott, what do you know of The Crown of Thorns?'

'Worn by Christ? Not a lot, why?'

'You humour an old man, please. In 1238 the King of France, Louis IX, was offered a collection of artefacts; Holy relics, remnants and curios, you understand? These include The Crown of Thorns, thought, as you say, to have been worn by Jesus Christ upon his crucifixion. The king did not buy the crown as that would have been un-ecumenical, I think this is right, but he did entrust a sum believed to be equivalent to half of France's worth at the time. Lot of money. Have you ever been to Saint-Chapelle, Scott?'

'No,' Hunter replied.

'You ought to. It is possibly the most extraordinarily beautiful building in the world. King Louis had it built to house Crown of Thorns

185

and that is, by and large, where they have remained ever since, under the protective custody of the church and seldom if ever seen.'

Hunter stared into his glass and wondered where the Russian was headed.

'Every once in a while, to impress a visiting member of nobility perhaps, or buy influence with a foreign power, Louis would snap off a thorn from the crown and present it to his guest. They were now in his debt and he had fortified his often fragile position with them.'

The man on the other side of the wooden partition coughed a chesty cough and Hunter watched a liver spotted hand reach for his drink.

'I believe your British Museum has one such thorn.' He coughed again. 'And now I reach the part of my story which may interest you, Scott. Whilst it is touching to believe all of this, the overblown pageantry, the romance, there is other side to this tale. Currently, I believe the crown reside in Notre Dame where it has been since 1806, which, personally I think is shame, as that was never intended to be its home, but that is church's business, not mine. However, there are those who believe not only that the incomplete crown currently in Notre Dame is fake, but real Crown of Thorns is intact and hidden deep within the vaults of Saint-Chapelle. Never lost its thorns. Was never bartered away or corrupted to curry favour or advancement.

'King Louis, these people believe, buy influence, placate enemies, bolster allies, with falsehoods. Fakery.'

Was Kadnikov referring to Bayer's largely redacted report, Hunter wondered, a report he claimed not to have written and never to have seen? A fake and a forgery. And if he were, how did Kadnikov even know of its existence? Only someone within The Service could have told him and the only contact Hunter *knew* Kadnikov had had with The Service was with George Wiseman.

'How was America?' Hunter asked.

'Ah, yes. America,' the Russian scoffed. 'Another thorn from our crown. Let me ask, do you believe everything you are told, Mr Hunter?'

'That depends on who's doing the telling.'

'Does it? I shall have to remember that. George never had the slightest intention of allowing me to speak with Americans. I'm not ashamed to say, but I'm too valuable.'

'What are you doing here then?'

'At present? Having most...' he hesitated, perhaps considering Hunter's reaction to his next statement, '*pleasant* drink with David Hunter's son.'

The Russian's last sentence ought to have shocked Hunter more than it did.

'How do you know my father?' he asked.

He waited for an answer, but when Hunter looked down at the counter he no longer saw the corner of the dark hat with the silk band. He turned on his barstool in time to hear the door of the adjacent booth swing shut. To run after the enigmatic Russian or to leave him be? Hunter returned to his perch, ordered himself another drink and considered Aleksei Kadnikov's Crown of Thorns. He should probably drop into Bedford Place, fill out a contact report detailing this latest conversation. But then, if Alperton and Davenport had used *him*, they had almost certainly used Sandy Harper and Hunter was struggling to imagine quite how pissed off he might be as a result. More prudent perhaps to stay put and keep quiet.

13

'Scott!' Fairchild called after Hunter, 'What the hell is going on? I've just seen John Alperton swanning around on the third floor like he owns the place?'

Hunter was curiously taken aback. He'd never seen Fairchild look anything other than composed.

'He never left,' he said, enjoying himself a little too much.

'What?'

'Alperton. He never left, Sam.'

'But Davenport more or less handed him his papers, or that's what I heard.'

Hunter shook his head.

'And Harper,' Fairchild continued indignantly, 'he told us he'd gone. You remember, at the pub?'

'Afraid not, Sam. And I think Sandy Harper may have been as taken in by them as the rest of us.'

'Why?'

'Alperton realised if he wanted to get Tikhonov to do his dirty work, he'd have to be out of the picture.'

'What about Davenport? She never sanctioned that?'

Hunter smiled. 'I'm not even sure it wasn't her idea, Sam. A touch of quid pro quo. She allowed Alperton to close the book on a particularly grubby chapter of his career.'

'In return for?' Fairchild asked, looking expectantly at Hunter.

'Sorry, Sam, not this time.'

'Patzuk?'

'Don't you read the papers? Dmitry Patzuk's dead.'

'How?'

'Nailed to a cross in an abandoned West London warehouse.'

'Tikhonov?'

'That would be my guess.'

'And where is *he*?' she asked.

'No one seems to know. Vanished. Gone sailing, perhaps? Who knows?' Hunter replied, trying not to recall his conversation with Aleksei Kadnikov.

Fairchild smiled. 'That's cool. I kinda liked him.'

'Yeah, me too,' Hunter said sadly.

'I guess all this means you found the file then?'

'Tikhonov must have had it the whole time,' Hunter said, remembering the signature he'd seen scrawled in Palgrave's little black book.

'I don't think so, Scott. I asked him, at your father's place, repeatedly. I'm pretty sure he knew nothing about it.' And then, somewhat to Hunter's relief, Samantha Fairchild broke off. 'Does this mean laughing boy's back too?'

'I'm afraid it does,' Hunter said grinning broadly, 'I'm afraid it does. Traitors?'

'What?'

'For a drink?' Hunter said before he'd really thought it through.

'You're not worried I may try and drug you?'

'No, I don't think I am.'

'Or blow you up?'

'No.'

'Good. Listen, thanks Scott, but I'll have to pass.'

'Oh, okay.'

'I've got a kind of... prior engagement.'

'With K?' Hunter asked.

'With *what*?' Fairchild replied.

'K. On your keyring, there's a large letter K.'

She laughed, quietly and to herself. 'Not that it's any of your business, but no, not with K.'

'You're right, none of my business, sorry.'

'See you around, Scott Hunter.'

'Just before you go, Sam. Were you in my flat the other day, nosing around?'

Fairchild smiled. 'Harper told me to. I did the crappiest job I could.'

'Yeah, I noticed. What were you looking for?'

She turned to face him. 'Anything out of the ordinary.'

'Find anything?'

'In your flat?! Just about everything.'

'What did you tell Harper?'

'That you need a cleaning lady. What about you? Harper ever ask you to check my place out?'

'I don't even know where your place is, Sam.'

'Good. Let's keep it like that, shall we?'

✳✳✳

Since their move to London, Dmitry Patzuk and Oleg Lobanov had resolved to become distant friends of financial convenience. They'd swapped one lax authority in a country with little extravagance to offer for a capital promising much but at a price. In London, Patzuk and the people he'd worked for had discovered that not everybody could be bought or intimidated. Oddly, he'd found the higher up you were prepared to climb, the more corruptible people had become, which, for a nation priding itself on tea, cricket and an antiquated predisposition towards fair play, seemed remarkably un-British to the man from the Ukraine. Small men with little or no real power were often stubborn, bureaucratic and uncooperative but go to their bosses or, better still, their bosses' bosses and they could be bought as easily as any Russian peasant. The very people who were preaching to the British public on everything from moral probity to financial austerity could be sweetened with anything from a bag of cocaine to the promise of a long January weekend on a luxury yacht in the Caribbean. Hypocrisy, it transpired, knew no bounds.

Consequently, the realities of London had come as quite a shock. But once Patzuk and Lobanov had established their routines and settled down with new passports, they'd agreed, socially at least, to go their separate ways. They would not consort together, avoid the same expensive restaurants, night clubs and cocktail bars. But their affairs continued, conducted through intermediaries, intermediaries like Evgeny

Tikhonov. He had been crucial to their operations, laundering their money, often through a string of vacant black hotels on the coasts of Spain before dividing up the spoils and distributing them equitably through totally legitimate banks in England or more questionable ones in Switzerland. And now, with Patzuk gone, Tikhonov had been summoned in the dead of night. Tikhonov hadn't been summoned like this since Moscow. Patzuk would have to be replaced. Someone who could be trusted to move huge amounts of money to and from the motherland without attracting unwanted attention.

Reassured that he had ascertained the purpose of his visit and excited by the prospect of increased responsibilities and the resultant financial rewards, Evgeny Tikhonov closed his eyes and settled back into the Mercedes's soft leather interior whilst Lobanov's driver negotiated his way through central London and out to Chelsea.

Shoppers are urged not to panic buy

It was a chilly morning, the sky a perpendicular slope of cirrocumulus stripes. Hunter walked through dewy glades of bluebells, relieved, at least for a while, to be done with his father's car. As he approached Marcus Bayer's refuge in the woods and savouring the smell of wild garlic spring had delivered, he brooded over his previous day's meeting. If Sir John Alperton had indeed killed Clive Somerset, as Evgeny Tikhonov was insisting, what did that make him? At best a traitor working beyond the fringes of The Service. At worst, a dangerously loose cannon verging on the psychotic, taking lives seemingly without motive or reason and who surely should be held accountable for his crimes.

But then there was something about Tikhonov's story which still didn't quite stack up. Something Hunter had read in the Parisian press cuttings. When the police had arrived and attended to Somerset's body, there had been a coat. An expensive Italian overcoat, according to the news reports, which had been laid over the dead Englishman's head. Not carelessly thrown, in an act of wanton deception, but reverentially laid. Would a murderer stop to do such a thing? What if Tikhonov had been wrong and this had not been a callously executed crime, but the scene of an unfortunate accident and Alperton's actions were not calculating and mendacious but almost piously remorseful?

Hunter stepped from the woods and began looking for Marcus Bayer. Only John Alperton would know the real answer and there was no way he would be sharing it with Scott Hunter. He found Bayer kneeling over a clump of young, pink rhubarb. 'Did you forget to mention you knew Aleksei Kadnikov?' he asked, passing the disgraced Russian analyst a supermarket bag.

'Yes, I suppose I must have,' Bayer replied without looking up. 'What's this?'

'Coffee, pasta, bog roll. Try not to use it all at once, it's like gold-dust. I'll put the coffee on, and then you can tell me all about Paris.'

Bayer looked up. 'Gold-dust?'

'You really have no idea what's going on out there, do you?'

'I've never found it does me much good.'

'There's some bacon and eggs in there too and something for Anushka, if you'll get a fire going?'

'I assume you're here to tell me your problem's gone away? Because you should know, I have nothing further to say on the matter,' Bayer said bluntly.

'Neither does Dmitry Patzuk,' Hunter replied, throwing him the previous day's copy of *The Mail*. 'Page 6.'

'Ah, well,' Bayer said, casting a dispassionate eye over the copy, 'we've all got to go some time, I suppose. Best not to dwell on it. I notice there's no mention of Lobanov?' he concluded, handing the paper back.

'Last seen boarding his private jet, according to your friend.'

Bayer nodded. 'That's probably as close to a result as you can expect, I'm afraid. The Russians have a saying for moments such as this, *Little thieves are hanged, great ones escape.*'

Hunter helped Bayer get the fire going and erect the heavy metal cooking tripod.

'So,' Bayer said, 'why are you here, Mr Frost?'

'It's real, isn't it, Blackmore's locker? Perhaps not in the way *I'd* imagined, but it does exist?'

Bayer half nodded, half shrugged.

'And if the file Alperton destroyed *was* genuine, because I think we have to accept that it could all have been an elaborate spot of theatre put on for my benefit, but assuming it wasn't and the page he burnt was real...'

'Well, it must have come from somewhere,' Bayer said, 'that's true.'

'Blackmore's locker,' Hunter said again, patting Anushka. 'But that's not it, is it? You've never doubted its veracity or its existence.' Bayer didn't reply, just smiled to himself, allowing Hunter time to think. 'It's the nature of the intel you're questioning. Not a glorified wastepaper basket full of lost or misplaced files. Something much more damning.' Hunter shifted uncomfortably on his makeshift seat, hoping for Bayer to fill in the gaps. 'Palgrave's the gatekeeper?'

'Yes,' Bayer smiled, 'and no.'

'He keeps everything,' Hunter continued, thinking out loud, 'Topographical, thematic and cadastral.'

'Possibly, but think of him more as a custodian. He handles *some* of the books, even knows where they're kept, may have read a few of them, but none of that means he comprehends their significance or understands their true worth.'

Hunter tried to imagine quite how offended Julian Palgrave might have been to hear this.

'Just think about this for a second,' Bayer continued. 'He remains one of the few people in Bedford Place with complete access to all of that information. Or at least, that's how it might appear.'

If what Bayer was saying was true, Hunter thought he was beginning to understand at least a little of the antipathy shared between Palgrave and Sandy Harper, although, knowing Harper, there was almost certainly bound to be more to it than Palgrave's ability to distribute intelligence as and when he saw fit.

'If Palgrave's the only one controlling all that intel, surely that would make him one of the most influential people in The Service,' Hunter concluded.

'It should do, shouldn't it. Unless, of course...'

Was Marcus Bayer implying there were *other* files? Files beyond even Julian Palgrave's overprotective custody?

'You're saying that whatever was in that report, the unredacted report, was so incendiary even Palgrave couldn't be trusted with it?'

'Bravo, Mr Frost.'

'Kadnikov told me a story, about The Crown of Thorns. It's what we've been talking about all along, I just never realised it. Blackmore's locker isn't some chaotic dumping ground where random pieces of misfiled reports wind up, it's a reliquary.'

'A what?' Bayer asked, looking up from the fire.

'Where the holiest of the holy reside.'

'Ah. And not just them,' Bayer said chuckling, 'but the filthiest secrets too. The sort of secrets that would bring down the Lord God Almighty.'

'Or John Alperton?'

Bayer smiled again.

'Why did you lie to me?' Hunter asked, carefully avoiding Bayer's gaze.

'Who says that I did?'

'Alperton.'

Anushka moved off, seeking the attentions of her suddenly speechless master.

'Alright then,' Hunter continued, 'shall I tell you what I think happened in Paris?'

'What would you say if I said no?'

'I think you handed over a package to Evgeny Tikhonov otherwise known as Samphire, a package containing British passports paid for with Russian secrets. I think for doing so you were paid by GDLC Holdings, just as Fraser was paid for her silence. I think that when I turned up you went straight to Alperton and I think it's more than likely that you're still working for him now.'

'You're wrong,' Bayer replied after a moment's thought 'about the money at least.'

'You're still active?'

'It's a great story, but I'm afraid that's all it is. I left The Service on April Fool's Day, 2015, remember?'

'What exactly did happen when you got back from France?'

'I was met off the train at St Pancras. I'd been expecting that. They drove me down to a safehouse in West Norwood.'

'Boden Road?' Hunter asked, picturing the tatty green front door and newly installed lock. Marcus Bayer didn't disagree.

'There were three of them waiting for me. Sandy Harper, John Alperton and a third man I didn't recognise. Alperton I'd been expecting, Moscow was his op after all. Harper I could have predicted. Always on the sniff if there was even the hint of a misstep.

Between them they put me through it for a couple of days. What had made me follow Kadnikov? Was I working for the Russians? Was I a double? Had it been a rendezvous Tom stumbled into? Was that why...? With hindsight all reasonable questions I suppose. I tried to explain about Paris, that I'd been sent to Pont des Arts to meet Samphire, but Alperton kept steering me back to what had happened in Moscow.'

'And the other man, the one you didn't recognise? What was his role in all this?'

'Took a backseat mostly. Kept a written record of everything I'd said, content to let Sandy Harper do the hatchet work. Seemed rather pleasant actually, although I got the distinct impression the other two weren't exactly delighted to have him on board.'

Hunter nodded, picturing the scene and recalling that sloppy signature. Pleasant. Yes, of course he is.

'And do you think Alperton killed Somerset?' he asked, perhaps subconsciously eager to move the conversation on.

'It doesn't really matter, does it? My debrief was filed a few days later. The Home Office slapped a D notice on it as soon as they caught wind of the situation and someone had it redacted. Then it was left to rot in the file of a recently disgraced ex-operative who happened to have been in Paris at the time. No one would ever bother to look there. Or so they thought.'

'But the paper file was a copy,' Hunter put in. 'So Alperton must have realised the original was floating around somewhere, like one of Kadnikov's bloody thorns. If Alperton wasn't able to find it, that can only mean that he doesn't know the whereabouts of Blackmore's locker.'

'And with good reason, wouldn't you say?'

Hunter had one last question, but Bayer beat him to it. 'You're wondering who copied, then redacted the original report.'

Hunter nodded. 'Tobias Gray,' he said with confidence. 'Lovely bit of leverage to hold over someone, particularly if you're worried they may be after your job. Then, once Gray's gone and Davenport's taken over...'

'Taken over?' Bayer said cutely. 'We'll see about that. I think that when Gray left what would have shocked John Alperton more than anything was the realisation that, after all those years of power plays and dreaming of the top spot, he was actually going to get it and that for the first time in his life there was a danger he'd be held truly accountable.'

'You're saying Alperton allowed Davenport to succeed him because he got stage fright?'

'Something like that,' Bayer replied.

'On the condition that she do him one favour in return, find the original file and locate The Crown of Thorns.'

'That would be my guess,' Bayer replied. 'What do you know about her?'

'Not a lot.'

'Exactly. I think you might want to look a little closer at exactly who it is you're really working for.'

'But The Crown of Thorns is still out there somewhere, isn't it?'

Bayer laughed. 'I shouldn't waste your time thinking about it. Even if it does exist, you'll never find it.' He hesitated. 'Listen, do you never wonder what the point of it all is?'

'I did have it explained to me once,' Hunter replied.

'Lucky you.'

***

Aleksei Kadnikov ran a fat finger between collar and throat. He tugged at his tie. He wasn't enjoying the heat. He couldn't smoke. His precious hat lay in a crumpled heap on the pine seat next to him and the hot thick air was aggravating his cough. He made a promise to himself. Once this business was concluded, providing it was concluded successfully of course, he would step outside and smoke a cigarette, probably two. He'd never enjoyed this aspect of his work, had never taken pleasure in ending another man's life, unlike some of his contemporaries. Dmitry Patzuk had simply been another casualty of the breakdown of law and order in Russia. That his murder had occurred two thousand miles from home, that his family would probably never know how or why he'd died was simply symptomatic of the sickness sweeping through the motherland.

There had been a time, when Kadnikov had first taken the decision to leave Russia and move to England, when he'd struggled with the sadness considering the land of his birth had provoked. He'd tried to help. He'd tried to help a nation which seemed determined not to help itself. He'd given up all his secrets to George Wiseman, a man he'd never met but whom he trusted implicitly. He'd told Wiseman everything he felt able and hoped the old man would, in return, use the information not to further cripple an already hobbled regime but to try and save it from itself. And George had been as good as his word. But then George had killed himself and so now he felt duty bound to continue his work alone. Was he responsible for Dmitry Patzuk's death? In one sense, the most direct sense, certainly he was. He'd placed the call to Oleg Lobanov warning him that Patzuk had been seen consorting with a man thought once to have worked with the British Secret Service. Yes, he'd made that call and his recently acquired contacts in The Service had taken care of the rest. After all, he'd only been trying to protect the motherland. Everything he'd ever done had been to protect the motherland.

***

'Does the name Anna Kuznetsov mean anything to you?' Hunter asked, sipping his coffee and recalling his conversation with Aleksei Kadnikov.

'It's a common enough name in most parts of Russia,' Bayer said, 'but yes, it does ring a bell.'

Hunter had a feeling it might.

'Do you remember me telling you about a young woman who lost everything to one of Lobanov's Ponzi schemes?'

Hunter nodded. 'She killed herself in the foyer of one of his offices.'

'Her name was Kuznetsov.'

Hunter looked at him. Who was this man? he wondered. This self-confessed orphan with a hole in his life that even the redoubtable Service hadn't been able to fill. This expert analyst with a first-class Oxbridge education but poor at paperwork. This dishonourably discharged spy, sent home after only two days of interrogation but with a direct line to Sir John Alperton. A man who, on a whim, could follow his enemy to the ends of the earth for a cosy little chat about nothing in particular and in the next beat kill his best friend.

'Why do you ask?'

'Oh, just trying to remember what the point of it all is,' Hunter replied, forcing a smile.

Bayer took a stick and prodded at the fire, sending embers leaping into the sky. 'I'm intrigued,' he countered, 'you never did ask me who wrote the original report. Is that because you already know?'

'Like I said,' Hunter replied, patting the flimsy plastic bag which lay between them, 'like gold-dust.' He stood and brushed the ash from his trousers. Anushka immediately circled him, sniffing at his pockets. 'I should be going. There are still people I need to talk to and it's a long drive home.'

'Goodbye, Mr Frost.'

✱✱✱

'Where's Lobanov?' Tikhonov asked the hulking bodyguard in the ill-fitting suit who held open the Merc's heavy passenger door for him.

'Banya. Follow me.'

'Why does he want to see *me*? He's never asked to see me before.'

'Ask him for yourself. Banya.'

The bodyguard led him past the front of Oleg Lobanov's magisterial country home, through a crackling gravel car park, littered with sports cars and brooding SUVs. He'd done as Sandy Harper had instructed, hadn't he? He'd waited patiently for the phone call from Lobanov and then he'd murdered Dmitry Patzuk and sent a message too, just as he'd been instructed. It had never crossed his mind to question the order to kill his boss. That was simply the way of things in the old country. Whether it be the FSB or the Vory giving the orders, if you were wise and wished to keep your head on your shoulders, you did as you were told, no questions asked. But now he was beginning to wonder what Lobanov had in store for him. Would it be presumptuous to suppose that, with a gap in his organisation opening up, Oleg Lobanov might be about to make him an extremely lucrative offer? The path turned sharply, heading down the side of Lobanov's massive home to a small, purpose built, single storey building clad in long, broad wooden beams. The other man held open the door for Evgeny Tikhonov and ushered him inside. At the end of a corridor, tastefully lined in the most expensive pine, a single glass door, opaque with steam.

'Take off your shoes.'

Tikhonov did as he was told, slipping out of his comfortable leather deck shoes before easing open the door and disappearing inside.

'Mr Lobanov?' Tikhonov registered the lukewarm water on the soles of his feet, heard each awkward slap as he walked further into the baths. 'Mr Lobanov?'

Suddenly the steam moved around him, swirling past, pushed from behind. He heard the other man approach. It entered his mind to spin, to counter, to feint, to parry, but by then it was too late. The crude metal wire had already slipped over his head, instantly tightening around his neck.

'Goodbye, comrade Tikhonov. Try not to struggle. Dead men don't repent.'

✱✱✱

Sunday, 22nd March 2020
Public advised to stay at home on Mothering Sunday.

That evening, Frances Verity found herself splitting a couple of bottles of cheap Rioja with a pair of spies, one retired. Scott was learning to enjoy the happiness she brought his father. That was why he'd wait for her to leave before he asked the question which had been burning inside him all weekend.

'It's getting late,' she said in a gap between drinks. 'I should probably call a cab. I'll swing by tomorrow and pick the car up, if that's alright?'

David got up and Scott could see he was moving towards the phone. 'Why don't you stay?' he said. 'That would be okay, wouldn't it, Dad?'

'But I don't have anything with me,' she protested weakly.

'That's okay,' Scott continued, 'there's bound to be one of Dad's old shirts you can borrow?'

She looked at David Hunter. He smiled back, offering an awkward shrug.

'Okay,' Frances said, enjoying his discomfort, 'well, I'd better go and see if your father runs to a spare toothbrush too!'

Then, perhaps suddenly aware that she was about to incautiously slip into another woman's bed, Frances left quietly, already decided she would not return. They watched her go and David was about to thank his son when Scott spoke up.

'What were you doing in Bedford Place?' he asked.

'When?'

'How about the 4th April 2015, for starters?'

David Hunter put down his glass and stared at his son. 'Really, Scott, I haven't the faintest idea. What were you doing five years ago?' he countered, mediocre Tempranillo failing to mask his irritation.

'I expect you were just trying to do the right thing?'

His father sighed and went to top up their glasses. 'Yes, I expect I was.'

'I saw your signature in Palgrave's book,' Scott said, unable to help himself.

'Really? Then I hardly know why you're asking.'

'I know you interviewed Bayer and I know you wrote that report too.'

'I interviewed a tremendous number of people in my relatively short career, Scott.'

'He'd just returned from Paris.'

'Lucky him.'

'Where he'd played a bit part in a much larger drama. A drama in which John Alperton reluctantly took centre stage.'

David Hunter shook his head and raised his glass. 'That sounds like John.'

'He may have been responsible for the death of an English civilian.'

'Now that, if true, is regrettable.'

'And I think the whole episode might have been long forgotten, had it not been for one of Bayer's interrogators.'

'Oh, really?'

'A quietly spoken, yet honourable third party.'

'Sounds painful.'

'Who made sure that Marcus Bayer's testimony from Paris remained in his typed-up notes.' Hunter stared at his father across the table. 'The report was later redacted to within an inch of its life, but what its author must have understood was that, by then, it had entered Julian Palgrave's unfathomable system. Once in the system a record of its existence would always remain, along with the signature of its creator.'

David Hunter's expression settled and he listlessly pushed an empty glass across the table. 'If the report *was* redacted, it's not going to be much use to anyone, no matter who wrote it,' he said.

'You'd think so wouldn't you,' Scott continued, 'and I'd given up ever seeing the original.'

'Understandable, I suppose.'

'Until I mentioned it to you the other day.'

'I'm not sure what you're driving at, Scott? I'm a long time retired and certainly unable to produce such material out of thin air, even if I wanted to.'

Scott smiled. 'Must have been in Blackmore's locker all along then.'

David Hunter looked across the table at his son and nodded slowly. 'Yes, yes I guess it must have been.'

❋❋❋

Frances glanced at his side of the bed. David had remained downstairs, talking with his son, and so she'd been asleep when he'd joined her, but now the duvet lay thrown back, his brief presence leaving barely an impression in the mattress. The clock radio informed her it was twenty past three. He had lain next to her, wide eyed and awake for over an hour whilst she had tried to get back to sleep. Then, at two o'clock, David Hunter had slipped from their bed without a word and left. She knew his son suffered from insomnia, it was one of the few things she did know about him. Perhaps his father was a sufferer too. She stayed in the half empty bed and waited for him to return. But then there were strange noises from outside and suddenly, all alone and in unfamiliar surroundings, Frances Verity felt quite terrified.

When she'd met and fallen in love with David Hunter, she'd never imagined their relationship would become such a complex one. He'd seemed disarmingly straightforward, a trifle shy perhaps, reticent even, but kind, gentle and funny. Then he'd introduced her to his son, his odd son who was clearly clever, had been to Cambridge but had no job. She had not found Scott easy to love and, whilst that feeling appeared mutual, she'd known, deep down, that there had to be more to his antipathy toward her than an unfortunate clash of personalities.

Eventually, after much gentle persuasion, David had felt able to open up to her about his wife. He'd explained that she'd taken her own life and Frances had begun to understand a little of Scott's psyche, his pain and how with that one awful act, his absent mother still informed his life.

She tried to put the noises emanating from outside to the back of her mind, to think about something different. She struggled to convince herself that David would be back soon. Once men hit a certain age, she recalled, they were forever disappearing in the middle of the night for one reason or another.

But David Hunter did not return and the noises coming from his back garden only persisted. Unable to stifle her curiosity, Frances got up, pulled on a sweater and carefully drew back a corner of curtain. David, still in his pyjamas, stood halfway up the garden, like a miner, a small camping torch strapped to his head, digging eagerly at the base of a shrub with a well-loved old spade. She squinted. It was a hardy little succulent he was fussing over, with long tear-shaped leaves, inch-long spines and balls of small poppy shaped pink flowers which were just about to come into bloom. Her first husband had been quietly obsessive over their rose garden but nothing like this. She watched as David pushed his foot down firmly on the spade's shoulder and removed another sod of turf before stopping and dropping to his knees. With her sleep irrevocably disturbed, she decided to go downstairs and see if she could get a better look at what he was doing.

Frances stood at the kitchen window, hugging herself against the cold, and watched in confusion as David Hunter, this man she thought she loved, finished wrapping a rusty, metal biscuit tin in clear, thick plastic before placing it reverentially in the hole he'd just dug. Then he reached for his spade and carefully filled it back in, burying the tin. He stretched his arms above his head, turned off the glowing head-torch and walked towards the house.

✳✳✳

The United Kingdom records its highest number of coronavirus deaths in one day

Arriving at Peterborough Station, Samantha Fairchild bought a simple spray of delicate wildflowers, not realising how self-conscious they would make her. In the taxi she clutched them awkwardly to her chest and hoped they would be enough, whilst worrying they were too much. She suggested the driver drop her at the entrance to Cathles Hill

Court, sparing him the bother of turning the car in the narrow cul-de-sac's dead end.

She paid, pressing an extra couple of pounds into the driver's hand without explanation, swung her legs out of the passenger seat, removed her facemask, smoothed down her skirt and pulled the flowers to her, still anxious of the gesture.

Margaret Fratton's house, along with the rest of the street, lay eerily quiet. There is something quite straightforward and unmistakable about an empty house, which one knows almost immediately. Fairchild took the step up and into the porch and just as quickly rang the antiquated bell. She waited, wondering if the flamenco dancer had ever found her polka-dotted papier pinafore or if Lenin had ever been reunited with the other Matroyoska heads of state. She rang the bell again, and again, all the while wondering what had become of Mrs Margaret Fratton.

The house remained dark. No sounds came from within.

✳✳✳

The United Kingdom enters full lockdown

Read the series from its beginning.

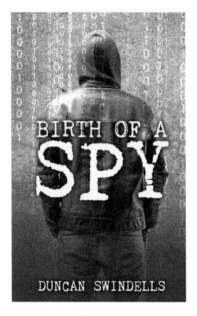

The Scott Hunter Spy Series Book 1

Out of work Cambridge graduate Scott Hunter breaks Second World War Enigma codes. His girlfriend is desperate for him to find a job and settle down, so when a fresh code lands unexpectedly on Scott's doorstep, he promises it will be his last, little realising that revealing the dark secrets it has protected for over fifty years will shatter their lives forever.

Praise for Birth of a Spy

A modern take on the classic spy novel.

Absolutely fantastic read... a plot and sub-plots that will keep the reader page-turning until the very end

The world created by the story became more deliciously dark with each chapter

As good, if not better, as any John le Carré story.

If you like a thriller packed with drama and shady characters this is the book for you!

When all your friends have gone, who can you really trust?

The Scott Hunter Spy Series Book 2

Istanbul on the eve of the millennium and a pair of British spies are sent to rendezvous with the most valuable asset out of the East since the Second World War. But when a dismembered corpse washes up on the banks of the Bosphorus and one of Britain's finest young agents defects, heads must roll.

Twenty years on and with the events of that night long forgotten, Scott Hunter is suddenly ordered to Hong Kong to find an American journalist and track down a traitor believed by many to be dead. All he knows; that Landslide is the key to everything.

Absent Friends is the sequel to Birth of a Spy and the second book in the Scott Hunter Series. In his first assignment for the mysterious "service" Scott Hunter travels the world in this high-paced thriller laced with espionage and intrigue.

"Brilliant!"
⭐⭐⭐⭐⭐

"a great story-teller"
⭐⭐⭐⭐⭐

"I read it in two long sittings broken only by work and sleep. What a great story."
⭐⭐⭐⭐⭐

About the Author

Success as a writer of short stories led to the creation of the Scott Hunter Spy Series where the globe-trotting Swindells cleverly combines factual knowledge with fiction and a main character thrown unwillingly into the strange, murky world of Britain's Secret Service.

Buoyed up by critical acclaim for Birth of a Spy, Absent Friends and A Crown of Thorns, quickly followed, continuing Scott Hunter's burgeoning career as an agent in The Service.

A fifth-generation classical musician, Swindells studied at The Royal Academy of Music. Following a successful free-lance career in London he is currently Principal Bass Clarinet with the Royal Scottish National Orchestra.

In 2022 he established Ex Libris Digital Press, a company aimed at aiding self-publishing authors format their paperbacks and ebooks prior to publication.

He lives with his wife, two sons and a couple of demanding black and white cats in a small village outside Stirling.

Printed in Great Britain
by Amazon